The Paradise Trap

The Paradise Trap

Catherine Jinks

EGMONT
USA
New York

EGMONT

We bring stories to life

First published by Egmont USA, 2012
443 Park Avenue South, Suite 806
New York, NY 10016

3 5 7 9 8 6 4 2

www.egmontusa.com

Library of Congress Cataloging-in-Publication Data

Jinks, Catherine.
The paradise trap / Catherine Jinks.
p. cm.
Summary: Eleven-year-old Marcus is spending a week at the beach with his mother
in a tiny old travel trailer, but boredom turns to terror when a new friend discovers a
cellar that has magical doors through which people keep disappearing.
ISBN 978-1-60684-273-7 (hardcover) -- ISBN 978-1-60684-283-6 (ebook) [1.
Supernatural--Fiction. 2. Sirens (Mythology)--Fiction. 3. Robots--Fiction. 4.
Vacations--Fiction. 5. Family life--Fiction. 6. Horror stories.] I. Title.
PZ7.J5754Par 2012
[Fic]--dc23
2011025300

Printed in the United States of America
Book design by ARLENE SCHLEIFER GOLDBERG

CPSIA tracking label information:
Printed in May 2012 at Berryville Graphics, Berryville, Virginia

To James Jinks,
the latest addition

1.

"Our best holiday ever . . ."

Marcus didn't want to spend his summer vacation at the beach.

He wasn't a beach person. His skin was pale and freckled, so it burned easily. He wasn't a bodybuilder, so he didn't like taking off his clothes. And he wore glasses, which had to be removed in the surf.

Marcus would have been quite happy sitting in his bedroom all summer long, playing computer games. His favorite game was Cruising for a Bruising. Even though he was only eleven years old, he had already reached the lowest first-class deck on the SS *Midas*. There were just five decks to go. Once he'd fought his way past the angry chefs in the gourmet kitchen, dodged the fat people bouncing off each other on the dance floor, and pushed all the armed lifeguards into the heated pool, he would be within easy reach of the bridge.

He was looking forward to his life-and-death struggle with Captain Creap. Defeating this evil despot would mean conquering the world's largest, richest luxury liner. Marcus couldn't wait to do that. He had plans for all the stewards who'd been throwing deck chairs at his stowaway avatar.

But Marcus's mother didn't care about his plans. She had plans of her own. That was why, on the last day of school, he arrived home to find an unfamiliar trailer attached to his mother's car outside their house.

"It was cheaper to buy this old trailer than to hire a nicer one for the week," explained his mother, whose name was Holly Bradshaw. "I got a great deal, because it was taking up valuable space in the lot. No one wanted to hire it."

"I'm not surprised," Marcus muttered. The trailer was small and dirty and covered with dents. There were dead flies on all its windowsills. Inside its poky living area, the two-burner stove was encrusted with grease, as were most of the benchtops. The curtains were in shreds. The linoleum was sticky.

"It's a bit small," Marcus pointed out, just in case his mother hadn't noticed.

"That doesn't matter," she said. "There's plenty of room for the two of us. Besides, just look at all the cupboard space!" She yanked open one of the cupboard doors, which came off in her hand. "Don't worry about that," she added, hastily propping the door shut. "I'll fix everything before we go. And I'll give the whole place a good scrub, too."

"Will scrubbing get rid of the smell?" Marcus sniffed suspiciously. "It smells like sweaty gym clothes in here."

"Really? *I* think it smells like moldy baked beans." When Marcus screwed up his nose, Holly tried to reassure him. "We'll air the place out. I'm sure it's not permanent. Maybe the little old lady used to smell a bit."

Marcus was confused. "What little old lady?" he asked.

"The little old lady who used to live here."

Gazing at his mother in alarm, Marcus squeaked, "She didn't *die* in here, did she?"

"Of course not."

"How do you know?"

"Because the man at the lot told me she didn't."

Marcus wasn't convinced. "I hope she didn't die in here," he mumbled. "I hope it's not haunted."

Holly laughed. "Don't be silly," she rejoined. "Whoever heard of a haunted trailer?"

Marcus shrugged. He adjusted his glasses and looked around the cramped, grimy, battered space. He didn't want to spend a whole week in it. Though his

3

home was quite small and shabby, at least it wasn't a rat cage on wheels.

"Most of the time we'll be outside," Holly promised, watching his face. "When *I* was eleven, and *I* went to Diamond Beach, I spent every day in the open air from dawn till dusk. It was fantastic. I made lots and lots of friends and had the best time ever." She smiled her encouragement. "I know you will, too, Marcus."

But Marcus didn't believe her.

"I don't like the beach much," he said.

"You'll like this one," Holly assured him. "I told you before—there are fish and rock pools and barbecues and lagoons and heaps of great kids and a fantastic playground. It's magical." Her eyes softened as she remembered her long-ago visit to Diamond Beach. "We don't have many treats, so we deserve this," she insisted. "You'll love it. You won't want to come home."

Marcus didn't bother asking if his dad would be coming, too. His dad lived on the other side of the country and never took trips with Marcus. They hadn't laid eyes on each other for nearly five years.

Instead, Marcus asked an even more important question. "Can I bring my laptop?"

"*No.*" Holly was firm. "You spend too much time on that computer. I want you to get out and enjoy the real world while you're still a kid."

4

Marcus sighed.

"But the real world isn't any fun," he objected. "It's not as good as a fake world."

"Yes, it is. At Diamond Beach, it really is." Holly put an arm around his shoulders. "You wait," she said. "I guarantee Diamond Beach will be more fun than any computer game. It'll be our best holiday ever."

2.

. . . or maybe not

When Marcus and his mother finally reached the Diamond Beach Trailer Park, they couldn't see the beach. Not from the entrance gates, anyway. All they could see were rows of trailers, stretching as far as the distant horizon under a blazing sun.

There wasn't a tree—or a rock pool—in sight.

"It's changed," Holly murmured as she hunted for lot WW6842. "It's grown so much. . . ."

Marcus stared out the car window as they bumped past trailers that were squished together like chocolates in a box. He saw crying babies, flapping laundry, potholes, power poles, and lots of lines. There was a line at the snack bar, where flies swarmed around the overflowing rubbish bins. There were lines in front of the nearby vending machines. There was a line at the bathrooms and showers, which were in a low gray building made of concrete. And there was a line for every slide and swing in the grubby little playground near the barbecues.

"I don't get it," said Marcus, staring in amazement at all the fretful, sticky, sunburned toddlers. "Why isn't everyone down at the beach?"

"Because the beach is such a long way from here," his mother replied. "This is the cheap section of the park, remember?" When at last they reached their designated campsite, she was crestfallen. "I owe you an apology, Marcus," she said with a sigh. "This isn't what I expected."

Marcus felt sorry for her. "But there *are* heaps of kids," he pointed out. "Just like you promised."

"Ye-e-es . . ."

They both gazed at a mob of yelling, squabbling children who rushed by in pursuit of a football. Marcus could just make out a tangle of arms and legs through all the dirt that was being kicked up. He couldn't tell how many kids there were, or how old they might be.

They were soon out of sight, having bounced down the road like tumbleweed in a whirlwind.

"You're bound to find *someone* who's nice," Holly said without conviction. When Marcus didn't answer, she tried gamely to reassure them both. "Once we get to the beach, none of this will matter. We'll be so busy swimming and building sand castles, we won't notice how crowded it is. You'll see."

Marcus shrugged. Then he helped unpack the car and settle in to the trailer, which still smelled bad despite his mother's efforts. She had sprayed the greasy walls with detergent, aired the musty cushions, scrubbed the blackened stove, wiped down the rickety cupboards, mopped the peeling linoleum on the floor, thrown out the threadbare rug, and replaced the ragged curtains with new ones made of old sheets. She had even washed the light fixtures.

So why did Marcus's skin crawl whenever he stepped inside?

"Did you leave the cupboard doors open on purpose?" he asked his mother. Every cupboard gaped like a mouth, ready to engulf whatever he might choose to feed it.

"No." Holly was standing right behind him, carrying a box of food. "Those latches are really old. They obviously couldn't cope with all the bumping and swerving."

"Maybe," said Marcus. "Or maybe we've got a poltergeist."

It wasn't meant to be a joke, but his mother laughed anyway.

"There's no room for a ghost in here," she rejoined, dumping her box on the table. "There's barely enough room for *us*!"

She was right. After only ten minutes inside the trailer, Marcus could hardly breathe. The walls were closing in, and the smell seemed to be getting worse. He kept bumping into Holly as they filled the cupboards with plates and pots and jars. "Oops!" they said over and over again. "Sorry!" "Watch out!" "My fault!"

Though he knew it was impossible, he could have sworn the windows were shrinking.

So when at last he'd finished his share of the chores, Marcus didn't curl up in a corner with his Nintendo. Instead, he set off for the beach with his mother. He couldn't stay put—not in a haunted trailer that smelled like sweaty gym clothes. At least there would be fresh air at the beach, even if it was fresh air full of sand and Frisbees.

Luckily, there were signs pointing in the right direction—otherwise Marcus and Holly might have got lost. Holly said she didn't recognize anything. All the old landmarks had disappeared, swallowed up by row upon row of trailers. At first the trailers were small and dilapidated. Then Marcus noticed a change; as he and Holly drew closer to the sea, the trailers became bigger and flashier, with satellite dishes and screened porches and basketball hoops. Some had flower boxes under their windows. People had set up picnic tables and picket fences.

But the most lavish trailers of all were at the very

edge of the beach. The Bradshaws couldn't believe their eyes when they reached the park's dress circle, where the richest tourists had parked their luxury cars on massive lots. There were two-storied trailers with Juliet balconies and carports, waterslides and plastic hedges, portable kiddie pools and Astroturf lawns that had been rolled out like rugs. There were blow-up gazebos and fold-out tennis courts. There were people lolling on deck chairs under striped umbrellas, sipping icy drinks served to them by servants in uniform.

"Wow," Marcus said reverently. "I wish we were staying *here*."

Holly opened her mouth. Before she could speak, however, one of the deck chair people suddenly sat bolt upright and cried, "Holly? Holly Bradshaw? Is that *you*?"

The Bradshaws stopped in their tracks, staring in amazement at a plump little woman with piled-up hair, jeweled sunglasses, and very long polished fingernails.

"It's Coco!" the woman continued. "Coco della Robbia! Don't you remember me? You haven't changed a *bit*!"

3.
An old friend

At first Holly couldn't remember Coco, who had to explain that they'd met years before, as children.

"It was right here at Diamond Beach," Coco recalled. "You were older than me, and you had a sequined bikini and bubble gum–flavored lip gloss. I was *so* envious, because I was wearing my sister's old swimsuit. It had a purple hippo on it."

"Oh, yes! The purple hippo!" Holly exclaimed. "I remember now!"

"What about the crabs? Do you remember feeding the crabs?" asked Coco.

"Of course!" said Holly. "Do *you* remember when Jake sat on the jellyfish?"

Both women shrieked with laughter. The other

people in deck chairs glared at them.

"Who's Jake?" Marcus wanted to know.

"Oh, Jake was one of our friends," Holly told him. "Jake was the loveliest boy. Wasn't he, Coco?"

"He sure was. He was *gorgeous*."

"I had such a crush on Jake," Holly admitted. "I wrote him a letter when I got home, but he never replied."

"He never came back to Diamond Beach, either," Coco said regretfully. "I've been here every summer since then, and he's never shown up. I was always hoping that he would. I was always hoping that *you* would, Holly. And you did!" Coco beamed up at the Bradshaws. "And you brought your family as well! Or is this just a friend?"

"This is my son Marcus," Holly replied. "I'm divorced."

"Oh, so is my husband," Coco said comfortably, patting the empty deck chair beside her. "Why don't you both sit down and have a drink with me? We've got so much to talk about."

Holly and Marcus exchanged glances. Then they looked at the golden strip of sand that was barely visible beneath all the towels and umbrellas and milling bodies. "Well," said Holly in a hesitant tone, "I'd love to, but I promised to show Marcus the beach. . . ."

"Oh, no!" Coco shuddered. "Not the beach! It's

12

so dirty and crowded! I never set foot on the *beach* anymore!"

Holly blinked. "But—"

"You don't *need* the beach," Coco went on. "Not with all the amazing computer programs these days. You can go scuba diving no matter where you are!" She waved at the palatial trailer behind her, which had a pop-up second story and three satellite dishes. "My stepchildren are in there right now, on their laptops, surfing or water-skiing or deep-sea fishing—"

"I'd like to do that," Marcus interrupted. "I'd like to go inside your trailer."

"Well, of course you would!" Coco jumped to her feet, wrapping herself in a filmy pink robe. "What was I thinking of? Come on in and I'll give you a tour! My husband's *very* proud of this trailer. He's always tinkering with it."

As she moved toward the trailer's front door, taking tiny steps in her high-heeled sandals, Coco explained that her husband was a techno-wizard who liked inventing things. "You may have heard of him," she chirped. "His name is Sterling Huckstepp."

Holly's eyes widened. "As in Huckstepp Electronics?" she asked.

"That's the one," said Coco. "He's very clever."

She led the Bradshaws along a vinyl pathway, up a flight of fake-marble stairs, and into a small collapsible entrance hall. The walls were covered with mirrors that could be pulled down like roller blinds; from the ceiling hung a disposable chandelier made of crystallized mineral salt. ("It's completely soluble," Coco revealed. "When you're packing up to go, you just wash it down the drain.") Under this chandelier stood a little white robot with the smooth, triangular, almost featureless head of a praying mantis. It had stubby hydraulic fingers and caterpillar treads on its feet.

Coco addressed it imperiously.

"Prot," she instructed, "bring us some iced tea, the bowl of cashews, diced ham with cheese, lemonade, and three glasses."

"Yes, ma'am," the robot buzzed. Then it spun around and rammed straight into one of the walls before reversing, adjusting its coordinates, and trying again.

This time it managed to pass through a doorway without banging into anything.

"I'm afraid Prot is one of Sterling's prototypes," Coco explained fretfully. "Sterling likes to test out his early models at home, but sometimes they don't work very well."

"Goodness!" Holly was amazed. "Would you look at that, Marcus? A talking robot!"

"Cool," said Marcus.

"He's a pest, I'm afraid. More trouble than he's

worth." Coco suddenly brightened as a gray Persian cat slunk into the vestibule. "And here's my little Choo-choo," she purred, pouncing on the cat. "*She's* not clumsy. She's Mommy's little girl, aren't you, angel? Yes, she is. She's a good little girl. . . ."

It was obvious that Coco loved cats. Her living room was full of cat statues, cat cushions, cat lamps, cat paintings, cat books, and cat hair. Four real cats were lolling around on the overstuffed couch and matching ottomans. There were photographs of the same cats sitting on the mantelpiece—which was made of plastic, though it looked like stone.

Apart from the fireplace and the cats, everything in the room was pink, including the curtains, cushions, and carpet.

"Where's the TV?" Marcus inquired. "Is it hidden somewhere?"

"It's out the back." Coco waggled her fingers at the rear wall. "In our rumpus room."

"There's a *rumpus room*?" Holly squeaked.

"It's just a little lean-to. You can dismantle it in about ten seconds flat," Coco assured her before turning back to Marcus. "Why don't you go and find the other kids, sweetie? They'll show you how the equipment works. It's no good asking me; I'm hopeless."

"Okay." Marcus was keen to explore the rest of the trailer. "So where *are* the other kids?"

"Heaven knows. Upstairs, probably." Coco waggled her fingers again—at the ceiling this time. "Either that or they're in the gym."

"There's a *gym*?" cried Holly.

"It's just an inflatable thing, like a jumping castle. It comes in a box," Coco replied. To Marcus she said, "Keep looking—you'll find them somewhere. It's only a trailer, after all. It's really not *that* big. . . ."

4.

A new friend

Marcus's first stop was the kitchenette. Here he found Prot trying to open the fridge door, which kept hitting the robot's caterpillar treads and springing shut, over and over and over again.

"Hey, Prot," said Marcus as he came to the rescue, "is there an Xbox in this place?"

"You want eggs?" Prot droned. "In a box?"

"No, no. An *Xbox*. Or a Wii console. Something like that."

"You have a weakened sole? You require a shoe repair?"

Marcus rolled his eyes just as a gruff little voice behind him warned, "It's no good talking to Prot. He never understands *anything*."

Turning, Marcus was surprised to see a small boy in a suit of armor. The armor had been constructed out of tinfoil, flowerpots, kitchen utensils, and computer equipment. The boy underneath it had unruly hair and no front teeth.

"I'm Edison Huckstepp," the boy announced. "Who are you?"

Marcus introduced himself. "Your mom and my mom are friends," he explained. "Your mom said I could look around."

"She's not my mom," Edison said, correcting him. "She's my *stepmom*."

Marcus shrugged. "Whatever," he replied. "So can I have a look around or what?"

"Sure." Edison made for the dining nook. "See that table?" he asked, pointing at a square table with rolled edges. "Well, check out what happens when I push this button."

As Edison pushed—and Marcus watched—the table unfurled like a length of carpet.

"It goes from four people to twelve people," Edison continued. "And if I push *this* button, you get flowers." A holographic centerpiece suddenly appeared on the tabletop: pink roses in a nest of cherry blossoms. "You can change them, too," he added, pressing the wall-mounted button again and again.

The roses flicked off, to be replaced by lilies, then orchids, then peonies, then carnations.

"Yeah, but where are the computer games?" asked Marcus, who wasn't very interested in flowers.

"Upstairs," Edison replied. "I'll show you."

He led Marcus back into the vestibule, where they encountered a fat, balding, red-faced man wearing a vivid Hawaiian shirt. Marcus guessed that this man was probably Sterling Huckstepp.

"Hi, Ed," the man said cheerfully, pausing on his way to the front door. "What are you doing?"

"Hi, Dad." Edison's greeting confirmed Marcus's suspicions; the man definitely *was* Sterling Huckstepp. "I'm going to play a game with Marcus. What are *you* doing?"

"I'm off to show the people next door my new pocket-size barbecue." Sterling Huckstepp waved a small black box at the two boys, then opened it like a book so that two halves of a metal grill fitted neatly together. "See?" he went on. "You can plug it into a dashboard cigarette lighter and stow it away in a glove box!"

"That's great, Dad."

"The grills are detachable. You store the tongs and the spatula underneath." Grinning with delight, Sterling glanced from Edison to Marcus. "Guess how many sausages you can fit on this."

"Umm . . ." Marcus was confused. He didn't know if Sterling meant fat sausages or skinny sausages.

"Four?" Edison hazarded a guess.

19

"Six!" his father cried. "Six sausages or two steaks!"

"Wow," said Marcus.

"Or four chicken drumsticks. Or eight kebabs." Sterling smiled down at his invention. "You can barbecue anything on this baby."

Without another word he departed; the front door banged shut behind his retreating silhouette. Marcus stared after him, openmouthed, but Edison seemed unfazed. "My dad invents things," the younger boy volunteered.

He guided Marcus up a circular metal staircase, which punched its way through an even sturdier metal ceiling before delivering the two boys into an air-conditioned hallway made of canvas. On one side of the hallway were plastic windows hung with frilly pink curtains. On the other side was a series of hard plastic doors, each with a lightweight aluminum knob.

"That's my room," Edison informed Marcus, pointing at the last door in the row. It was shut. "All my games are in there."

Marcus nodded. He followed Edison down the hallway before stopping outside an open door.

"Who's she?" he inquired, staring at the girl in the room next to Edison's. She was a black-haired teenager with a jeweled stud in her nose, wearing lots of tattered Lycra over very short shorts. Her room was hung with dark, brooding posters; she was sprawled across a velvet beanbag chair, muttering into a cell phone.

"That's my sister," Edison declared. "Her name is Newton, but we all call her Newt."

Marcus thought Newt looked interesting. She certainly didn't look like a beach person. "Do you think she'll play a game with us?" he asked.

Edison shook his head. "Nah. She's on the phone."

Marcus suppressed an impatient sigh. "I don't mean right now," he said very slowly and clearly. "I mean when she gets *off* the phone."

Edison gawked at Marcus. "Are you kidding?" the younger boy scoffed. "Newt *never* gets off the phone."

5.
Past and present

"...and she never gets off the phone," Coco said to Holly, who was sitting beside her on the couch. "She spends the whole day in her room, chatting or texting. And when she *does* go out with her friends, half the time she's on the phone to her other friends!" Coco massaged the bridge of her nose, as if she had a headache. "I don't know what to do. It's as if she can't talk face-to-face anymore. She certainly doesn't talk to *me*."

"At least Newt has friends," Holly replied sadly. "Marcus doesn't seem to. He's always on his computer, playing games."

"Oh, he's probably doing that with his friends," Coco assured her in a comforting tone. "You can play online games with other people."

"Yes, but they're not real friends, are they?" Holly objected. "Not like the friends you and I had. That's why I brought him to Diamond Beach—because I remember how easy it was to make friends here." Her forehead puckered as she stared out the living room window, which was angled to give anyone sitting on the Huckstepps' enormous pink couch a perfect view of the ocean. "But it's changed so much," she lamented. "There are so many people here now."

"Which is good for Marcus," Coco chirped, stroking her fattest, fluffiest cat. "With so many people, he's bound to have a bigger choice of friends."

"I guess so." Holly heaved a weary sigh. "The trouble is, even if he does make friends, there's nothing much to do. You just told me yourself that it's too crowded to kick a ball around and too dirty to go swimming. And if there isn't enough wilderness left for a game of stowaways . . ." Trailing off, her eyes misty with nostalgia, she allowed herself a wistful little smile. Then she snapped out of her daze, adding, "Marcus is always telling me that his computer games are better than real life—and I'm beginning to wonder if he's right after all. I mean, just look at this place! It used to be paradise, and now it's awful!"

"It's not so bad," said Coco.

Holly, however, wasn't convinced. "How can you bear it?" she asked. "I bet you can afford any kind of holiday you like. Doesn't it *depress* you, coming here?"

"Oh, no!" Coco looked shocked. "I love coming here."

"Why?"

"Because it makes me happy." Seeing Holly's puzzled expression, Coco tried to explain. "The first time I visited Diamond Beach, I thought it was perfect. And whenever I come back, I remember how I felt the first time. All these memories pop into my head. Like Jake's treasure map, or the dancing dog. Or that little old lady who used to play us nursery rhymes on her antique phonograph—remember her?"

Holly nodded. "They were the prettiest songs I'd ever heard."

"That's just what I thought!"

"And the weather was perfect," Holly said, reminiscing. "And the sea was always warm."

"And no one argued."

"And there were no flies or mosquitoes." Holly gave an embarrassed little laugh. "Sometimes I think I'm delusional. I keep telling myself that it can't have been *that* great. But it was, wasn't it? You think so, too."

"Of course," said Coco. "It was perfect. Everyone felt the same. Jake didn't want to leave. He packed a knapsack and told me he was going to run off and hide when his family went home." She clicked her tongue and shook her head. "I don't think his parents were very nice to him," she concluded.

"They weren't," Holly agreed. "He told me they weren't. So did he run off and hide in the end?"

"I don't know. We left before his family did. And he wasn't here when we came back the next summer." It was Coco's turn to indulge in a nostalgic smile. "My mother always loved this place," she said. "Sterling and I used to bring her every year before she died. And Sterling doesn't mind where we go, as long as he gets to tinker with his trailer. He loves to show off all the new gadgets he's installed to make it better. He's a handyman at heart—that's why his first wife bailed. She had champagne tastes, but there was nothing for him to *do* with himself at the Ritz Hotel in Paris. She didn't seem to realize that you can live the high life everywhere, if you try hard enough."

"So it's the memories that draw you back here?" Holly asked sympathetically.

Coco shook her head. "Oh, no!" she rejoined. "It's because the service here is so good. And so *cheap*. Diamond Beach isn't like the city, you know." She began to count off the local attractions on her lavishly manicured fingers. "There's a fabulous beautician, and an excellent massage therapist, and a hairdresser, and a pet groomer, and a whole tribe of personal trainers, and a really nice jeweler who sells door to door. Not to mention the tradesmen, who are desperate for work. Nobody says 'I can't make it for another three weeks' in *this* neck of the woods, let me tell you!"

She was cut short as Prot hummed into the room, bearing a pink lacquered tray laden with (among other things) three pairs of spectacles.

Coco gave a little shriek.

"For goodness' sake!" she quavered. "What's *that*?"

"Some mice teeth, a bowl of cash, used ice ham, with cheese lemonade and three glasses," Prot replied in a toneless voice.

"Oh, you stupid machine!" Coco's voice became shrill and waspish. "I asked for some *iced tea*, the bowl of *cashews*, diced ham with cheese, lemonade, and three *drinking glasses*." She threw a cushion at the robot. "Get out! Go on! And take that hideous stuff with you!"

Prot's upper portion swiveled around on its caterpillar treads, which began to reverse out of the room.

"And don't bother coming back!" Coco yelled. Then she turned to Holly. "Sterling insists on encumbering me with every harebrained invention he comes up with. The freeven was bad enough, but this thing is worse."

"The freeven?" Holly echoed, at sea.

"It was a combined freezer–microwave oven. Sterling wanted a vending machine that would deliver a roast dinner at the push of a button. But all he got was a great big mess." Coco pushed the cat off her lap as she stood up. "I've told him time and again I don't want a robot maid. You can hire local staff at Diamond

Beach for *practically nothing*. He won't listen, though. So I end up doing everything myself." Suddenly her pinched expression was replaced by a brilliant smile. "Maybe we should just forget about the lemonade," she concluded, "and have something a little stronger instead . . . ?"

6.
Ghost hunters

In Edison's room Marcus was admiring the bunk beds, which could be pulled out of the wall. Every fixture and fitting was either retractable or collapsible, including the wardrobe. A brightly colored box in one corner could be endlessly reconfigured. It could be folded into a chair, a bedside cabinet, a storage chest, a stepladder, a desk, or a partition.

"This is fantastic," Marcus said with a sigh. "I wish *we* lived here."

Edison shrugged. "It's okay, I guess," he said. "But I'd rather live in a teepee. Or an igloo."

"You should try living in our trailer." Marcus pulled a face. "It's really old and smelly."

"Eww."

"Yeah. Some old lady used to own it. I think she might have died in there." Grimacing, Marcus examined Edison's Nintendo. "It's probably haunted."

"Really?" The younger boy perked up. "Why?"

"Oh, the cupboards keep popping open," Marcus observed. "And the whole place feels funny. Like it's shrinking in on you."

"Wow!" Edison was growing more and more excited. "Can I go see it?"

"There's nothing to see. It's just a dirty old trailer."

"Oh, *please*?" Edison whined. "If it's haunted, I wanna see it."

"Why?" Marcus asked, trying to be patient. "You can't see ghosts in the daytime."

"Maybe I can, if I use my infrared goggles." Edison plunged into his wardrobe, emerging seconds later with something that looked like a pair of strap-on binoculars. "Dad made these," he announced. "If they work, we might be able to *catch* the ghost."

"With what?" Marcus's tone was skeptical, to say the least. "A jam jar?"

Edison frowned, chewing on his bottom lip as he surveyed his possessions. "I guess a butterfly net wouldn't work," he mused.

"Not in a million years." Marcus spoke firmly. "And neither would a mousetrap. Or a mosquito zapper."

"We've got an infrared camera, but it's at home," Edison continued. Suddenly he brightened. "Hey!

You know what? Newt's got some spray-on green hair color!"

"Huh?"

"If I see the ghost through my goggles, I can spray it with green stuff! And then *you* might see it, too!"

Marcus swallowed a snort of derision. "You think hair color is going to stick to an invisible ghost?" he said. "You've gotta be kidding."

But Edison ignored him. The younger boy picked up a backpack and began to stuff it with supplies: goggles, a flashlight, a pair of scissors, a half-eaten granola bar. "We'll get some flour from the kitchen," he said. "If you put flour on the floor, sometimes ghosts will leave footprints. I saw that in a movie once."

"Edison, that trailer is filthy enough. My mom will have a *fit* if you put flour all over the floor. . . ."

Edison, however, was already charging across the threshold, shedding bits of armor as he went. Marcus followed him into the next room, where Newt was still lolling on the beanbag with her phone pressed to her ear.

"What is it?" she asked, scowling at her brother.

"Hey, Newt!" he cried. "You wanna see a haunted trailer?"

"Nope."

Edison was amazed. "But I thought you liked ghosts!" he protested.

Newt rolled her eyes as she covered the mouthpiece of her phone with one hand.

"What have I told you about coming in here?" she said sternly. She was aiming all her comments at Edison, as if Marcus didn't exist. "You know perfectly well you shouldn't come in here without an invitation. Now get lost."

"Can I have your green hair dye? The stuff in the spray can?"

"No."

"Please?"

"*No!*" the girl snapped. "Go buy your own hair dye!"

Edison shrugged. Then he turned to Marcus and said, "Shaving cream is probably just as good."

"I'll count to five," Newt growled. "One. Two. Three . . ."

"You are *so* going to regret not coming," Edison warned her.

"And you are *so* going to regret not going. Especially if I have to get up and make you," was his sister's testy response.

"Come on, Edison." Marcus felt like a complete fool. He tugged at the younger boy's arm. "Leave her alone, eh? She's not interested."

With another shrug, Edison gave up. As he stomped out of the room, his sister uncovered the mouthpiece of her phone.

"This place is bad enough," she muttered to the person at the other end of the line, "without total strangers bursting in on me. . . ."

Marcus cringed.

"I guess your sister really hates it here, huh?" he said on his way downstairs. "I don't blame her. I'd rather be at home, too."

"Really?" Edison was obviously taken aback. "Why? Do you have a dog at home?"

"No."

"A tree house?"

"No."

"A ride-on mower?"

"Don't be stupid."

"Well, what's so good about your place, then?"

"Nothing," Marcus said impatiently. "I just don't like the beach, that's all."

Edison pondered this remark for a moment, but couldn't seem to make much sense of it.

"If your trailer's really haunted, you'll have a *great* time here," he pointed out with the air of someone offering comfort. "It'll be the best holiday you ever had. Especially if we manage to catch that ghost."

Then he turned on his heel and went in the bathroom to look for shaving cream.

7.

A buried secret

It was a long walk from the beach to the Bradshaws' trailer. Marcus and Edison trudged on and on, their eyes screwed up against the glare. They had to dodge a lot of balls and Frisbees and puddles of melted ice cream. Dogs were barking, and radios were blaring. Onions sizzled on barbecues. Pigeons and seagulls strutted around, pecking at all the squashed chips and discarded wrappers that littered the landscape.

At first the two boys passed crowds of sandy people carrying wet towels and surfboards. Gradually, however, the sand disappeared. Marcus saw one little kid making a dirt castle while her mother sunbathed on the hood of the family car. Nearby, an old man had set up a deck chair and a beach umbrella so he could sit and stare at another old man doing exactly the same thing across the road.

By the time Marcus and Edison reached their destination, they had been joined by a small white dog wearing water wings and swimming goggles.

"Shoo!" said Marcus, flapping his hands at the dog. "Go home! Go on! *Get!*"

But the dog wouldn't leave him alone. It trotted after him into the trailer, where it began to sniff around suspiciously.

Edison was sniffing, too.

"Wow," he said, wrinkling his nose. "This place smells just like my grandad."

"You think?" Marcus was surprised. "*I* think it smells like sweaty gym clothes. Does your grandad smell like sweaty gym clothes?"

"No," Edison replied. He dumped his backpack onto the floor. "It's not very big, is it?" he added, gazing around. "There isn't much room to hide a skeleton."

"A *skeleton*?" Marcus gaped at him. "What skeleton?"

"That old lady's skeleton." Yanking open a cupboard, Edison hunkered down to peer inside. "Did you check for hidden wall panels?"

Marcus snorted. "You're nuts," he said. "Why would an old lady's skeleton be stuffed inside our wall?"

"Who knows?" Edison shrugged. "Maybe she was

34

murdered. Maybe that's why she's haunting the place."

Marcus shook his head in a long-suffering way as Edison kept poking around in search of bones, or bloodstains, or paranormal activity. Meanwhile, the little dog followed its nose along the kickboards and beneath the table, where it sat down and gave a sharp yap.

"Swimming goggles can't be good for dogs," Marcus observed, eyeing the animal doubtfully. "Maybe we should take them off."

Edison didn't seem to hear. "Hey, Marcus," he inquired, "do these seats lift up?"

"Huh? What?"

Edison explained that in *his* family's trailer, all the bench seats were storage units. By raising their hinged, padded tops, you exposed the cache of flippers or picnic rugs or fishing equipment underneath.

Marcus pursed his lips.

"These are extra beds," he replied. "You take the cushions off at the back so you can lie down."

"Yeah, but have you checked *under* the cushions?" Edison wanted to know. When Marcus shook his head, the other boy grinned. "We should take a look. Maybe the skeleton's in one of those seats. . . ."

The seats wouldn't budge, though. Not at first, anyway. Marcus tugged and strained and nothing happened.

"I told you," he said, panting. "They don't open up."

35

"Wait . . . hang on. . . ." Edison wriggled under the table so he could examine the lower halves of the two benches. Luckily, he was small enough to squeeze into such a restricted space. "Just pass me the flashlight, will you?"

Marcus shuddered; he knew how dark and greasy it was under the table. As he fished around in the younger boy's backpack, the little white dog began to lick Edison's face.

"Aha—stop—get off!" Edison giggled, then gasped. "I knew it!" he cried.

"What?"

"There's a hook-type thing! It's holding the seat down!" After a moment's silence, Edison gave a grunt. "It's really stiff."

"Here. Let me," said Marcus.

But Edison needed help with the dog, not the latch. "He won't leave me alone," Edison explained. So Marcus had to eject their little white visitor as Edison fiddled with the rusty hinge.

"Go home," Marcus ordered, dumping the dog outside. "Go on! Get!"

But it wouldn't move. It just stood on the front steps, wagging its tail.

"Gotcha!" yelped Edison. When Marcus glanced around, he saw that the other boy was on his knees, opening one of the benches like a toy box.

"You don't live here," Marcus informed the dog

before slamming the door in its face. He felt guilty when he heard it scratch and whine.

"Hey, Marcus." Edison was peering into the deep, dark hole he'd just uncovered. "Guess what."

"You've found your skeleton," Marcus replied. He was joking, of course.

Edison, however, took him seriously.

"No. At least . . . I dunno." He looked up. "It depends what you've got in your cellar, I guess."

8.

"This is crazy. . . ."

It was true. Edison had discovered a cellar.

"That's—that's impossible," Marcus protested. He stared in disbelief at a long, narrow flight of wooden steps that descended into some kind of musty, shadowy, subterranean region. "This trailer is on wheels," he croaked. "It *can't* have a cellar."

Edison peered downstairs. "It sure looks like a cellar to me," he said.

"But—"

"It's big, isn't it? You're lucky. We don't have a cellar in our trailer." While Edison rooted around in his backpack, Marcus stood gawking, unable to believe his eyes. Was it an optical illusion? Was it done with mirrors? How could there possibly be a cellar when the trailer was sitting on wheels, off the ground?

Could Holly have parked over an abandoned cellar and not have noticed it?

"We should get another flashlight," Edison remarked crisply. He had strapped on his infrared goggles but hadn't dragged them over his eyes. "Is there one around here somewhere?"

"I—uh—yeah." Marcus couldn't help sounding dazed. "Are you—I mean, are we going down to have a look?"

"Of course!" Edison seemed taken aback. "Don't you *want* to?"

"I guess. . . ."

"We should take something to drink, as well," Edison solemnly recommended. "Just in case we get thirsty."

He waited until Marcus had retrieved a flashlight from one of the kitchen cupboards. There were no sodas, but Marcus found a bottle of water instead. He stuffed it into the backpack, which was now hanging off Edison's shoulders. Outside, the little white dog was still whining and scratching.

"Okay," said Marcus, "I'll go first."

"No, I will."

"No, *I* will." Marcus refused to give an inch. "It's my trailer, and I'm the oldest. I'll go first."

So it was Marcus who ended up in front, with Edison close behind him. Very slowly and carefully they advanced down the stairs, which creaked under their weight and wobbled slightly with every footstep. By the time they reached solid ground, they had already switched on their flashlights. The wavering beams flickered across a stone floor, a vaulted ceiling, and damp brick walls hung with cobwebs.

"Oh, wow." Edison's tone was reverent. "This is *fantastic*. It's like a dungeon."

"But what is it?" Marcus demanded faintly. "Why is it here?"

"Hey! Look at that!" Edison pointed. The beam from his flashlight had come to rest on a closed door with a shiny brass knob. "Let's see where that goes!"

"Hang on," said Marcus, whose own flashlight beam had picked out another, identical door. The two doors were placed side by side.

There was nothing else in the room, just the doors and the cobwebs.

"This is crazy," Marcus faltered. He felt as if he were in a dream—or perhaps a computer game. Lots of computer games were played in virtual dungeons.

"Which one looks safer to you?" Edison asked him. On receiving no answer, he nodded at the left-hand door. "Let's try that one."

He darted forward eagerly before Marcus could pull him back.

"Wait!" Marcus shrilled. But it was too late. Edison

had already turned his chosen knob and yanked open the door attached to it.

Instantly, the air was filled with carnival music.

The two boys stared. Their jaws dropped in perfect unison. Beyond the threshold lay a vivid, sunlit amusement park. There were striped tents and fluttering flags and rides and booths and banners, but no people. No one was shrieking on the roller coaster or chomping on cotton candy. No one was throwing hoops at targets or buying novelty baseball caps.

Though it was full of noise and movement, the entire park was empty of life.

"Oh, *wow* . . . ," Edison breathed.

Together he and Marcus stepped through the door onto a smooth stretch of green lawn. To their right, an enormous carousel was spinning on its mirrored axis, pumping out a cheerful, chiming song. To their left, a row of painted clown heads swung from side to side in front of a wall hung with alluring prizes: plush toys, Kewpie dolls, inflatable aliens. Ahead was an arena filled with bumper cars; beyond that stood a slowly revolving Ferris wheel. Wherever Marcus looked, there were flashing lights or moving parts or happy, painted faces.

Everything was bright and clean and colorful under a cloudless blue sky.

"This is crazy," Marcus repeated, his voice hushed.

"Yeah," Edison agreed, "but it's *great*."

And then, just as Marcus opened his mouth to suggest that perhaps they shouldn't stay very long, the six restless clown heads swung around to smile at Edison.

"Hello, Edison!" they chorused. "Do you want to win a stuffed blue gorilla?"

9.
"Hey, Edison!"

Suddenly the whole fairground sprang to life.

"I'd love to go home with you, Edison!" the stuffed blue gorilla pleaded.

"Edison! Oh, Edison! Please come for a gallop!" neighed the pastel ponies on the carousel.

"Hey, Edison! Over here!" an enormous voice boomed. Glancing around, Marcus saw that the octopus ride was beckoning with its long, steely arms, each of which had a two-seater car attached to it. "Come on!" urged the octopus. "You'll have a wonderful time!"

Marcus swallowed.

"I bet we've been gassed," he said hoarsely. "There must be a leak in the gas bottle under the stove." Not that he could smell gas—only fried fat and hot sugar. "We've got to get out of here," he insisted. "I think we're having hallucinations."

Edison, however, wasn't listening. His face was flushed and his eyes were bright.

"Oh, man!" he exclaimed. "Those bumper cars are *so cool*!"

"Edison—" Marcus began. But he stopped when something tugged at his T-shirt.

Looking down, he nearly had a heart attack. A plywood policeman was grinning up at him with painted teeth. The policeman held a sign that said YOU MUST BE THIS TALL TO GET ON.

"You're too big for these rides," the policeman announced, plucking at Marcus's T-shirt with his uplifted measuring hand. "But Edison isn't. Edison can stay."

"Get off!" Marcus gave the creepy little thing a shove. "Don't touch me!"

At that moment, it occurred to Marcus that you shouldn't be able to touch a hallucination. Then he found himself wondering how he and Edison could be having the *same* hallucination—unless Edison himself wasn't real.

"Hey, Edison," said Marcus, whirling around to see if he could grab his friend's arm. It was too late, though. Edison was already streaking toward the bumper cars, his legs pumping wildly.

"Hey! Wait! Edison!" yelled Marcus, leaping forward. The little plywood policeman tried to hold him back. But even Marcus had more than enough muscle to deal with a sheet of painted wood. He slapped the policeman aside just as the clowns revealed that they weren't disembodied heads on boxes after all.

One by one they stood up, displaying their glossy fiberglass shoulders, arms, chests, stomachs, hips . . .

Marcus pounded past them on his way to the bumper cars. *"Edison!"* he screamed, wide-eyed with fear. The clowns followed him, as clumsy and hesitant as newborn foals on their long, skinny, stiff-jointed legs. Behind them swarmed a teeming mob of plush toys, Kewpie dolls, and inflatable aliens, all of whom had wriggled off their hooks and dropped to the ground so that they could chase Marcus.

"Edison! Come back!" Marcus cried. But Edison had already jumped into a shiny red bumper car. There must have been about a dozen cars sliding around in their fenced arena, which Marcus reached just ahead of the first plush animal. He slammed into a brightly colored perimeter fence, then stretched out an arm toward the younger boy.

The bumper cars, however, weren't about to let go of Edison. Cursing and muttering, they jostled their way between Marcus and his friend, nudging Edison's bright red car until it had been pushed to the other side of the arena. Trying to catch up with Edison was impossible; every time Marcus moved, the cars moved along with him, making sure that Edison was well out of his reach even as they plowed into each other. "Ow!" the cars snapped. "Look out!" "Get off!" "Watch where you're going!"

They seemed very bad-tempered.

"Edison!" Marcus bawled, trying to make himself heard over the jangling carnival music—which grew louder and louder as he raised his voice. Edison was laughing. The bumper cars were snarling and swearing. Sideshow patter was blaring through a loudspeaker: "Step right up, Edison! Try your luck and win a buck. . . ."

By this time the plush animals had caught up with Marcus. He had a blue gorilla wrapped around one leg and a snow leopard hanging off one arm. The clowns were spitting Ping-Pong balls at his head. The inflatable aliens were arming themselves with hoops and popguns. Off in the distance, a crowd of gibbering fluorescent skeletons had spilled out of the ghost train.

"Edison!" Marcus bellowed. "You can't stay here! It's a trick! It's not real! *Edison!*"

He swatted away the fluffy pink kangaroo that was trying to plaster itself to his face. Plush animals were piling up around his body like a multicolored snowdrift; there were sheep and tigers and dolphins and zebras and ducks and bees and teddy bears, all snuggling up to each other.

It occurred to him that if he didn't move, he was going to suffocate under half a ton of fake fur. So he retreated a few steps, kicking kittens and punching puppies.

That was when he spotted the Ferris wheel, which was rolling across the grass toward him.

"Bye, Edison!" Marcus squawked before dashing away at top speed. He didn't think twice. He didn't look back. He simply charged along, shaking off fluffy animals and telling himself that this was all a bad dream—that the Edison he'd left in the bumper car didn't really exist.

Then a dreadful thought struck him: would the exit still be there?

Oh, please, he prayed, *please, please let it still be there!*

And it was. As he careered past the cotton candy stand, he caught sight of a shadowy rectangle piercing the brick wall up ahead. Marcus recognized this wedge of darkness as the door to the cellar when he spotted a rickety staircase just beyond its battered wooden frame. So he swerved toward it, dimly conscious of the heavy rumble pursuing him.

He was short of breath. His heart was thumping. His legs were hurting. On finally reaching the threshold, he threw himself across it in a diving tackle.

WHOMP! The door slammed shut.

Marcus lay on the cellar floor. "Aah . . . aah . . . aah," he panted. Everything was dark and silent. He could smell only damp earth and mold.

It took him a moment to realize that he'd dropped his flashlight somewhere inside his hallucination.

10.

Getting help

Marcus didn't dare open the cellar door again. Instead, he staggered upstairs, looking for Edison. Surely the *real* Edison hadn't been left behind in that bright red bumper car? Surely he was lying unconscious near the gas leak, gripped by hallucinations of his own?

But the trailer was empty. There was no smell of gas. And when Marcus checked outside, he couldn't see Edison anywhere.

The only familiar face he *could* see belonged to the little white dog.

"Oh, man . . . ," Marcus groaned as the white dog yipped and grinned and danced about. It followed him all the way back to the beach, never once stopping to lift its leg or sniff at a car tire. Even though

Marcus ran the whole distance, from one end of the park to the other, his little white companion somehow managed to keep up.

By the time Marcus reached the Huckstepps' place, he was shaking and sweating. "Is Edison home?" he demanded when Prot answered his knock.

"You are not authorized to receive that information," the robot replied.

"Edison!" Marcus shouted, desperate to hear the younger boy's voice. *"Hey, Edison!"*

"Please wait here," said Prot. But Marcus ignored this request. He lurched past the robot into the vestibule. *"Edison!"* he cried. *"Can you hear me?"*

"No dogs," the robot warned. "No dogs allowed." At that very instant, a cat emerged from the living room; there was a volley of angry barks, followed by a feline hiss of outrage.

Marcus grabbed the dog before it could launch itself at the cat.

"Choo-choo?" Coco's high-pitched call drifted into the vestibule. "Darling? What's wrong?"

"No dogs allowed," Prot repeated.

"I know that! I heard you already!" Marcus grappled with the dog, shoving it back outside just as Coco entered the room. Prot shut the front door so quickly that Marcus nearly lost a hand.

"What's going on?" asked Coco. "Was that a dog I heard?"

"Don't worry. It's gone," Marcus assured her. His breathing was still ragged. "Is Edison here?"

"Edison?" she said vaguely, as if she'd never heard of him. Then she addressed the robot. "Is Edison here?"

"Edison left the trailer exactly forty-three minutes ago, using this exit," Prot reported. "He has not yet returned."

"Are you sure?" Marcus pressed. "Are you *absolutely positive*?"

"What's the matter?" Holly interrupted from the bathroom doorway. For a split second Marcus didn't recognize her, because her face was caked with green goo and her hair was tucked into a shower cap. A pink towel had been draped around her shoulders. "Are you all right, Marcus?"

"Edison didn't come back." Marcus spoke in a strangled whisper. "He—he must still be down there."

"Down where?" said Holly.

Marcus swallowed. He sensed that no one would believe what he was about to say.

"Down in the cellar of our trailer," he croaked.

There was a brief, stunned silence. The two women stared at him.

"I know it sounds crazy, but there's a cellar under our trailer," Marcus continued. "We found it. And we went through one of the doors at the bottom of the stairs, and there was this fairground full of talking rides, and the bumper cars kidnapped Edison, and I had to get out or I would have been squashed by a runaway Ferris wheel. . . ."

He trailed off as Coco glanced nervously at his mother. But Holly didn't look frightened, astonished, or even mildly concerned. She just smiled and nodded.

"That sounds like a nice game, sweetie," she said. "I'm glad you're having so much fun."

"But—"

"I'm kind of busy right now, though. When I'm done in the bathroom, you can tell me all about it. . . ."

"Wait! Mom!"

Holly, however, wouldn't listen. She suddenly vanished, leaving a heavy herbal scent in the air.

Coco pursued her with many anxious words of advice. "Now don't just peel that off, Holly—you have to *soak* it first. Let me do it, or you'll ruin your nails. . . ."

Defeated, Marcus hurried upstairs.

"Hey, Newt!" he yelled. "You've got to help me!" Knowing that Edison's sister wouldn't want to be pestered—and that she would scoff at the very idea of a talking bumper car—he didn't mention fairgrounds at all. "Edison's stuck!" he exclaimed, bursting into her room. "He's trapped under our trailer! You've got to come quick!"

Newt was still lying on her beanbag chair. When

Marcus appeared, she simply rolled over to face the wall.

"It's nothing," she muttered into her phone. "It's just one of Edison's stupid friends. . . ."

"Hey!" Marcus didn't have time for diplomacy. "Your mom won't listen! We've got to help your brother!"

"Go away," she said crossly. "I'm on the phone."

Marcus stood for a moment, gazing helplessly at the back of her head. He didn't want to be a nuisance. He could sympathize with her point of view. But something was very wrong and he couldn't fix it by himself.

So he snatched the phone from her ear.

"Hey!" She whipped around. "Give that back!"

"You've got to come," he replied. "Edison needs you."

"Give that back *right now!*" she roared, throwing herself at him. Marcus retreated. She lunged again.

Then he turned on his heel and ran, heading downstairs and out the front door.

11.

Back to the cellar

As Marcus burst out of the Hucksteps' trailer, Newt was close on his heels. But her bare feet slowed her down. So, despite Marcus's growing fatigue, the distance between them gradually lengthened.

He didn't want it to lengthen too much. He was hoping that by staying just ahead of her, he would lure her all the way back to his own trailer—where he would show her the fairground in the cellar. Maybe *she* would know what to do about Edison. Because Marcus was stumped.

"You drop that *now*!" Newt screamed. Marcus, however, kept running. He soon left behind all the Astroturf lawns and expensive European cars. The trailers got smaller as the crowds grew, until clots of sunburned tourists started getting in his way. To avoid them, he dodged down a side street, narrowly missing the laundry lines and volleyball nets that were stretched across his path. He skidded on a spilled slushie and jumped over an inflatable pool. He passed a makeshift playground where some kids had constructed a slide out of a surfboard and a swing out of a hammock.

Behind him, Newt and the white dog jostled for position.

"*I'm going to kill you!*" Newt warned Marcus, her voice cracking. By this time she was red-faced and pouring sweat. With her pale skin and layers of black Lycra, she looked grossly out of place, like a bat in a dovecote. "You are *so* going to pay for this!"

In the end, though, Marcus didn't pay for anything. Because when Newt finally stumbled into his trailer, she was so exhausted that she could only collapse onto the nearest bench, gasping and moaning.

Marcus checked the other bench, which he'd slammed shut earlier. Sure enough, when he lifted the seat, he saw that the cellar was still there.

"Hey, Newt," he piped up. "Do you want to see this? You'll freak, I promise."

"It stinks in here," was her unexpected rejoinder. After gulping down a few more lungfuls of air, she added, "It smells like cat pee."

"Cat pee?" Marcus was puzzled. "*I* think it smells like sweaty gym clothes."

But Newt ignored him. "And what is that for?" she continued, staring at the little white dog. "Did *you* do that?"

"No," said Marcus.

"You shouldn't put goggles on a dog! It's cruel!"

"I know," said Marcus. "I didn't."

"Poor thing . . ." Newt reached for the dog, which didn't try to run away. When she picked it up, it licked her face enthusiastically. "What a cute little fella," she said as she peeled off its goggles.

"Uh . . . yeah," Marcus agreed. "But you should probably take a look at this."

"I'm more of a dog person than a cat person. Not like Mom." Having removed the dog's water wings, Newt glared at Marcus. "Now—are you going to gimme that phone?" she challenged. "Or do you want me to punch your head in?"

Marcus wasn't about to put up a fight. He raised his sweaty hands in submission. "You can have it! You can have the phone!" he promised, waving it at her. "Just as soon as you check out the cellar!"

"Huh?"

"There's a cellar under this seat." Marcus pointed.

"Really?" Newt seemed surprised, though not stunned. "You should tell my dad," she remarked. "He's trying to build a wine cellar underneath *our* trailer."

"Edison's down there," Marcus continued

doggedly, "and he won't come out. Not for me, any-way. So I figured he might listen to you."

Newt sniffed. "Oh, he'll listen to me, all right," she growled. Then she stood up and approached Marcus, still nursing the little white dog.

Marcus stepped aside so she could peer downstairs.

"Mmph." After a moment's pause, she cleared her throat. *"Hey, Edison!"* she shouted. *"If you're waiting to jump out and scare me, don't! Or Dad's going to know what you did to his portable wind turbine!"*

No one answered.

"He probably can't hear you," Marcus offered at last, in a very small voice. "He's behind a closed door. . . ."

Newt snorted impatiently. "You guys are such jerks," she snapped before scrambling over the side of the bench and stomping down into the cellar. Marcus followed her, using the pale glow of her illuminated phone screen to light his way. He was worried that she might hurt herself in the dimness. He was also concerned about the little white dog, which remained tucked under her arm. And he wanted to warn her about the Ferris wheel.

"Uh . . . Newt?" he began, then caught his breath.

There were now *three* doors at the foot of the stairs, and one of them was a cat flap.

Or was it a doggie door?

"Okay," Newt said to him. "So where's Edison?"

"Um . . ." Marcus hesitated. "Well, he *was* through there, but—"

"Edison!" Newt yelled, interrupting Marcus. *"You'd better come out!"*

"But last time I was down here, there was no cat flap," Marcus finished anxiously. "So I don't know if he's still behind the same door or not."

"Edison!"

"This is weird. It doesn't make sense. You'd better be careful."

Newt, however, wasn't the least bit concerned. She barged through the door Marcus had indicated, threatening her brother with every terrible fate she could think of. But her fierce harangue was cut short by the blast of noise that greeted her as she stepped across the threshold.

She froze so abruptly that Marcus ran into the back of her.

"Newton!" a girl's voice cried from somewhere in the heaving crowd that confronted them. "Newton Huckstepp! You *came!*"

12.

The world's best party

*O*oompa-ooompa-ooompa. The throb of a heavy bass note was audible under the roar of voices and the clink of glasses. Strobe lights flashed. Bodies writhed.

Marcus spotted a revolving mirror ball and said faintly, "This isn't an amusement park. . . ."

But Newt wasn't listening. "Is that *you*, Hayley?" she squealed.

She was addressing a blonde girl in a very short, very shiny red dress as the girl pushed through a crowd of tightly packed dancers. "Of course it's me!" the girl bellowed, straining to be heard above the noise. "Ben's here, too! And Seamus! And Jess!"

"You're kidding!" Newt peered around. "Where are they?"

"Over there!" The girl pointed, then staggered as someone slammed into her. She laughed. "Come and join us!" she exclaimed. "This is the world's best party!"

She flung out her arm, gesturing at the entire cavernous space. A mist of sweat and smoke hung so thickly in the air that Marcus couldn't make out how high the room was, though he *could* see balcony after balcony rising in tiers above him. The balconies were packed with people and hung with colored lanterns. A giant chandelier sparkled. More people were surging up and down two sweeping flights of stairs.

A curved wall nearby was lined with jewel-colored bottles; Marcus kept catching glimpses of a bar through the press of gleaming, gyrating bodies.

Ooompa-ooompa-ooompa went the music.

"Something's wrong!" he shouted, plucking at Newt's Lycra sleeve. "This shouldn't be here! We ought to leave *right now!*"

But Newt wasn't listening. "Isn't that the drummer from Strep Throat?" she yelled at Hayley. "I *love* that band!"

"Oh, you mean Zeke?" the blonde girl replied. "Yeah, he's here—and so is Vance Vigor!"

"You're *kidding!*" Newt was so excited that she squeezed the little white dog just a bit too hard.

It whined in protest, then growled as Hayley reached for Newt's wrist.

"Is that your dog?" Hayley demanded. "Or is it part of your outfit?"

"Uh . . ." Newt glanced down at the dog vacantly, as if she didn't know how she'd ended up with it. Marcus tried to catch her eye.

"Newt," he said. "Hey, Newt!"

"Oh, I don't believe it!" There was an undertone of scorn in Hayley's voice. "You actually brought your *little brother* with you?"

"I'm not her brother—" Marcus began, but he was shouted down.

"He is *so* underage, Newton!" the blonde girl continued. "He'll have to leave!"

"Yeah, I know." Newt shoved the white dog at Marcus. "Here. Take this. I'm going to hang around for a few minutes."

"No!" Marcus protested. The dog wriggled in his arms, yapping at Hayley. "Newt, don't be stupid!" he cried. "These people aren't real! Vance Vigor's a famous singer—what would he be doing under our trailer?"

Newt, however, was already being dragged away. And when Marcus tried to follow her, the crowd closed in on her retreating back, swallowing her up and barring his progress.

"Newt! Hey, Newt!" he called. *"These aren't your real friends! They can't be!"*

"Okay, son." A giant hand closed around his arm. "Let's go."

Marcus looked up to see a hulking, tattooed bouncer looming over him. This bouncer had a shaved head and wore a tie but no shirt. His muscles were the biggest Marcus had ever laid eyes on outside a computer game.

"No kids in this club," said the bouncer. "You're not old enough. There's alcohol being served." His gaze shifted to the little white dog. "No animals allowed, either," he added.

"But my friend!" Marcus wailed. "I need to talk to her! She's just over there!"

"Sorry."

Hustled toward the exit, Marcus craned around to scream at Newt. *Newt! Look! I've still got your phone!* he told her. To the bouncer he said hoarsely, "My friend's underage! She's older than me but she's still too young! You should make *her* leave, as well!"

"Don't worry about your friend," the bouncer rejoined. "She'll be fine. You worry about yourself."

"But—"

"Kids like you don't belong in here. So I don't want to see you again." The bouncer suddenly leaned down and thrust his massive, rawboned, scarred, and tattooed face at Marcus. "Get out and stay out," the bouncer rumbled, "or I'll take you round the back and teach you a lesson you won't forget. Understand?"

Marcus nodded dumbly. The white dog barked. *Ooompa-ooompa-ooompa* went the music.

"Right." The bouncer straightened. Then he yanked open a heavy steel fire door. "Off you go. And don't come back," he snarled, giving Marcus a mighty shove.

Whomp! The door banged shut behind Marcus, who tripped and nearly fell. The music stopped. Darkness descended. Newt's phone bounced off a familiar stone floor.

Once again, Marcus found himself in the cellar of his trailer. And Newton Huckstepp was nowhere to be seen.

13.
Moms to the rescue

"Well, that's just awful," Coco was saying. "If you ask me, you're better off without him."

"I know," Holly agreed. "I am. Only I worry about Marcus sometimes." She reached for a chocolate but had trouble picking it up because her new fake fingernails were so long. "He must feel rejected, even though he doesn't talk about his father much."

Coco gave a nod. "It *is* very difficult," she observed, peering up at the sky with a puckered forehead. She was lying on an inflatable lounge chair, holding a tall, icy drink in one hand and a remote control in the other. Holly lay beside her on a matching lounge; both women had retired to the Hucksteps' back veranda, where they were basking in the sun as they gazed across Diamond Beach.

But there was a bit too much sun. As Holly tried to peel the wrapper off her chocolate, Coco waved her remote control at some well-disguised piece of electronic gadgetry overhead.

A striped canvas awning immediately began to unfold above them.

"Men are hopeless," Coco went on. "What *I* always say is that they're just children at heart." The words had barely left her mouth when a strange object suddenly writhed into view. It was Prot's disembodied left arm, which had somehow dropped to the floor and wriggled its way onto the veranda like a snake or a worm. "Oh, for heaven's sake!" Coco snapped, then raised her voice. *"Sterling! I thought I told you to fix that robot."*

"I am fixing it." Her husband popped his head around the side of the French door, screwdriver in hand. "That's why I had to take its arm off."

"Well, don't just leave the horrible thing scuttling around," Coco said crossly. "We have *guests* here."

"Sorry, my love."

"If it's not fixed by dinner, I'm hiring a proper maid," Coco finished. "And don't, for heaven's sake, let the cats anywhere near it!"

"I won't," Sterling promised, snatching up the runaway arm. As he shuffled out of sight, Coco pursed her lips at his receding figure, her expression formidable. But when she turned back to Holly, she looked smug.

"It's for his own good," Coco declared. "If I wasn't firm, he'd never finish anything. He's always getting distracted." She sipped at her drink. "Now. Where was I?"

"You were saying that all men are children."

"Yes. Exactly. I rest my case."

Holly heaved a sorrowful sigh. She was still fumbling with her chocolate wrapper. "I don't think Marcus is very childish," she lamented. "He spends all his time hunched in a chair like a little old man. He never talks, he never runs around, he never gets excited about *anything* except his wretched computer games . . ."

"*Mom!*" It was Marcus. He burst into view, panting and red-faced and clutching the little white dog. His glasses were so warm and sweaty that they'd misted up. "I couldn't . . . call you . . . ," he rasped. "No signal . . . dropped the phone . . ."

"Marcus?" Holly exclaimed, stiffening with alarm. "What's wrong?"

"Newt . . . ," he groaned. "Edison . . ."

"What about them?" Coco asked sharply.

"They're both . . . stuck in . . . the cellar. . . ."

"What cellar?" Holly rose from her inflatable lounge chair, which made squeaky, rubbery, fartlike

66

noises. "Sit down, sweetie, you look terrible. What happened to you?"

"Nothing," said Marcus. Suddenly he noticed his mother's glossy nails, false eyelashes, and caramel-colored fake tan. Her hair was its usual sandy shade, and her eyes were still green, but . . . "What happened to *you?*"

"I had a makeover," Holly admitted.

Meanwhile, Coco was struggling out of her own inflatable lounge chair. "Now listen, Marcus." She sounded impatient. "What *exactly* is going on?"

"I told you," Marcus replied. "Newt and Edison are stuck under our trailer."

Coco gasped. Her eyes widened with horror as she clapped a hand over her mouth.

"They're *what?*" Holly shrieked. Glancing from face to face, Marcus suddenly realized that he hadn't been clear enough.

"Oh—I don't mean they're *squashed* or anything," he added quickly. "I don't mean the trailer's *fallen* on them. They're in the cellar, that's all. And they won't come out."

"But, Marcus—" Holly began. Marcus, however, wouldn't let her continue.

"There's a cellar, Mom! I swear!" he insisted. "If you don't believe me, come and have a look!"

"Marcus—"

"I thought I was hallucinating, only I wasn't!

Because Newt saw the same thing I saw! And so did Edison!" Marcus blinked back tears, cleared his throat, and fixed his pleading gaze on Coco. "You've got to come," he begged. "They won't listen to me. The whole thing's so weird—I didn't know what to do."

"It's all right, Marcus. I'll come." Coco shoved her manicured feet into her high-heeled sandals. "I'll come and I'll give them both a piece of my mind, since they've obviously played some dreadful trick on you."

Marcus considered this theory for a moment, then dismissed it. "I don't think so . . . ," he mumbled.

"I'll come, too," said Holly. "If there's anything wrong with our trailer, the buck stops with me."

"How far is it? A long way?" asked Coco.

Holly hesitated. Marcus bent his gaze to Coco's high heels.

"I don't think you'll be able to walk there," was his conclusion.

"Then we'll take the golf cart." Coco teetered toward the living room. *"Sterling!"* she called. *"Where are you? I need the keys to the golf cart!"* Over her shoulder, she added, "No dogs in the house, Marcus. Meet me out front. . . ."

14.
The first door on the left

Marcus was tired. He'd been rushing around so much that he sank into Coco's pink golf cart with a sigh of relief. But the golf cart was painfully slow. And Coco refused to accelerate when he asked her to.

"How can we go any faster?" she rejoined. "This place is crawling with people—we'll crash into someone if I go any faster than this."

"Yes, we have to be careful, Marcus," Holly concurred. "There's a speed limit around here, you know."

So they chugged along at a leisurely pace, carefully avoiding old men, mooching seagulls, and toddlers on tricycles. At one point the little white dog jumped down from Marcus's lap, sniffed at a discarded sandwich wrapper, peed on a car tire, and jumped back into the golf cart again—all without having to rush.

"We would have got there quicker if we'd walked," Marcus complained.

At last they reached the Bradshaws' trailer, which looked dirty and battered and surprisingly small. Even next to the golf cart it looked small. And when Marcus squatted down to check for evidence of a cellar staircase, he saw nothing beneath the trailer except dirt, shade, spiders, and a squashed Styrofoam cup.

"I don't believe it," said Coco. She was sitting behind the wheel of her golf cart, staring in amazement at the grubby little trailer. "Isn't this where Miss Molpe used to live?"

"What?" Holly frowned at her. "What are you talking about?"

"Your trailer," Coco replied. "It looks *exactly* like Miss Molpe's."

"No, it doesn't," Holly said quickly. Then, after a moment's hesitation, she added, "Who's Miss Molpe?"

"You *know*. The old lady who used to play us those phonograph records!"

"Oh! That's right." Holly turned to study the trailer. "You really think so?"

"I'm not sure." Cocking her head, Coco appeared to be ticking off a mental checklist. "Hers was spotless, of course, but it was the same shape . . . with the same blue stripe . . ."

"Come on!" Marcus urged. He was already hovering on the doorstep. "What are you waiting for? We've got to hurry!"

"The curtains are different," Coco went on, ignoring him. She began to climb out of her golf cart. "I remember Miss Molpe's curtains. They had red flowers on them."

"Really?" Startled, Holly raised her eyebrows. "I had to replace the old curtains," she revealed. "They certainly had flowers on them, but the flowers were pink, not red."

"They could have faded," said Coco, teetering toward Marcus across the uneven ground. "Is it the same layout inside?"

"I don't know," Holly confessed. "I can't remember much about Miss Molpe's trailer."

"Can't you? Goodness! I remember it *so well*. It had a sort of banquette with striped seats, and speckled Formica on the table, and frosted glass wall sconces with a painted gold trim . . ." Coco caught her breath as Marcus opened the door for her. "It *is* the same place!" she squealed. "It *must* be!"

"But—"

"Except that it never used to smell like this." Coco pinched her carefully sculpted nose between her lacquered talons. "No offense, but it smells like a septic tank in here."

"*I* think it smells like sweaty gym clothes," said

Marcus. He had followed Coco across the threshold, his mother close behind him. "The staircase is under that seat," he pointed out, "which is why we didn't spot it at first."

He ushered Holly to the seat in question, lifting its lid to show her the mysterious cellar. Coco, however, didn't seem very interested in the cellar. She was gazing around, awestruck. "It's the same one," she murmured. "I know it is. I remember those cushion covers. And those benchtops, and that funny little oven."

But Holly wasn't listening. "This can't be true," she croaked, staring down into the dimness. "This—this is impossible."

"I know," Marcus said solemnly.

"There can't be a cellar!" She rounded on him, as white as salt. "How can there be a cellar?"

Marcus shrugged.

"The man at the lot didn't mention a cellar," Holly continued, oblivious to the fact that Coco had joined them. So had the little white dog, which would have jumped into the stairwell if the sides of the bench hadn't been so high.

Defeated, the dog fell back, barking furiously. Marcus picked it up.

"Well, this is very impressive," Coco observed. She leaned forward, peering downstairs. "Sterling will want to see this, for sure. He'll be *so* jealous."

"It doesn't make sense, though." Holly sounded almost panic-stricken. "How can this trailer possibly have a cellar?"

It was Coco's turn to shrug. "Don't ask me," she replied. "Ours has a gym and a home theater, but I've no idea how Sterling managed it." She shot an inquiring glance at Marcus. "Are my kids down there?"

He nodded.

"Newt!" she cried. *"Edison!"*

"They can't hear you," Marcus explained. "The doors are closed."

"Doors?" said Holly. "What doors?"

"I'll show you." Marcus climbed into the stairwell, then made his way carefully to the bottom step. He could hear Coco's cork heels clomping after him.

"Is there a light switch?" she asked. "It's awfully dark down here."

"I don't know," Marcus replied. He hadn't bothered to pull Newt's phone out of his pocket, because it didn't seem to be working anymore. "I haven't seen one."

"Luckily I've got my key ring flashlight," said Coco as a thin pinkish beam pierced the shadows. It flickered across three full-size doors and a small plastic flap.

"What on earth . . . ?" Holly squeaked. She was bringing up the rear. "You mean there's *more* cellar?"

"Um . . ."

"Newt! Edison!" Coco brushed past Marcus and headed straight for the nearest door. *"This isn't funny! You'd better come out before I have to come in and get you!"*

"Wait—Mrs. Huckstepp?" Marcus grabbed her. "There's just one thing. . . ."

"Which room are they in?" asked Coco, shaking him off.

"I'm not really sure," Marcus admitted. "The whole layout's changed since I was here last."

"Edison!" Coco was fast losing patience. *"I'm coming to get you!"*

"No! Wait!" cried Marcus, who had suddenly worked out what was going on. But it was too late. Coco had already opened the first door on the left.

15.

The Crystal Hibiscus

"**W**elcome, Mrs. Huckstepp!" a soft voice purred. "Welcome to the Crystal Hibiscus Health Spa and Beauty Retreat! We're *so* happy to offer you our holistic relaxation-and-energy-balancing experience this afternoon!"

A wave of perfumed air hit Marcus with the impact of a hurricane-force wind. At the very same instant, his ears were assailed by hysterical barking as the dog in his arms began to thrash around madly.

Then he saw that Coco was being addressed by a giant pink cat.

"We'll begin with a full-body pamper session, incorporating a five-senses therapy approach," the cat continued. Standing on its hind legs, it was almost as tall as Coco. It had golden eyes and a silver bow around its neck. "This will include a degustation aroma-therapy menu, a music massage, a color-spectrum light bath, and a head-to-toe feather wrap."

"Oh, my goodness," Holly whimpered. Together, she and Marcus gaped at the tropical paradise that lay in front of them. Huge scented flowers bloomed against a backdrop of palm trees and distant lagoons. Marble fountains bubbled in the foreground, their gentle plashing barely audible above the tinkle of wind chimes and the ripple of a recorded harp. Thatched pavilions were scattered between clumps of thick jungle foliage and white cane furniture. An artificial waterfall cascaded into a mosaic-encrusted plunge pool, which was ringed by cushions and bisected by a row of stepping-stones shaped like lily pads.

"Oooo!" Coco exclaimed, breathless with enchant-ment. "This is *heaven*!"

"We like to think so," the cat replied suavely, ushering her over the threshold. Other giant cats were padding between various pavilions, carrying fluffy pink towels and glass jars full of cotton balls. "Welcome!" they murmured. "Come in and put your feet up!"

Coco advanced like a sleepwalker as white doves cooed in a nearby coconut tree and butterflies as big as pigeons fluttered overhead. A white cat in a pink kimono presented her with a pair of slippers. Another cat offered her jasmine tea. Giant felines were converging from every direction, some on their hind legs, some on all fours.

It was too much for the little white dog, which wriggled out of Marcus's grasp and jumped to the ground, yapping fiercely.

"Whoa!" cried Marcus. When he darted forward to restrain the dog, his mother stumbled after him, onto a paved terrace dotted with statues.

"Marcus?" Holly quavered. "Am I losing my mind?"

"No," Marcus assured her. He held the writhing dog in a modified headlock. Meanwhile, Coco was being led toward the nearest pavilion—where a bath shaped like a clamshell was filled to overflowing with iridescent bubbles.

"After your cleansing and relaxation routine, you can take advantage of our beauty bar," the pink cat was saying to Coco. "There's a wide range of options, including our complete manicure package, our organic face-lift, and our hair-enhancement program."

"Mrs. Huckstepp!" Although Marcus had to shout over the dog's frenzied yelping, neither Coco nor the pink cat seemed to hear him.

"I'm hallucinating," Holly whimpered. "I'm seeing pink cats."

"So am I," said Marcus.

"We must have breathed in some kind of toxic

fumes." His mother's tone became more and more hysterical. "It must be that stuff I used on these stupid fake fingernails!"

"It's not fumes," Marcus insisted. "It's magic." Then he raised his voice again. "You can't stay here, Mrs. Huckstepp! It's a trap! It's not real!"

The pink cat rounded on him, its hackles raised. "Excuse *me*," it hissed, "but you don't have a *booking*, little boy."

"Mrs. Huckstepp!" Marcus shoved the dog into his mother's arms before trying to run after Coco. Unfortunately, he didn't get far. His path was blocked by a big black cat wielding a syringe.

"Botox?" the black cat inquired, its fangs bared and its green eyes narrowed. "Or would you prefer a laser treatment?"

"Mrs. Huckstepp!"

"Perhaps a spell in our isolation tank . . . ?"

"Mrs. Huckstepp!" Marcus dodged the black cat as it lunged for him. Almost immediately, however, he was slapped in the face by a hot towel. A second hot towel was thrown over his head. By the time he'd freed himself, some other supersize cats were bearing down on him with acupuncture needles and electric hair irons and bowls of steaming hot wax.

"Do you *really* want a chemical peel, little boy?" they yowled. "Do you *really* want a deep-tissue massage?"

Marcus retreated a step or two. At the same time, his mother lost her grip on the white dog, which shot toward the black cat like a guided missile. The cat unsheathed its painted claws. It swiped at the dog; there was a fierce spitting sound, followed by a high-pitched yelp.

Suddenly the dog turned tail and bolted between Marcus's legs on its way to the door.

"Run!" Holly cried as a looming wall of fur bore down on her.

Marcus ran.

16.

"We need the robot!"

Holly was just behind Marcus when he stumbled into the cellar. She slammed the door behind her, then tried to hustle him toward the stairs. But Marcus dug in his heels.

"Wait!" he protested. "Where's the dog?"

His mother couldn't reply; she was out of breath. As they scanned their dimly lit surroundings, Marcus spied the plastic flap, which was swinging back and forth. *Squeak-squeak-squeak*. Each swing revealed a brief glimpse of emerald-green grass bathed in a golden light.

"Oh, no." Marcus tried to pull away from Holly, whistling frantically. "Here, boy!"

Holly yanked him back again.

"No," she snapped.

"Just let me—"

"*No!*"

She half dragged, half pushed Marcus upstairs. Only when they had reached the safety of the trailer did she finally let him go.

As she collapsed across the table, gasping and moaning, Marcus tugged at her sleeve.

"We need the robot," he insisted.

"Huh?"

"We have to get Prot down here. Can you call Mr. Huckstepp? Can you tell him to bring his robot?" When Marcus saw Holly's blank expression, his tone became even more urgent. "Robots don't *have* dream holidays!" he cried. "Not like people! We need Prot to open one of those doors!"

"But—"

"It's magic, Mom. They're magic doors. Every one of them leads to somebody's dream holiday. That's why we can't go back—if we do, we'll get sucked into our *own* dream holidays. And we won't want to come out again."

Still Holly didn't react. She just stared at him, looking shell-shocked.

Marcus sighed impatiently.

"Do you have Mr. Huckstepp's number?" he demanded. "Did you put it in your phone? Because if you didn't, we'll have to go and get him."

Holly groped for her hip pocket, but Marcus was way ahead of her. He seized his mother's phone and began to check the contents of her electronic directory.

As it turned out, Coco had supplied Holly with a generous list of Huckstepp contact numbers. Together with a home number, there were two office numbers, a fax number, a ski chalet number, and five cell phone numbers, one of which belonged to Sterling.

Sterling answered on the seventh ring. "Hello?" he said.

"Mr. Huckstepp?"

"That's right. Who's this?"

"It's Marcus Bradshaw."

"Who?"

"I'm with Mrs. Huckstepp. She needs your robot." There was a long silence. "Hello?" said Marcus. "Mr. Huckstepp? Are you there?"

"Sorry, I . . . Who am I talking to?"

"Hang on a minute." Marcus shoved the phone toward his mother. "Mom, you've got to talk to Mr. Huckstepp!" he pleaded. "Tell him to bring his robot, or he'll never see his family again!"

"Who . . . ?"

"It's *Mr. Huckstepp*! He won't listen to me!"

Gingerly Holly took the phone. Then she pressed it to her ear, almost poking herself in the eye with a false fingernail as she did so. "Hel-hello?" she stammered. "Oh, hello, Sterling. It's Holly Bradshaw."

"Tell him to bring the robot," Marcus softly reminded her.

"The thing is, Sterling, we've . . . um . . . we've got a problem. A very strange problem." Holly's voice broke. "No, I— It's hard to explain. But we need you here. Coco needs you here."

"Ask him to bring his robot!" Marcus hissed.

Holly, however, was busy describing her exact whereabouts. Only after she'd given Sterling a set of precise directions did she instruct him to bring his "little robot" along.

"There's a door that needs opening," she quavered. "Coco's stuck behind a door, and—well, you just have to come and see. It's very peculiar." Sterling must have asked something at this point, because Holly hesitated briefly. Then she said, "Well, to be honest, it's downstairs. In the cellar. What? That's right, there's a cellar." Her taut face slowly relaxed as she listened to the booming assurances at the other end of the line. "Oh, thanks," she croaked at last. "Thank you *so* much, Sterling. See you soon."

"And don't forget the robot!" Marcus piped up.

"And don't forget the robot," his mother finished. "Thanks. Okay."

She signed off.

"Well?" Marcus demanded.

"He's coming," Holly replied. "He wants to look at the cellar."

"And the robot?"

"He's bringing the robot."

"Good." Marcus gnawed at his thumbnail, thinking hard. "If we can get that robot to open a door, we might not end up walking into our own dream holidays," he mused. "We might be able to get back into Coco's spa. Or Newt's nightclub. Or maybe we'll see what's *really* behind those doors!" For a moment he considered the vast range of possibilities, his eyes widening. Then something else occurred to him. "Unless it doesn't work," he added glumly. "Those doors might not open for a robot. They might disappear when a robot tries to touch them. Maybe you need to actually *have* some kind of dream holiday before you can open any of the doors down there."

But Holly wasn't listening.

"Sterling will know what to do," she mumbled in a distracted kind of way. "He'll work out what's going on."

"I told you what's going on," said Marcus. "It's magic. This is a magic trailer."

His mother shook her head.

"Things always look like magic when you don't understand them," she rejoined. "Sterling will understand, though. He's a brilliant engineer. When Sterling arrives, he'll be able to explain everything."

17.

The disappearing doors

It was half an hour before Sterling finally showed up. He had warned Holly that there might be a delay while he reassembled his robot; by the time his two-seater dune buggy appeared at the end of the street, a glorious sunset was tinting the sky red and gold.

"My *word*!" Sterling exclaimed as he braked behind his wife's golf cart. "What an absolute *classic* you've got there! It's an old Airstream, isn't it? About 1965?"

"Uh . . ." Holly swiveled around to look at the trailer. She had been sitting on its front steps but had jumped to her feet at Sterling's approach. "I'm not sure. . . ."

"It's a beauty," Sterling continued. "I love vintage trailers. Are the fittings original?"

Marcus gave a snort, then rushed forward to unclip the harness Sterling had wrapped around Prot. "They're original, all right," Marcus growled. "They're about as original as you can get."

"Fantastic!" Sterling beamed at him. "You'll have to give me a tour."

"Yes, but we shouldn't *need* to give you a tour! Not in a place this size!" Holly wailed. "That's the whole problem! We shouldn't even *have* a cellar! It doesn't make sense!"

Across the road, a woman hanging up wet laundry peered over the top of her clothesline at Holly, who flushed and fell silent when she realized that she was being stared at. A small sun-dazed crowd had already gathered to inspect Sterling's dune buggy, which had a slightly homemade look about it, as if Sterling had thrown it together one afternoon using bits of jet aircraft and a ride-on lawn mower.

Three bare-chested teenage boys whispered to each other as they poked at the car's supersize wheels.

"I like it when things don't make sense," Sterling remarked. He climbed out of his own seat and helped Marcus extract Prot from the other one. "It gives me more to think about."

"Hey," said the boldest teenager, "is that a robot?"

"Affirmative," Sterling replied in his best robotic drone. Then he set Prot down on a patch of dirt and pointed at the trailer. "Inside," he ordered.

When the robot began to move, there was an admiring murmur from the crowd. Marcus immediately decided not to mention giant cats or talking bumper cars. Not for a little while, at least. Not until he could do it in private.

Holly must have reached the same conclusion, because she didn't speak until she and the others were safely over the trailer's threshold. Then she closed the door and said, "Our cellar is under that seat over there. Maybe it's been done with mirrors or holograms—I don't know. But I'm sure *you'll* be able to figure it out, Sterling."

"Let's hope so." Sterling rubbed his hands together, his blue eyes twinkling with excitement. He looked fatter than ever in the cramped, crowded, dingy space; his glowing sunburn and vivid Hawaiian shirt made everything around him seem colorless in comparison. "I've always wanted a portable wine cellar, but I've never been able to build one. I could certainly use a few tips." Lowering his voice, he leaned toward Holly. "If you want *my* advice, though, you should invest in a couple of air fresheners. It smells like a fish-processing plant in here."

Marcus heaved an impatient sigh. "You can't build something like this," he argued. "It's magic. You'd need to be a magician."

Sterling wasn't listening. He had shuffled forward and was goggling into the open seat, his eyebrows raised. "Good lord!" he said, marveling. "You've got stairs and everything!"

"I told you, it's a cellar," said Holly.

"Yes, but I thought you were talking about a subfloor storage area slung between the axles," Sterling confessed. He was sounding more and more enthusiastic. "This is amazing! It's a masterpiece! I've never seen anything like it!" With a laugh, he added, "Bit of a squeeze, though. I hope I can fit through that hole."

"It doesn't matter if you can't," said Marcus. "Prot's the one we need down there—if he can manage it."

"Marcus!" Holly snapped. "Don't be so rude!"

"Oh, there's no need to worry about Prot," Sterling remarked breezily, as if she hadn't spoken. "Prot's hydraulics are state-of-the-art. He can handle a few measly stairs."

Sterling was right. Prot descended into the cellar without difficulty, using a built-in head-mounted light to plot a course. It was Sterling who found the stairs troublesome—and not just because the entrance hole was so narrow.

"These treads aren't very wide!" he cheerfully announced. "When you've got a gut like mine, you need wide treads or you can't see where you're going!" He nearly came a cropper several times, thanks to his poor night vision and intense curiosity. "This feels like the genuine article," he would comment, abruptly stopping to examine a wall or a stair rail. Whenever that happened, Marcus would bump into him.

It was a miracle that they reached the bottom of the staircase in one piece.

"Good lord!" Sterling gave an admiring whistle. "Just look at the *size* of this place! It's so *solid*!"

"Yeah," Marcus said. "It is, isn't it?"

He noted that there were now three full-size doors, clearly visible in the glow of the robot's headlamp. The doggie door had vanished—perhaps because the dog had vanished?

"There's no end to the thing, either," Sterling continued in amazement. "What's through here? Cupboards? Cellars?"

"Wait!" Marcus yelped. He grabbed Sterling's hand, which had been reaching for the nearest doorknob. "Don't *you* open it, Mr. Huckstepp! Prot has to do that!" Turning to his mother, Marcus added, "The doggie door's gone. That can't be good. If the doggie door's gone, then Coco's door might have gone, as well. These doors might be for *us*."

Holly blinked. "Oh dear," she said weakly.

"And if these doors are for us, they won't lead to the Crystal Hibiscus," Marcus went on. "We might never get back into that spa, unless Prot can help." Leaning down, he addressed the robot. "Hey, Prot," he asked, "can you open one of those doors for me?"

Prot's head swiveled so that Marcus found himself

shading his eyes from the robot's spotlight.

"Please specify," came Prot's flat rejoinder.

"No." Marcus was firm. "I can't specify. Just choose one. Any one. We can't choose it for you."

"Random selection, Prot," Sterling suggested helpfully. "There's no correct answer."

For about five seconds, Prot remained motionless. But as Sterling opened his mouth again, the robot trundled forward.

Marcus caught his breath and crossed his fingers.

18.

Pick your dream

Prot chose the middle door, which didn't vanish when the robot turned the knob. *Click* went the latch. *Cre-e-eak* went the hinges.

Marcus wasn't expecting much. He wouldn't have been surprised by a blank brick wall, or a mirror image of the cellar, or even another door, leading to another door, leading to an infinity of identical doors, with never an end in sight.

To his astonishment, however, there was a room behind the middle door: a drab, windowless room containing a beige carpet, a wooden desk, a high-backed chair, a banker's lamp, a telephone, and lots of display shelves. Stretched across the rear wall, above a modest-looking elevator, was a sign that read SIREN SONG TRAVEL.

"Wow," Sterling breathed.

Marcus, however, wasn't impressed. "I knew it," he said glumly. "We can't get back into that spa. *Or* into the nightclub."

"But where's Coco?" His mother fretted. "I don't understand. . . ."

"Neither do I." Marcus was stumped. Surely they couldn't have stumbled on *Prot's* dream holiday? "Do you recognize this office, Mr. Huckstepp?" he asked, wondering if the robot's circuits contained an image of the place where it had originally been assembled.

Sterling shot him a puzzled glance. "Of course I don't recognize it," he replied. "How could I? I've never been here before."

"Maybe this is a different *part* of the spa." Holly appealed to Marcus. "Maybe we'll find Coco if we take the elevator."

"I don't see how," said Marcus. "There's no up button. Or down button."

"You're right. There's no control panel." Sterling seemed both amused and delighted. He bustled across the threshold, heading straight for the back of the room. "Is this elevator a fake?" he inquired. "Could there really be more *levels* down here?"

Marcus shrugged. Having cautiously advanced, he suddenly found himself within easy reach of a display shelf—which was stocked with row upon row of travel brochures. There were hundreds of brochures, some for fishing and skiing holidays, some for more peculiar holidays.

"'Cakeland Cruise,'" he read aloud. "'Toy Store Safari.' 'Chocolate Farm Stay.'" He screwed up his nose in bewilderment. "This is weird. . . ."

"'Jumping Castle Weekend,'" his mother said. She too was now scanning the array of titles. "'Space Vacation.' 'Dolphin Jockey Training Camp.'"

"Some of these are really ancient." Marcus eyed a yellowing pamphlet that sported black-and-white engravings. "'Antarctic Balloon Expedition—join doughty explorer Alfred Repton-Kinshaw in his quest to conquer a final frontier.'"

"This one's in German," Holly pointed out.

"'Pilgrimage to Jerusalem'?" Marcus had picked up a parchment scroll tied with red ribbon and inscribed with Gothic lettering. "What kind of a holiday is *that*?"

"Oh my goodness!" Holly shrieked. Marcus and Sterling both spun around to gape at her; Prot simply stood in a corner, circuits humming.

Holly was waving a crisp, colorful brochure.

"Look!" she cried, stabbing at the brochure with one long, glossy fingernail. "'The Crystal Hibiscus Health Spa,'" she quoted. "'Pamper yourself in kitty-cat heaven.'"

Marcus squinted at the cover, which showed

Coco Huckstepp lolling on a massage table under a palm tree. "I don't believe it . . . ," he mumbled.

"Look, Sterling!" Holly pushed the brochure into Sterling's hand. "This is where we left Coco. See? In a spa. And *here she is!*"

"And here's Edison!" Marcus squeaked. His gaze had been snagged by another brand-new brochure—this one featuring Edison's photograph under the words *Happy Friends Amusement Park*. Edison was shown laughing on a roller coaster in the company of a giant plush panda that was eating ice cream.

"How did you do this?" asked Sterling. He glanced from brochure to brochure, looking dazed. Meanwhile, Marcus was searching for Newt's dream holiday. He finally spotted a Never-Ending Dance Party pamphlet with her face on it.

"Gotcha!" he crowed, snatching it up. "Here's Newt! That's all of them now."

"Sorry, guys—you've lost me," said Sterling with a puzzled half smile. "What's the joke?"

"There's no joke," Marcus replied. He was inspecting Newt's brochure, wondering if it might contain any clues to her exact whereabouts. Unfortunately there was very little text—just picture after picture of young people dancing, drinking, kissing, laughing, and sprawling in great heaps on low, squashy couches.

"I don't believe it," Holly suddenly croaked. Marcus glanced up and saw her clutching a slightly faded brochure as if she'd found a long-lost diamond necklace. "This can't be true."

"What?" asked Marcus.

"It's—it's Jake." She whirled around, thrusting the brochure in his direction. "It's Jake—Jake Borazio! *It's that kid I had a crush on!*"

19.

"Please enter your code . . ."

Marcus frowned. "What do you mean?" he asked.

"Don't you remember? I told you about Jake." Holly pointed at the brochure in her hand. "That's him there. And that's the rock pool where we used to hunt crabs. And that's the old snack bar." Holly's voice broke; she had to swallow before adding, "This is Diamond Beach the way it used to be, twenty-five years ago."

Marcus scanned the pictures in front of him. He saw a dark-haired kid about his own age wearing board shorts and zinc cream. He saw a marshy lagoon, a run-down shack with *Snack Bar* painted on it, a modest cluster of trailers and tents, an almost deserted stretch of white sand.

"'Diamond Beach Paradise,'" he read.

"You don't think *Jake's* down here somewhere, do you?" Holly faltered. And Marcus shrugged.

"I dunno," he replied. "Maybe. Mrs. Huckstepp recognized our trailer—she said it used to belong to a little old lady called Miss Molpe." Squinting at the sign above the elevator, he murmured, "I wonder if Miss Molpe's got anything to do with this."

"Hey," said Sterling. His tone, though mild, was plaintive. "Could someone please tell me what this is all about? It's very clever but I'm not sure what you want me to do."

Holly didn't seem to hear. She was mooning over the Diamond Beach Paradise brochure.

Marcus sighed. "This place looks like the control room," he informed Sterling. "We must have got in here because Prot doesn't have a dream holiday. Now we just need to find a way into Mrs. Huckstepp's spa." His roving gaze settled on the desktop. "Do you think that phone works?" he wondered aloud.

Holly was muttering to herself. As Marcus trudged over to the desk, Sterling examined the Crystal Hibiscus brochure. "It doesn't say here where the spa actually *is*," Sterling announced. "I can't see a map or an address or anything. . . ."

Marcus lifted the phone receiver. It was heavy and old-fashioned. When he put it to his ear, there was an audible *click* at the other end of the line. Then a recorded female voice said, "Please enter your code number."

Code number? Marcus scowled. "What code number?" he demanded.

"Please enter your code number," the recorded voice intoned again. "Please enter your code number. . . ."

"They want a code number," Marcus informed Holly.

"Who does?" she asked.

"I dunno. It's a recorded message."

"Can you dial out?" was Holly's next question, which puzzled Marcus. Why would she want to know that?

"It's not very magical, is it?" he observed, confused by all the technology. At which point Sterling remarked, "Maybe *this* is a code number." He held up his Crystal Hibiscus pamphlet, tapping at something Marcus couldn't see. "It's in very small print, but it's a number. Eight-zero-three-four-four-seven-one-one."

Marcus hesitated. The recorded voice was still chanting in his ear.

"Maybe we should be careful," Holly warned faintly. But Sterling said, "Go on. Don't stop now— we're really getting somewhere!" There was an expectant gleam in his eye.

Squaring his shoulders, Marcus punched Sterling's mystery number into the phone. Eight. Zero. Three. Four. Four. Seven. One. One. As the final digit was keyed in, there was a noisy *clank* from the back of the room.

The elevator door was sliding open.

"Lovely." Sterling tucked the Crystal Hibiscus brochure into his hip pocket. Then he marched into the elevator, with Holly at his heels.

After a moment's hesitation, Marcus followed them both.

"Wait!" cried Holly. "What about Prot?"

"Come along, Prot." By wedging his foot against the door, Sterling stopped it from shutting. "Hurry, please."

"There are buttons in here," said Marcus. "Should we push one?"

"Not if it's red," Sterling joked. He released the door once Prot had chugged past him. "Let's wait and see what happens," he advised.

The door closed gently, but the elevator didn't stir. It just sat. It was a very ordinary elevator, with worn carpet and wall-mounted buttons.

Marcus had never seen anything less magical in his life.

"Maybe we should key that code number in again," Sterling suggested. "What was it? Eight-zero-three-four-four-seven-one-one?"

Marcus nodded. "Prot had better do it," he said. "Just in case."

So Prot keyed the code into the control panel,

using one of his retractable fingers. There was an immediate response. With a shudder, a bounce, and a painful grinding of gears, the metal box in which they stood began to move—up, not down.

"Oh dear," said Holly. "This doesn't seem right."

"Don't tell me we're going back upstairs!" Marcus protested. He had a horrible feeling that the elevator was about to deposit them in the trailer again.

As their journey stretched on and on, however, he changed his mind.

"This can't be one floor up," he said at last. "It's taking too long."

"Is there an emergency stop button?" Holly queried, her voice shaking.

"Yes. But who's going to help us?" Marcus couldn't even tell what floor the elevator was passing, because the numbered buttons on the control panel weren't illuminated. "What if it's not going anywhere?" he asked. *What if we can't get out?*"

"It's all right." His mother took his hand. "Don't worry. We'll get out."

"It's clever, isn't it?" Sterling remarked cheerfully. "You'd swear we were in a twelve-story building." The words had barely left his mouth when the elevator lurched to an abrupt halt. "Ah!" he said. "Here we are. I'll be interested to see this."

Ping! The door chimed and trundled open, admitting a great rush of warm, perfumed air. Marcus could hear the splash of water and the tinkle of harp strings. He could see gleaming marble and glossy foliage.

It was all reassuringly familiar.

"Oh, wow!" he said, exulting. "We're here! We actually did it!"

Once again, they were on the threshold of the Crystal Hibiscus Health Spa.

20.

The Crystal Hibiscus revisited

"**W**ell, I'll be darned." Sterling shook his head, awestruck. "This is unbelievable. I've never seen virtual reality like *this* before."

"We should have brought cat food. Or maybe a stick." Holly was peering suspiciously at the bright, balmy, unpopulated scene in front of them. But there were no giant cats around—just enormous blossoms, towering palm trees, and multicolored birds of paradise. "What are we supposed to do if we get chased again?"

Marcus figured that this was probably a rhetorical question, since the answer was obvious. If they got chased, they would run.

"We should leave Prot here to hold the door

open," he suggested. Though he had spotted an up button beside the door, he no longer trusted doors—*or* buttons. "We don't want the elevator leaving without us."

"Good point," said his mother. Then she turned to the robot. "Prot, you should stay, please, to keep our escape route clear," she ordered. "Understand?"

"Clarification required," was the robot's toneless, plodding answer. "I do not understand how I must staple east to key power escape route clear."

"Just *stay here*, Prot," Marcus instructed, very slowly and precisely. "Hold the door open. And wait until we come back. Okay?"

"I will hold the door open and wait until you come back," Prot concurred.

"Good." Looking around, Marcus saw that Sterling had already wandered out of the elevator. "Mr. Huckstepp! Hold on!" Marcus squeaked in alarm. "We have to be careful!"

He and his mother rushed to join Sterling, who was reverently patting a white wicker chair. Holly explained in a low voice that they couldn't linger, that they had to find Coco, that the Crystal Hibiscus Health Spa was a very dangerous place. But Sterling seemed more interested in the flowers, and the fountains, and the fact that the elevator was embedded in a caretaker's hut.

"Isn't that neat?" he gabbled before dipping his

hand in a stone basin to test the water. "Hey! Check this out! It feels like the real thing!"

"Shh! Not so loud!" hissed Marcus.

"Will you look at that!" Sterling pointed through an archway toward the distant view of whitecaps on a sapphire sea. "Is that a back-screen projection of some kind, or what?"

"Sterling. Listen to me," Holly begged in the softest of whispers. "We have to find Coco. She came here and wouldn't leave—"

"I'm not surprised!" Sterling boomed just as two giant cats rounded the nearest bend in the path. One cat was pink and one was gray; both were carrying trays laden with tropical fruit, chocolate-covered nuts, manicure equipment, and vials of nail polish in every shade of pink known to humanity.

Sterling gave a shout of laughter.

"I don't believe it!" he exclaimed. "It's Coco's dream come true! She must be having the time of her life."

His voice echoed off the sweeping expanses of white marble like a thunderclap. Holly and Marcus both winced as the two cats froze. Four identical golden eyes swiveled in Sterling's direction. A pair of tails began to twitch.

"No wonder she's hiding out," he continued. "I don't blame her for not wanting to leave; I'd like to stay, too!"

The two cats exchanged glances. Though they didn't exactly shrug, Marcus somehow sensed that they wanted to. They then proceeded on their way quite calmly, as if nothing had happened.

Holly's jaw dropped.

"What was that all about?" asked Marcus.

"I—I'm not sure. . . ."

"They didn't attack us. Why didn't they attack us?"

"I don't know."

"I do." The answer had come to Marcus in a flash. "It's because of Mr. Huckstepp. He keeps saying how wonderful everything is—"

"And how Coco would never leave!" his mother finished. "Which is exactly what the cats want to hear."

"Yup."

"So he's not regarded as any sort of threat." Holly frowned as she watched Sterling trot after the two cats. "Oh dear. What's he up to? You shouldn't touch a cat's tail—cats hate it when you do that."

"It moves!" Sterling called back to her, gesturing at the fluffy pink tail that had just jerked away from his reaching hand. *"It's got some kind of hydraulic system built into it!"*

Marcus sighed and tugged at his mother's sleeve.

"Come on," he muttered. "We'd better stay close, or he's bound to do something stupid. Anyway, those cats will lead us straight to Mrs. Huckstepp. There's no one else around here who'd be wanting mangoes; cats eat fish."

So they set off in pursuit of Sterling, who was following the cats. Their path led them through coconut and hibiscus groves, beneath flower-studded pergolas, over mosaic terraces, and around tiled pits full of bubbling goo. ("Oooh!" said Holly. "Mud baths!") All the while, Sterling continued to marvel at every little thing, working himself into a state of feverish admiration. "Who did this?" he would cry. "This is fantastic! Hey—will you check out the *definition* on that *visual field*?"

Thanks to his obvious enthusiasm, not one of the busy, bustling cats they passed on their journey spared them so much as a curious sniff.

At last they arrived at a circular pavilion with open sides and a palm-frond roof. The Corinthian columns holding up this roof seemed to emerge like mighty reeds from a pool of azure water; in the center of the pool was a raised platform, on which several giant cats were attending to Coco Huckstepp.

She was draped across a couch, wrapped in a pink bathrobe and reading a glossy magazine. Her face was covered in green gunk. One cat was buffing the nails on her left hand while another was giving her a scalp massage (claws retracted). A third cat was pouring tea. A fourth was flapping a huge fan made of pink ostrich feathers.

Marcus was puzzled by the antics of cat number five, which seemed to be spraying Coco's feet with jets of water from a trigger nozzle at the end of a long, flexible hose.

"Hydrotherapy," Holly murmured before he could ask. She sounded wistful. "You aim the water at pressure points on the soles of the foot." With a sigh, she added, "I love a good foot massage."

Sterling raised his voice to shout across the narrow stretch of water that separated him from his wife. "Coco! Sweetheart! Isn't this something?" he bellowed, waving both arms. "Boy, you must feel like you've died and gone to heaven!"

In response, Coco sat bolt upright.

"Sterling!" she shrilled. "What are *you* doing here?"

"Why, I came to see what all the fuss was about!" her husband rejoined. "And now that I've had a look— well, I just can't believe my eyes! This is the *greatest feat of computer engineering in the history of civilization.*" He made a dramatic gesture that encompassed the entire spa. "So what do you say? Should we get the kids in here for a virtual swim? Edison will *love* this, I just know it!"

21.
Trigger point

The only way onto Coco's little island was a short bridge made of white marble. Since the island was already crowded, Coco rose from her couch, shuffled into a pair of slippers, and crossed the bridge just ahead of her attendants, who immediately swarmed after her. "We're not finished, Coco!" they yowled. "What about your herbal lava pack? What about your hot-stone massage?" They seemed surprised and anxious, though not yet angry—perhaps because Coco hadn't yet tried to leave. And there was no point getting mad at Sterling—not while he was busy heaping praise on everything in sight.

"Isn't this great?" he demanded. "Isn't it a masterpiece? And it's *tailor-made* for you, Cokes!"

"I guess it is." Coco sounded slightly lost, as if she'd just emerged from a coma. "What was all that about the kids again?"

"They'd love it here. Don't you think?" Throwing an arm around his wife, Sterling fingered a fold of her bathrobe. "Did you bring this with you," he asked, "or was it supplied?"

"Uh—Mrs. Huckstepp?" said Marcus. He'd been keeping a close eye on the cats, some of which were now rubbing themselves against Coco's body, purring endearments and promising all kinds of delightful bonus offers: steam baths, vibration therapy, a seaweed wrap. Though every claw was sheathed, Marcus knew that the cats might take offense at any moment.

He therefore remained fully alert, choosing his words with great care. "Newt and Edison are in their own dream holidays, right now," he informed Coco, "and they wouldn't leave when I asked them to. So if you want to show them how great it is here, you'll have to bring them back yourself."

"That's right." Holly butted in, lying through her teeth as she faked a carefree smile. "Newt wouldn't listen—would she, Marcus? We kept telling her what a wonderful time she'd have in this place, getting her legs waxed and her energies aligned, but she refused to come."

"And she's at a dance party," Marcus added. "Where everyone's drinking alcohol."

"*What?*" Suddenly Coco snapped back to life. Her back straightened. Her eyes widened. She impatiently pushed a cat's head off her shoulder. "What dance party? Where?"

"Oh—um—it's not far," said Marcus, pointing in the general direction of the elevator. "It's back that way. . . ."

"Show me." Coco set off at a brisk pace, much to everyone's surprise. The cats padded along behind her, protesting that she hadn't finished her therapy. Sterling seemed astonished that she didn't want to stay put. Even Holly said, "Aren't you going to change first, Coco? You're still in your robe and slippers. . . ."

"So what?" Coco retorted. To Marcus, who was trying to keep up, she said, "Is Eddie with Newt? She didn't take *him* to her party, did she?"

"No," Marcus replied. He was slightly out of breath. "Edison's gone to this really dangerous amusement park—"

"Oh, for heaven's sake." Coco cut him off, her tone crisp. "As soon as I get a moment's peace, those two start carrying on like hooligans. . . ."

"But, sweetheart," wheezed Sterling, who was beginning to sweat as he waddled after her, "why not let *me* go and get them? You can always stay here, if you want."

"Yes! Yes! You can always stay here!" the cats howled. They were growing more and more alarmed;

Marcus could see their tails twitching. "You're booked in for a pedicure!" they wailed. "You haven't had an ozone bath! You'll age ten years if you don't finish your treatment!"

"I'll age ten years if I have to worry about Newt," was Coco's response, which didn't go down well with the cats. One of them hissed, and another glared balefully at Marcus. A third slipped past Coco and planted itself in front of her. "You mustn't go yet," it argued. "If you stay for a detox sauna, we can offer you a free set of mink eyelashes."

"Get out of my way," Coco said crossly.

The cat's tail began to lash back and forth. "At least let us remove your conditioning mask," it wheedled.

"No. I can do that myself."

"But you can't," the cat growled. "You'll require a special alkaline toner."

Marcus had had enough. He knew that any further delay would simply mean a buildup of feline reinforcements. So he lunged at the cat, pushing it into a nearby mud bath.

"*Run!*" he yelled.

Holly didn't need any encouragement. She grabbed Coco's wrist and leaped forward. Marcus was right behind her. Sterling followed their example, though he looked rather bewildered and had a hard time matching their pace.

"Ouch!" he complained, fending off a cuticle probe.

"Hey, guess what. That really hurt! These things can really hurt you!"

Marcus glanced back. Only a couple of cats were now in pursuit; the rest had paused to pull their thrashing, squawking, traumatized friend out of the mud bath. But Marcus was getting worried. It wouldn't be long before the fastest cat (a snow-white Persian) caught up with Sterling and brought him down like a baby antelope in a nature documentary.

"Nearly . . . there . . . now . . . ," Holly panted. Sure enough, the elevator was in plain sight, about a hundred yards ahead. As he measured the distance with his eye, Marcus noticed something else that was even closer: a plunge pool with hydrotherapy attachments.

He veered toward it.

"Go! Go!" he screeched.

His mother pounded past, dragging Coco. Sterling, however, was beginning to slow down. Red and sweaty, gasping and staggering, he was no match for the snow-white cat, which was down on all fours now and closing in like a cheetah, its ears back and its hackles up.

Marcus didn't delay. He hurled himself at the little cluster of shiny chrome taps, pipes, and jets beside the plunge pool. Snatching up a deadly looking trigger nozzle, he pointed it straight at the white cat.

Then he unleashed a high-pressure stream of hot water.

"Bull's-eye!" he crowed as the white cat fell back. It turned tail and ran screeching, while the pink cat behind it hesitated. But when Marcus adjusted his aim, the pink cat didn't stick around for a dose of extreme hydrotherapy. It took off like a bullet.

"Come on!" Marcus bawled. He threw down the trigger nozzle, grabbed Sterling's arm, and galloped toward the elevator, where Holly and Coco were already waiting. Coco was beckoning frantically. Prot was still holding the door open.

Holly rushed to her son's aid; together they yanked a breathless Sterling into the cramped steel box. Marcus caught a last glimpse of about two dozen snarling, spitting tiger-size cats hurtling toward him.

Then the elevator door clanged shut, blocking out the awful sight forever.

22.
Gate-crashing

There was a brief stunned silence.

"It's a good thing cats hate water so much," Holly said at last. She'd barely finished speaking when a sudden *thump* was followed by a frantic scratching on the other side of the door.

Marcus quickly pulled the dance-party brochure out of his pocket.

"Let's key in this code number," he panted. "Six-zero-zero-eight-two-three . . ."

Once again, Prot was given the job of pressing buttons. And as soon as Newt's code had been entered, the scratching noise stopped.

Then the elevator began to move.

"It's going up again," Holly remarked. "How can it be going up again?"

No one answered. Sterling was too busy trying to get his breath back; he was doubled over, puffing and blowing, with his hands on his knees. Coco was looking around in consternation. "Where did this elevator come from?" she demanded. "I don't remember an elevator."

As for Marcus, he was wondering what to do about the enormous tattooed bouncer at the door of Newt's club.

"By the way," he said, "last time I tried to get into Newt's party, a bouncer threw me out. Because I'm underage."

Holly frowned, but Coco seemed unconcerned.

"That's all right," she assured Marcus. "You can wait right here with your mom. Sterling and I will go and get Newt." Cutting an uncertain look at her breathless husband, she added, "Unless you want to stay here, too, sweetie."

"Nuh-uh," Sterling gasped. "I'll be fine."

"Are you sure?"

"I'm sure." He straightened up, as if to demonstrate how fit he was. "I want to see this club. I want to see what it's like."

Marcus thrust the brochure at him.

"It's kind of like the spa, only without all those cats," Marcus warned. "No one in there will want Newt to leave. They'll try to stop you from taking her. And there are *hundreds* of people." After a moment's reflection, he said glumly, "I hope they don't start throwing bottles at you."

"Oh dear. So do I." Holly sounded nervous. Once again, however, Coco was completely unfazed.

"I've had more than enough practice making Newt leave parties," she said with complete confidence. "A few hundred drunk teenagers never stopped me before." Then she turned to her husband. "This is taking an awfully long time. How many floors *are* there?"

Sterling shrugged. He was examining the dance-party brochure. "'Join Newton Huckstepp and her friends at the world's hottest venue,'" he read aloud. "'Meet all her favorite bands and movie stars. . . .'"

Suddenly the elevator stopped. The door opened. They heard the throb of muffled music: *ooompa-ooompa-ooompa-ooompa*. In front of them were a brick wall and a cleaner's bucket.

Coco blinked. "Is this it?" she asked.

"I think it may be around the corner. . . ." Holly stuck her head out the door, craning to her left. "Oh, yes. Looks like we're here, all right."

"Then off we go," Coco muttered. She seized Sterling's hand and took a step forward.

"Be careful, Coco!" Holly begged. "Remember— if you're worried, we can always come back with the police!"

Marcus stared at his mother. The *police*? His mind

boggled; how on earth was she planning to explain all this to the police?

Coco seemed equally unimpressed. She waved the suggestion aside. "I'm not worried," she said. "I used to hang out in worse places than this when I was young." As she disappeared around the corner, Marcus could hear her voice floating back toward him. "If there's a ladies' room in here, I might be able to wash this mask off. . . ."

Marcus hoped fervently that she wasn't going to *linger*.

"They'll have trouble finding Newt in a mob like this," Holly commented. She was still leaning out the elevator, squinting at the dimly lit dance floor. "And what if there's a dress code? What if Coco gets thrown out because she isn't dressed properly?"

Marcus sniffed. As far as he could recall, many of the dancers he'd seen on his previous visit had been wearing what looked like strips of silver duct tape. "I doubt there's a dress code," he mumbled, then joined his mother at the door of the elevator. By stretching their necks, they could just make out a swirling, swaying, steaming crush of bodies. At one point Holly started. "Look!" she exclaimed. "Isn't that the latest James Bond?" Before Marcus could even shift his gaze, however, James Bond was sucked back into the swarm from which he'd emerged.

After about five minutes—just as Marcus was

beginning to feel uneasy—he became aware of a slight commotion at one end of the smoky, cavernous dance floor. Someone was shouting. The movement of the crowd in that particular spot had become less rhythmic and more jagged. Then Marcus spied the tattooed bouncer, who stood head and shoulders above everyone else. Though the strobe lights made it hard to work out exactly what was going on, it appeared that the bouncer had become involved in some kind of argument.

"Oh dear," said Holly. "I hope that's not Coco."

Heads turned. The high-pitched yells grew louder. There was a disturbance in the tightly pressed throng around the bar, where people were being roughly pushed aside.

Marcus squinted into the crush. He was expecting to see Coco and Sterling being escorted out of it by the club's security team. Instead, Newton Huckstepp came stomping toward the elevator. She was red-faced and furious.

"I'm going!" she screamed. *"How can I stay when you've ruined everything? You always ruin everything with your big, fat, stupid mouths!"*

It took Marcus a couple of seconds to realize that she was talking to her dad and stepmother.

23.
Party poopers

"**W**ait! Newt! Don't go!"

About half a dozen teenage girls were chasing Newt, begging her to reconsider. Marcus recognized Hayley, the blonde girl in the shiny red dress.

"Everyone's got embarrassing parents!" Hayley cried. "And nobody cares that you're in love with Ryan. . . ."

"I'm *not*!" Newt shrieked. As she charged into the elevator, Marcus and Holly shrank against the rear wall—because it looked as if Newt's entire entourage was about to pile in after her. Even Prot began to trundle backwards out of the way.

But Newt was the only girl who crossed the threshold. Her friends all stopped short, as if blocked by an invisible barrier.

"You haven't finished your drink!" Hayley pointed out. "You haven't heard what that DJ said about you!"

"Like it even matters, now that everyone thinks I've been *stalking Ryan!*" Newt raised her voice to yell at Coco and Sterling, who were closing in fast. "Thanks to a pair of *total morons* with the *biggest mouths on the planet!*"

Sobbing with rage, she punched wildly at the control panel. Marcus cleared his throat.

"Ah—Newt?" he said. "I wouldn't do that if I were you. . . ."

"*Shuddup!*" she snapped.

"Excuse me, Newton." Holly was clearly annoyed. "Please don't talk to my son like that."

"Newton!" By now Coco was trying to push through the gaggle of teenage girls in her path. It wasn't easy; they kept stepping on her feet with their stiletto heels and spilling their drinks down the front of her bathrobe. "Newt, stop pushing those buttons or you'll land us in even *bigger* trouble!" she scolded. Then, when Newt ignored her, Coco turned to address her husband—who was busy fending off the tattooed bouncer. "Sterling! Hurry up, or she'll leave without us!"

"Coming, sweetheart . . ." Sterling had been shaking up a can of soda that he'd snitched from some innocent bystander. Now he yanked at its pull tab, blinding the bouncer with a spray of carbonated fizz.

Although there wasn't enough fizz to pick off the teenage girls barring his way, Sterling managed to force himself through them by using his belly as a battering ram.

"Scuse me . . . coming through . . . whoops-a-daisy!" he said.

Marcus, meanwhile, had made a reassuring discovery. "I don't think this elevator's going anywhere," he observed. "Not if Newt's pushing the buttons." He wondered why. Could it be something to do with the number she was keying in? Or did the problem lie in the fact that she wasn't a robot?

"Go away!" she bawled as her parents joined her. *"Leave me alone!"*

"Sweetie," Coco argued, "you're always on the phone to Ryan. That's why I figured that he had to be your new boyfriend. . . ."

"Shuddup!" Newt screeched, covering her ears and screwing up her eyes.

Marcus pulled the amusement park brochure out of his pocket. Then he leaned down to address Prot.

"Hey, Prot," he instructed in a quiet, careful voice, "I want you to press these buttons: eight-six-five-zero-zero-three . . ."

At that instant, a famous face appeared in the crowd that was building up outside the elevator. Though Marcus recognized the face, he couldn't put a name to it. He felt sure, however, that it belonged to a Hollywood actor. Only a Hollywood actor would have such perfect, shiny teeth.

"Where are you going, Newton?" the actor inquired. "I thought you were going to tell me about your poetry."

"Newt! Did you hear that?" Hayley squealed. "Get back here *right now*!"

But it was too late. Prot had keyed in Edison's code number—and the elevator door was sliding shut. Marcus caught a final glimpse of Hayley's agonized expression before the whole scene vanished behind a wall of steel.

Newt flung herself into a corner, folding her arms across her chest.

"There! Are you satisfied?" she spat, glaring at Coco. "You've made me look like a complete loser in front of all my friends! *And* you've completely wrecked my chances of ever going out with the greatest bass player in the history of the world! Thanks a lot!"

Coco sighed. She began to massage the bridge of her nose between her thumb and forefinger.

Marcus said, "None of those people were your real friends, Newt. The whole thing was a fake."

"So what?" Newt didn't seem to care. She just scowled at him. "How do *you* know?" she continued. "What makes *you* such an expert, anyway?"

Marcus shrugged. "You don't have to be an expert,"

he replied. "All you need is common sense." Before she could do more than flush angrily, he added, "Everyone has a dream holiday. Yours seemed real because there weren't any giant pink cats or talking bumper cars in it. But that doesn't mean it *was* real."

Newt eyed him as if he were insane. "Giant pink cats?" she echoed. "For pete's sake, what are you *on*?"

Sterling, however, was more interested in the bumper cars.

"Talking bumper cars?" His eyes lit up. "Where were they? *I* didn't see any talking bumper cars."

"Don't worry. You will," Marcus assured him—just as the elevator bounced to a sudden halt.

24.
Lost in the dark

Marcus didn't know what to expect from Edison's amusement park. Would the runaway Ferris wheel still be rolling around? Would the clowns be back in their boxes? Would the grouchy bumper cars have smashed each other to smithereens?

He was prepared for almost anything. But when the door opened onto a pitch-black interior, he couldn't believe his eyes.

"Are we—are we back in the cellar?" asked Holly, sounding worried.

"I don't know." Marcus checked his brochure again. Had he got the code number wrong? "We shouldn't be. . . ."

"Of course we're back in the cellar!" said Newt.

She had no sooner stepped forward, however, than a distant cackle of crazed laughter pulled her up short.

There was a tense silence.

"What was *that*?" she demanded at last in a high-pitched voice that echoed slightly, as if she were shouting down a tunnel.

Everyone listened. Marcus sniffed the air. It smelled of dust and damp and something else. Oil? Hot steel? As his eyes slowly adjusted to the darkness beyond the elevator, he began to pick out some vague shapes: a dense shadow, a thin gleam, a pale patch.

Then someone nearby uttered a long, deathly, gurgling groan.

"Let's get out of here!" Holly squeaked. Newt jumped backwards, reaching for the control panel. But before Marcus could remind her that she shouldn't waste her time pressing buttons, there was an enormous crash—followed by a drawn-out metallic squeal.

To the left, a set of double doors burst open. Light poured in as two rubbery flaps were slammed apart by a four-seater car on rails. At the same instant, a luminous green skeleton dropped from the ceiling, swaying and jiggling at the end of a hangman's noose. For a split second the skeleton's bony toes were dangling directly over the car's empty front seat. *"Haah-ha-ha-hoo-hoo-hoo!"* laughed a disembodied voice. Then the car changed direction and banged through another set of doors off to the right, its headlights briefly illuminating several plaster gravestones before it vanished.

There was a chorus of screams from everyone except Marcus, who heaved a sigh of relief.

"It's the ghost train," he declared. "Don't worry, it's only the ghost train. I *knew* I didn't get that code wrong."

"Ghost train?" Newt bleated. "What ghost train?"

"Edison's ghost train." Marcus was keeping a wary eye on the skeleton, which was close enough to hear every word he said. "This is Edison's wonderful amusement park," he went on, trying to sound enthusiastic. "It's the best place on earth, because all the bumper cars and things are actually *alive*."

Jerking his chin toward the suspended skeleton, he pulled a face at his mother—who immediately grasped the message he was trying to convey.

"Oh! Right!" she said. "Yes, of course. I've heard about this place. It's the kind of place you'd *never want to leave*."

Marcus wasn't impressed by his mother's acting abilities. He didn't find her forced eagerness at all convincing.

Newt, however, seemed completely fooled.

"*I* want to leave," she whined. "I want to leave right now."

"No, you don't," said Sterling. He was rubbing his

hands together in anticipation. "Why would you want to miss out on this? You won't find talking bumper cars anywhere else in the world."

"That's right," Coco chimed in. She, too, was now nervously watching the skeleton. "You're coming with us, Newt, because this is going to be . . . um . . . extremely interesting. And educational. And fun."

"And Prot can stay here," Marcus added. He began to spell out his orders very slowly and clearly. "Stay here, Prot. Hold the elevator door open until we come back. Understand?"

"I understand," the robot confirmed. "I will hold the elevator door open until you come back."

"But how are we going to get out?" Holly asked. "I mean—which way should we go? It's all so dark and dangerous. . . ."

"In a *good* way." Marcus corrected her hastily. "Dangerous in a *good* way. Because this is a ghost train and ghost trains are meant to be scary."

"Oh, yes. In a good way, of course." When Holly flicked another anxious look at the skeleton, Marcus had a sudden brain wave.

He cleared his throat.

"Uh—Mr. Skeleton?" he quavered. "Where do we go to see the rest of this magnificent and enjoyable park of yours?"

In the shocked silence that followed, Holly's acrylic talons closed tightly around her son's arm.

Newt stared at him in absolute disbelief. Coco winced, and Sterling raised his eyebrows.

Then the skeleton turned its naked, gleaming skull toward Marcus.

"There'll be a car along any moment," it announced, its jaw flapping. And as everyone gasped, the skeleton suddenly disappeared, yanked up into the shadows overhead.

A few seconds later, the promised car arrived. *Boom-CRASH* went the double doors. *Eeeeeek* went the wheels. "Haah-ha-ha-hoo-hoo-hoo," laughed the invisible maniac. Once again, the skeleton dropped from its hidey-hole in the ceiling.

This time, however, the car screeched to a standstill, planting itself directly beneath the rattling bundle of bones.

"Hop in," said the car. It had a tired voice and a jack-o'-lantern face. "I'm already behind schedule."

25.
All aboard

Sterling didn't hesitate. He jumped straight into the car's front seat.

"Come on!" he cried. "There's plenty of room if we all squeeze up!"

Coco and Holly exchanged apprehensive looks. Holly said, "Are you sure it's safe in that thing?"

"It'll be safer than getting knocked down by another one," Sterling retorted, "which is what will happen if we try walking along the rails."

"He's right," Coco had to admit. Meanwhile, Marcus was already climbing into the car, which had begun to make impatient hydraulic noises.

"All aboard," it droned. "All aboard who's coming aboard."

"Quick!" Marcus beckoned to his mother. "Before it leaves!"

Holly made up her mind then. She slid into the backseat beside Marcus, leaving a small wedge of space for Newt. But Newt wouldn't budge. She hung back, stubbornly resisting all Coco's efforts to coax her out of the elevator.

"I'm not going," Newt insisted. When the car released its brakes, signaling its imminent departure with a mighty hiss, Coco gave up and joined Sterling in the front seat. "Just stay there!" she told her step-daughter as the car started to move. "Don't, for heaven's sake, do anything you'll—"

Crash! Before she could even finish, the car slammed through the next set of doors, which opened onto a kind of fake tomb lined with Egyptian hiero-glyphs. A couple of bandaged mummies jerked to life; one sat up in its sarcophagus, while another stiffly raised its arms.

Though Marcus wasn't impressed by this creaky display, he didn't dare say so. Not while the mummies were listening in.

"I hope Newton's going to be all right," Coco fretted.

"She can't go back home," Holly pointed out. "Nothing happened last time she pushed those buttons."

"Yeah, but she could always tell *Prot* to push

them," Marcus weighed in. He was about to suggest that they send someone back when Sterling suddenly addressed one of the mummies in a booming voice.

"Hello there! How's life treating *you*?" Sterling inquired, then laughed and corrected himself. "Or perhaps I should say, how's death treating you?"

Holly cringed.

"Oh, for heaven's sake, Sterling!" Coco scolded. "Don't be so ridiculous!"

Marcus didn't think that Sterling's question was ridiculous. On the contrary, he wanted to hear what the mummies had to say. So he craned his neck and listened.

But the mummies didn't say anything. "Mmm-mm-mm," was all they could manage.

Their bandages were so thick that normal speech was impossible for them.

"Fantastic," said Sterling. Marcus noticed that the car gave a little sigh, though he couldn't work out whether the sigh came from its hydraulic system or its mouth. Then it banged through the next set of doors into a blaze of sunlight.

"All out. Prepare to disembark." Nothing could have been more listless than the car's tone. "All out, please. This is the end of the ride."

The car reduced its speed, grinding to a stand-still under a cavelike archway. The fake rock over-head was hung with cobwebs and toy bats. Halloween pumpkins were scattered everywhere. An upended coffin doubled as a kind of sentry box, inside which sat a skeleton wearing a ticket collector's uniform.

"Oh, now this is *really* impressive," Sterling remarked. He was looking through a pair of wrought-iron gates, beyond which lay the rest of Edison's amusement park: the striped tents, the snapping flags, the Ferris wheel, the roller coaster. "This is definitely the kind of place that Eddie would love."

"Where *is* Eddie?" Coco demanded—much to Marcus's dismay. He cut a quick, fearful glance at the nearby skeleton.

"Yes, we should probably ask Edison what his favorite ride is," said Marcus. "I bet it's *brilliant*. I bet we'll never want to get off once we're on it!"

By this time his mother was pushing him out of the car. "That's right!" she agreed. "Imagine how much fun we're going to have!" Then she put her lips to his ear and whispered, "Where did you last see Edison?"

"On the bumper cars," Marcus replied under his breath.

Holly gave a surreptitious nod before loudly remarking, "Let's go and have a ride on the bumper cars!" From the safety of the platform, she addressed Sterling, who still lingered in his seat. "Sterling?" she said. "What's the problem?"

"No problem," Sterling replied, a little wistfully. "I'd just love to have a poke around inside this thing—"

"No!" his wife snapped. She, too, was now standing on the platform. "We have to keep going! We have to find Edison!"

"So we can ask him which of these rides is the most fun," added Marcus, wishing that Coco wouldn't keep talking about Edison. It was dangerous. It was *thoughtless*. It was going to cause trouble.

Boom-CRASH! All at once, the double doors they'd left behind slapped open again. Everyone jumped. Coco screamed. But she soon relaxed when she spotted the car that was clattering toward her.

It had a goblin's face, a squeaky wheel, and a passenger sitting hunched in its backseat.

"Newton!" Coco exclaimed. "You changed your mind! Good girl."

Newt looked sulky. "I wasn't going to sit there in the dark all *alone*," she growled, as if someone had forced her to. Holly and Marcus rolled their eyes at each other. But Sterling seemed more interested in Newt's car than he was in Newt. He watched with interest as it decelerated.

When it gently bumped the rear of the car in front, Marcus distinctly heard a muffled "Ooof!"

"All out," Newt's car wearily announced. "Prepare to disembark."

"With pleasure." Newt stood up and stepped onto the platform. "So what now?" she asked. "Where's Edison?"

Holly flashed her a look of warning. Coco glanced warily at the ticket collector. Marcus opened his mouth to make yet another soothing remark about how Edison must be having the time of his life in such a wonderful place.

Before he could speak, however, Newt's car said, "Edison is on the giant slide. It's near the flume. He's been wishing you were here to play with him."

Then both cars moved off, steering back into the murky depths of the haunted tunnel from which they'd so recently emerged.

26.

In search of Edison

"What a wonderful place," said Coco. They were strolling through the amusement park, between clusters of rides and stalls. To Marcus everything looked picture-perfect: the twinkling mirrors, the gleaming toffee apples, the candy-striped awnings, the snow-white picket fences. The sky was a heavenly blue, the grass a lush emerald green. "It's just perfect," Coco went on, as if she were reading his thoughts. "Eddie would have taken one look at this and the first thing out of his mouth would have been 'I wish Dad were here.'"

"Maybe," her husband conceded.

"He'll be wanting to show you everything," Coco insisted. "And he'll be wanting Newt to try out all the rides with him."

"Yeah, sure," Newt scoffed. "Like *that's* going to happen."

"Shh!" Holly glanced over her shoulder. "Newt, will you keep your voice down? We're supposed to love it here, remember? If you keep talking like that, you're going to be heard! And then we'll really be in trouble!"

"I don't see why." Newt's tone was dismissive. "It's not like any of this is actually *real*. I bet the mummies can't even see where they're going. And the skeletons are a joke. And I could outrun the cars in that ghost train any old time." She flapped a disdainful hand at the scenery. "I mean, what can possibly happen to us in la-la land?"

"You don't know what you're talking about." Marcus tried to keep his voice low, despite the fact that he felt like snapping at Newt. "This place is really dangerous. The first time I came, I was nearly smoth-ered by stuffed toys. And then a runaway Ferris wheel tried to flatten me."

Newt gave a snort of laughter. "Stuffed toys?" she cackled. "You were attacked by *stuffed toys*?"

"Now stop it," said Holly. "We have to calm down and concentrate. We have to make sure we don't miss Edison."

Coco, meanwhile, was shaking her head in amaze-ment. "I've never seen such a clean amusement park," she said, marveling. "Not even Disneyland is *this* clean.

And the food smells delicious! And the lawn is so well kept!"

"The prizes are good, too," Newt had to admit, however grudgingly. "I wouldn't mind having a pair of those headphones myself."

"Yep, it's a real achievement," Sterling agreed. "If only I could work out how it's all put together . . ."

Marcus took a deep breath. He was about to point out, for the umpteenth time, that it was all put together with magic when something caught his eye.

"Hey," he said, stopping suddenly. "Look over there. Isn't that the flume?"

Everyone looked. It *was* the flume. Behind a towering stockade rose a series of chutes that carried fake wooden logs with seats in them up to the top of a man-made waterfall. As Newt observed these logs riding the rapids back to the ground, her grumpy expression became almost wistful.

"I'd really like to go on that," she muttered.

Marcus could see the attraction. But he could also see the giant slide.

"There it is," he announced. "There's the giant slide. Right next to the flume."

"And there's Edison!" Coco began to wave her arms. *"Yoo-hoo! Edison!"*

"Shh! Keep it down!" Holly begged.

Marcus could see Edison quite clearly. There were

three giant slides, all stuck together in a row, and Edison was at the top of the middle one. He was sitting on a blue mat, wearing what appeared to be a novelty pith helmet.

He must have spied his stepmother waving, because he waved right back. Then he pushed off and swooped down the massive inflatable slide, landing in a pit of multicolored foam balls positioned at its base.

WHOOMPH! The balls swallowed him up. Only his pith helmet remained, sitting on the surface of the ball pit.

Everyone—including Newt—laughed out loud.

"Woo-hoo!" Sterling cried, pumping the air with his fists. *"Go, Eddie!"*

Surging forward, he didn't seem to hear the thin patter of applause coming from the tent to their right. Marcus did, though. And when he peered in that direction, he saw a small gathering of clowns and plush toys clapping appreciatively.

"Well done, Ed!" Sterling exclaimed. He was standing over the ball pit. "Boy, that's a lot of balls, eh? I can't even see you!"

"Edison!" said Coco. "You can come up now!" Stooping, she retrieved the helmet, which had a miner's lamp built into its rim. To her evident surprise, however, she didn't uncover the top of her stepson's head. "Nobody's mad, okay?" she continued, softening her voice. "We're just happy we found you at last."

"In these fun and beautiful surroundings," added Marcus, just in case.

Holly had joined Coco and Sterling beside the ball pit. They all looked for a sign that Edison might be somewhere underneath the balls. But there wasn't the slightest hint of movement.

"Edison?" Now Coco was starting to sound worried. "Where are you?"

"Edison?" Holly squatted down and began to dig, snapping off one fake fingernail in the process. Coco immediately followed her example, scooping out handfuls of squashy foam spheres.

Soon everyone was kneeling and frantically searching for Edison. Even Newt pitched in. But the pit seemed to be bottomless.

"Oh no!" Coco wailed. "He'll suffocate in there!"

"He won't suffocate," Marcus assured her. "They won't let him. They love him too much." After a moment's reflection, he whispered, "They might try to keep him away from us, though."

"Edison!" yelled Newt. *"This isn't funny!"*

"What are we going to do?" Coco clutched at her husband. "Sterling! There must be something we can do!"

Sterling hesitated. "I—I guess you could lower me down on the end of a rope," he said at last. It was the first time Marcus had ever seen him look anxious.

"Ed's probably hiding," was Newt's theory. "I bet if

we bought a hamburger and waved it over the top of those balls, he'd pop up pretty quick."

"No, I wouldn't," a gruff little voice objected. "It's like quicksand in there. You can't climb back up—you have to keep going the long way round."

27.
Escape!

Edison was standing directly behind his stepmother. No one had noticed his arrival because all eyes had been on the ball pit. He seemed unchanged, though he was no longer wearing his backpack or his infrared goggles.

Everybody gasped. Then Coco cried, *"Eddie! Where have you been?"*

"Right here," he said. "I'm glad you came. Can I have my helmet?"

A shocked and speechless Coco handed it over. Edison immediately donned it again, as if nothing remarkable had happened. Marcus frowned.

"How did you get out from under those balls?" he asked. In response, Edison pointed at the nearby ticket booth, which was the size of a one-car garage and painted to look like a gingerbread house.

"I went through a tunnel," he replied. "It leads to a trapdoor that comes out just over there. I've done it about a hundred times. Do you want to see?"

"No," Coco rejoined with a bluntness that worried Marcus. He glanced nervously at all the clowns and plush toys.

They seemed to be closing in.

"Maybe later," he suggested.

"After we've explored a few other rides," Holly agreed quickly. "Your father wants to see the bumper cars, Edison, and we haven't had a proper look at the ghost train, either. *Have* we, Coco?"

"Huh?" It was a second or two before Coco caught on. Then she gave a start and said, "Oh! No, we haven't. That's a good idea, Holly."

Marcus thought so, too. He flashed his mother an approving look. Meanwhile, Sterling was asking Edison where the bumper cars were.

"They're over that way." Edison caught his father's sleeve. "I'll show you."

"Can I go on the flume instead?" Newt suddenly piped up. Marcus stared at her in astonishment. Didn't she understand what was happening? Evidently her stepmother thought not, because all at once Coco took charge of the arrangements.

"Not yet, Newt," she said, apparently oblivious

to the clowns and cuddly animals that were edging toward her. "First we'll have a proper ride on the ghost train. Then we'll look at the bumper cars. Then you and Marcus can go on the flume."

"And *then* you should try the roller coaster," Edison recommended. "It's great because the cars do whatever you tell them to."

He chattered away calmly as he followed his parents back to the ghost train, describing his encounters with singing carousel horses, crabby bumper cars, and a hectic hoopla stall. "The prizes kept running around," he explained to his father, "so it was really hard to throw hoops over them. . . ."

He seemed unaware of the rapidly growing crowd that had begun to trail after him. Marcus, however, was all too conscious of it. Every clown was in pursuit, as were most of the plush toys, two plywood policemen, a flock of plastic ducks, half a dozen inflatable aliens, and a miniature trackless train. Some of these creatures were carrying weapons (darts, paddles, popguns), and although they weren't yet angry, they were certainly anxious. Marcus could tell.

Luckily, Sterling said all the right things, oohing and aahing over his son's revelations. Coco was subdued. Newt didn't shoot her mouth off, either, though at one point she did yell, "Boo!" at a fluffy little ladybird that was hopping along in her immediate vicinity. When it squeaked and scurried away, she shot a triumphant look at Marcus, as if to say, "See? There's nothing to be scared of."

Marcus could only hope that she was right. Could they possibly coax Edison all the way back to the elevator without arousing suspicion? As they approached the wrought-iron gates to the ghost train, Marcus began to think that they might have a chance. He was particularly pleased when he heard Edison offer to whistle for a car. "They come when I whistle," Edison informed his parents. "It's really neat."

But then one of the clowns behind him said, "I don't think the cars *will* come just now," as if it didn't want Edison going anywhere near the ghost train exit. And Marcus realized that the game was up.

He shrank against his mother, wondering if he had the strength to disarm the nearest plush giraffe.

"Really? That's too bad." Edison's face fell before promptly brightening again. "Oh, well. Never mind," he chirped. "I guess we can always come back after we check out the roller coaster."

"No." Suddenly Coco put her foot down. "Now that we're here, we're finishing what we started. Tell the cars that they can have a late lunch." Ignoring Holly's frantic hand signals, she went on to say in a brisk, imperious tone, "If those cars don't come *immediately*, we'll *walk* into that tunnel."

Edison frowned. "But—"

"I refuse to be ordered around by the contents of

a dollar store. It's demeaning." She turned her back on the milling carnival creatures as if they were of no consequence; something about her flaking green herbal mask made her look quite scary. "Well?" she urged her stepson. "Are you going to call a car for us or not?"

Obediently, Edison whistled. Then one of the clowns stepped forward. "Can we come, too?" it asked.

"No," snapped Coco.

Marcus hastily added, "There won't be enough room."

"Yes, there will," the clown replied in a flat, tinny little voice. "You'll need two cars for six people. So there'll be plenty of space left over."

Edison looked inquiringly at Coco, who shook her head. "Sorry," she retorted. "No can do."

"Why not?" the clown asked softly, taking another step forward. "Don't you like us?"

Luckily Coco didn't have to answer, because at that moment the first car arrived. As she moved toward the platform, however, the head clown grabbed Edison's arm.

"*You* don't need to go, Edison," it pointed out. "You've already been on this ghost train six times."

Uh-oh, thought Marcus.

Edison shrugged. "That's okay," he said. "I don't mind doing it again."

"You should wait here with us," the clown insisted.

"We have something very special to show you."

"Yes . . . stay here . . . very special . . ." The other creatures sighed. Edison seemed torn. He hesitated, glancing at his father.

But Coco wasn't about to let anyone else take command.

"We're leaving," she snapped, seizing Edison's other arm. "Come on."

"Huh?" Edison stared at her, dumbfounded—as did Holly. Marcus couldn't believe his ears.

"You've had enough fun for today," Coco went on. "We can always come back tomorrow. You need dinner and a shower before you go to bed." She tugged Edison toward the car, which immediately began to back away. *"Stay right there!"* she barked, leveling a manicured finger at it. As the carnival creatures began to growl and mutter, she turned to address her stepson. "We'll stop for pizza on our way home," she promised, clearly under the impression that a pizza would make all the difference.

Much to Marcus's amazement, it did.

"Okay," Edison agreed with a sigh. "But can I have my own pizza? I don't have to share with Newt, do I?"

"You can have your own pizza," said Coco. Raising her voice over a sudden wail of protest from the crowd, she said to Holly, "I always promise pizza when I need to get him out of an amusement park. It usually does the trick. And if *that* doesn't work, I threaten him with a computer-game embargo."

Then she snapped her fingers at Sterling and marched onto the platform, with her resigned, speechless, acquiescent family shuffling along behind her.

28.
More Miss Molpe

But the carnival creatures weren't about to give up.

"Please, Edison, don't go!" they cried. "Don't leave us! We need you!" With despairing expressions they clustered around the car, where Edison was squeezing into the front seat between his father and sister. "It won't be any fun unless you're here! You *have* to stay, *please!*"

Though Coco ignored them, Edison sounded deeply apologetic as he promised to pay another visit. "I love this place," he said. "Why wouldn't I want to come back?"

"Let's go!" snapped his mother, who had wedged herself in behind Newt, next to Marcus. She was addressing the car. "Come on! Get a move on!"

Nothing happened. The car just sat there.

Marcus hazarded a guess. "I don't think it's going to move unless Edison tells it to."

"I'll play with you another time," Edison promised the nearest clown, which was clinging to one side of the car with its pasty white fingers.

"No! You don't understand! We're miserable here without you!" An inflatable alien pushed to the front of the crowd, wriggling between two giant teddy bears. Its voice was soft and sibilant, like air hissing from an open valve. "The hours are so long, and we're not even paid. . . ."

"And we'll get in trouble if you leave," the clown added, eliciting an immediate response from Marcus. He leaned forward, anxious to press for more details.

"Why?" he asked. "Is someone going to get mad at you?"

"*Edison!* Will you tell this car to move, please? We're *waiting!*" Coco wasn't interested in what the clown had to say. And Sterling felt obliged to back her up.

"Come on, Ed," he murmured. "We've really got to go now."

"Yeah, but where are we going?" Edison was obviously confused. "I mean, the door's not this way, is it?"

"There's an elevator," Marcus explained. And Newt moaned, "Can we *go*, please? I can hardly breathe, I'm so squashed!"

The car, however, wouldn't stir. "She'll get mad," it whimpered. "She'll punish us if you leave. . . ."

"Who will?" Marcus demanded.

"Miss Molpe," said the car, triggering a breathy, frightened chorus. "Miss Molpe . . . Miss Molpe . . . Miss Molpe . . . ," the creatures all echoed. Holly and Marcus looked at each other.

"Who's Miss Molpe?" Sterling queried. But before Marcus could explain that she used to own the Bradshaws' trailer, Newt barked, "She's one of the Sirens, okay? Now can we *get going*?"

No one moved a muscle. Even the creatures stood rigid, staring at Newt in astonishment.

"What do you mean?" Marcus finally managed to squawk.

"Molpe is one of the Sirens," Newt repeated. "You know—as in the band?"

"No, Newt, we don't know." Her stepmother's tone was long-suffering. "What band are you talking about?"

"It's an all-girl band called the Sirens. They're named after a bunch of ancient Greek monster-women who used to sing songs and kill people." Newt spoke impatiently, as if she couldn't *believe* how much ignorance there was in the world. "The drummer calls herself Molpe, even though her real name's Kym. The others are called Parthenope, Leucosia, and Ligeia."

"Siren Song Travel," Marcus whispered. Though

he wasn't addressing his mother, she responded with a groan.

"Oh my goodness," she said. "Oh my word, Marcus."

"Do you think . . . ? I mean, could this be . . . ?" Marcus trailed off, waiting for reassurance. But his mother had none to give.

"The sirens were those creatures who used to lure travelers to certain doom," she quavered. "They were in that book of Greek mythology I used to read you, remember? No one could resist their songs. Sailors would drive their ships onto the rocks and drown, or just lie around and die because they couldn't tear themselves away. . . ." She swallowed before adding hoarsely, "There are even stories that the sirens used to *eat* the people they trapped!"

For a brief, tense moment their gazes locked. Then Marcus said, "We've got to get out of here."

"Oh, we're getting out of here, all right." Coco had been impatiently drumming her lacquered fingernails on the door of the car; now she wagged a finger in the clown's face and warned, "There's nothing I hate more than bad service—especially in a tourist destination like this one. Bad service *really makes me mad.* And if you think Miss Molpe's scary, you should see what *I'm* like when some lazy, whining, incompetent loser tries to make excuses for unacceptable standards." As the clown shrank back, she raised her voice so that it cracked like a whip. "Unless you want to find yourself wishing that Miss Molpe was here to protect you, I suggest that you mind your own business, do your job, and *facilitate our departure!*"

Even Newt seemed impressed by this tirade. As for the ducks and the plush toys, most of them scurried away to hide, squeaking piteously. Several of the clowns began to sob.

Edison's forehead crumpled beneath the rim of his pith helmet.

"Poor things," he said. "Can't we do something to help?"

"Yes. We can," Marcus volunteered quickly, before Coco had the chance to explode. "What if we go straight to Miss Molpe from here," he suggested to the creatures, "and tell her that you guys weren't to blame? What if we tell her there was nothing you could do, because Edison had made up his mind to leave? She couldn't punish you then. She'd have to see that it wasn't your fault."

The creatures considered his proposal. There were two or three watery smiles. Then the biggest alien wheezed, "Do you promise?"

"We promise," Marcus said. "Don't we, Edison?"

"Oh, yeah." Edison nodded vigorously. "We sure do."

Marcus glanced at Newt, afraid she might make some caustic remark that would undermine all his efforts, like "How can we talk to this freak if we don't even know where she is?" But Newt had the sense to keep her big mouth shut—and next thing he knew, the car was rolling forward.

"Good-bye, Edison! We'll miss you so much!" the creatures cried, waving and blowing kisses while the tears ran down their shiny plastic or furry nylon cheeks. "Please come back! Come back soon!"

"I will!" Edison assured them, waving so energetically that he nearly knocked his own hat off. Marcus and Sterling waved, too. Then the car went crashing through a pair of swinging doors and all the bright, sunlit colors were swallowed up by darkness.

"Thank heavens for that," Coco muttered.

On their way to the elevator, they had to endure a crypt, a dungeon, and a haunted ballroom full of very clingy ghosts. At last, however, the car reached its destination—where Prot was still patiently holding open the door.

"Oh, wow," Edison remarked. "This is cool. This is better than the stairs, eh?"

"Not really," said Marcus. Holly, meanwhile, was shooing everyone out of the car, which had a mournful expression on its goblin face.

"Did Miss Molpe say you could use her elevator?" it asked. No one paid much attention except Marcus, who turned to look at the car.

"Miss Molpe uses this elevator?" he asked.

"Yes," the car replied.

"How often does she use it?"

"Whenever she needs to."

"Yeah, but how often does she come here?" Talking to the car was a little like talking to Prot, Marcus thought. He had to spell things out. "How often do you actually see her?"

"I've never seen her," said the car.

"What?" Marcus was flabbergasted. "But how do you know what she'll do if you've never even seen her?"

The car looked confused.

"I just know," it explained. "Miss Molpe is in charge. We have to do what she says."

"Marcus!" Coco beckoned from inside the elevator. "Hurry, will you?"

"Yeah, I'm coming."

Marcus squashed into the elevator beside Holly, who was reading aloud from the brochure in her hand. "'Eight-eight-two-two . . . ,'" she quoted as Prot tapped each digit into the control panel.

"Hey, Mom," Marcus asked his mother, "what do sirens look like?"

Holly didn't reply; she was too busy reciting code numbers. It was Newt who answered his question.

"They're supposed to be half woman, half bird," she explained. "They're not real, though. I told you—they're ancient Greek legends."

Marcus wasn't so sure about that. "Mom?" he said,

hoping to extract more information. Then his gaze was snagged by the familiar brochure in her tight grip. "'Diamond Beach Paradise'?" he read. "Are we going there? But that's not the *real* Diamond Beach. That's just a fake."

"I thought we were going home," Newt grumbled. Marcus was about to point out that they didn't yet know *how* to get home when Holly said, "I just want to make a quick stop."

"Why? So you can see Jake?"

"Maybe. If he's still there."

Then the door closed.

29.
Old Diamond Beach

"**A**re you talking about Jake Borazio?" Coco butted in. "That boy we used to know when we were all kids together?"

Holly nodded. She passed the Diamond Beach brochure to Coco, who gasped.

"It's him!" Coco yelped. "It's Jake! Look! Can you believe that?"

She shoved the picture under Sterling's nose. Marcus, meanwhile, had been struck by a disturbing thought. With a grimace he addressed his mother.

"If Jake's still down here somewhere," he said, "will that mean he hasn't grown up?"

Holly looked startled.

"Oh, I-I'm sure he has," she replied.

"But what if he hasn't? What if he's stayed the same age?" Marcus's voice dropped to a spooked whisper. "What if we're stuck in a time warp?"

Holly opened her mouth. Before she could reply, however, Coco said, "Holly, what's going on? Where did you get this?" She was referring to the brochure, which her husband was still holding. "Did you find it in your trailer?"

"No."

"You mean you've had it all this time?" Coco sounded amazed. "Since we were kids?"

"Uh—no . . ."

"It was in the office," Sterling supplied helpfully.

And when Coco gave him a blank stare, Holly mumbled, "It's complicated."

Then the elevator stopped.

"Oh, boy," said Marcus. "This is going to be weird."

He was right. It *was* weird. As the elevator door rolled back like a curtain, they all found themselves staring at the inside of a public restroom. The walls were made of brick; the floor was a slab of polished concrete. There was the usual array of basins, taps, and paper-towel dispensers, yet everything was sparkling clean. Marcus couldn't spot a single puddle, rust stain, cobweb, or graffiti tag.

The whole place smelled of flowers.

"Oh!" Holly exclaimed. And Coco said, "Is this . . . ?" before trailing off.

"Nice," drawled Newt, her voice weighted with sarcasm. "Just where *I'd* want to take my next holiday."

Holly ignored her, calmly stating, "It's the Diamond Beach toilet block."

"No, it isn't," Edison protested.

"Yes, it is." Holly spoke kindly. "It's the old one, not the new one. You've never been here before."

"But was the old one ever this clean?" Coco asked in a hushed tone. "It's so *clean*."

"I know. It is." Holly peered around. "I don't think I ever minded coming in here—did you? So it must have been *fairly* clean, back in our day."

"It's beautiful. Really beautiful," growled Newt without conviction. "It's the most beautiful grungy old restroom I've ever seen. I still don't want to stay here, though."

For once, Marcus agreed with Newt. "Let's get out before someone comes in," he begged.

So after instructing Prot to hold the elevator door, they ventured out of the restroom into the open. It was a beautiful day outside. The sky was cloudless. The temperature was perfect. The air was fresh and balmy and scented with seaside aromas: salt, fish, coconut oil, barbecued meat. Marcus was astonished at the landscape confronting him; it was familiar, yet at the same time utterly foreign. He recognized the curving sweep of white sand, the strip of navy-blue ocean, the silhouette of a rocky headland, the dark smudge of a distant lagoon. But the lagoon was wrapped in a thick cloak of trees. The headland had no houses on it. The white beach was deserted.

Only the ocean looked the same.

"Oh, wow," said Newt. "It's Diamond Beach. It really is."

They all gazed in wonder at the modest parking lot, with its small collection of vintage cars. These cars were parked beside a snack bar, which Marcus remembered from the brochure in Sterling's hand; beneath the big faded SNACK BAR sign were other signs, advertising ice cream, hot dogs, fish and chips. And beyond the snack bar lay a cluster of tents and trailers.

Holly let out a strangled squawk.

"That's—that's . . . ," she stammered, pointing. Coco had to finish the sentence for her.

"That's our trailer!" Coco squealed. "And that's your tent, Holly!"

"That's not our trailer," Newt objected. Sensing her alarm, Marcus decided to clarify things.

"She doesn't mean *your* trailer," he said. "She means *her* trailer. From when she was a kid."

Holly and Coco were clutching each other for support. Holly looked as if she was about to faint.

"Can you—can you see my mom and dad?" she whimpered.

Coco shook her head. Her lips were trembling.

"I can't see anyone," Edison complained. "There's nobody here."

"They're probably all inside," said Newt. But she seemed doubtful.

"Maybe there *are* no people." Holly was hoarse with emotion. "Maybe Jake's dream holiday was Diamond Beach without the people."

"Oh, yeah!" Edison's whole face lit up. "Wouldn't *that* be great!"

"There has to be an explanation," Sterling muttered, looking more and more perplexed. "I know there has to be a key to this somewhere. I just have to figure out what it is."

Marcus had been studying the trailers. One of them was big and yellow. One had stars and song lyrics painted all over it. Another might have been homemade; it was constructed out of wood, canvas, and plastic sheeting, like a slightly updated covered wagon.

But one trailer was small and beautifully kept, with flowered curtains and a blue stripe.

"Is that Miss Molpe's trailer?" he asked.

Then Holly screamed.

30.
Familiar children

A little girl had appeared in the distance, stepping out from behind one of the tents. Though her face was just a blur, Marcus could see that she was short and plump, with curly black hair. She was about eight years old.

Coco slapped her hands over her mouth.

"Is that *you*, Coco?" Holly croaked, gaping like a fish.

The little girl suddenly swerved in their direction. As she trotted toward them across the parking lot, Marcus began to feel scared. What would happen when the little Coco and the big Coco came face-to-face? Would one of them vanish in a puff of quantum physics? Would they merge together? Would they both go mad?

Big Coco was certainly shaken to the core. Gasping and reeling, she looked like someone about to have a heart attack. Little Coco, in contrast, was blithe and happy. She was also as cute as a button in her purple-hippo swimsuit, with her painted toenails and missing teeth.

"Hey!" she chirped. "Why are you here?"

She was talking to Edison—probably because they were both around the same age. It was Marcus, however, who replied.

"We're here to play," he said quickly. "Is there anyone here we can play with?"

Little Coco dimpled. "Sure!" she exclaimed. "There's me!"

"Anyone else?"

"Um . . ." Glancing over her shoulder, she wrinkled her brow in thought. "There's my big sister. And there's Abigail. And Holly . . ."

Marcus heard his mother squeak.

"Are there any boys?" he asked Little Coco, who answered him cheerfully.

"There's Paul," she offered. "And there's Jake. Only Jake doesn't play with us anymore, since he got so big."

Holly staggered. Her knees looked as if they were about to give way, but there was nowhere for her to sit down. So she slumped against the nearest rubbish bin (which didn't have any rubbish in it).

"Is that Miss Molpe's trailer?" was Marcus's next question. When Little Coco nodded, he asked, "Is she in there?"

"No. I haven't seen her for a *long* time." Little Coco cocked her head at him. "Why? Do you want some chocolate cake?"

"We want to talk to Jake Borazio," Holly bleated before Marcus could stop her. He knew that even mentioning Jake would ring alarm bells among those whose job it was to keep Jake well guarded.

Sure enough, Little Coco's expression became wary. "Jake's no fun," she said. "He won't play with you. Why do you want *him?*"

"We don't," Marcus assured her. Though he wasn't scared of Little Coco and her friends, he knew that there might be adults to contend with. "Are your mom and dad around?"

"*My* mom and dad?" Little Coco sounded vague, as if parents were a concept she'd hardly encountered before. "I dunno. I don't think so. . . ."

"Is your name Coco?" Edison piped up. He was obviously fascinated. Little Coco dimpled at him.

"Yeah," she said. "How did you know?"

"Because—ouch!" Edison jumped as Newt pinched his neck. "What's *your* problem?" he demanded.

"You are," Newt rejoined.

"I just wanted to tell her—"

"Yeah, well, *don't*. She'll freak." Newt jerked her

chin toward Big Coco, who was shaking and sniffing and wiping gobs of damp green gunk off her face. "We've already got a basket case on our hands. We don't want another one, do we?"

Sterling, meanwhile, was thinking aloud.

"Miss Molpe's got to be the code name for the command and control program that's running this system," he observed, tapping his front teeth with one finger. "There's a definite pattern here, don't you think?" When Coco failed to acknowledge his appeal, he turned to Marcus. "We should check out Miss Molpe's trailer. It might be an access point to the mainframe."

Marcus sighed. "There *is* no mainframe. It's magic," he groaned, wondering why Sterling couldn't accept that. He was about to suggest that *on no account* should they go anywhere *near* Miss Molpe's trailer when his mother leaned down to address Little Coco.

"Hey, sweetie," she quavered. "Are—are Mr. and Mrs. Bradshaw here?"

Little Coco looked puzzled. "Who?"

"Holly's mom and dad." Holly had to swallow before continuing. "The ones who live in that tent."

"I dunno." Little Coco squinted at the tent in question. Then her face lit up. "There's Holly!" she cried, madly waving. *"Hi, Holly!"*

Without warning she bolted, making a beeline for

the older, skinnier girl who was waving back at her. Marcus could see that the older girl was wearing a bikini. She had straight blonde hair.

"Oh my," his mother wailed. "It's me. It's *me*."

"I can't bear it." Coco's voice cracked. "We were so young. What happened?"

Edison eyed his stepmother in a bewildered kind of way.

"You grew up," he said. "Everybody grows up. They have to."

"Unless they die," Marcus mumbled. By this time he had spotted other children appearing from behind rocks, cars, and bushes. They were skipping out of the distant surf and crawling through tent flaps. They were climbing down trees and surging over sand dunes.

It was like watching the slow buildup of ants around a dead lizard—and he began to feel uneasy.

"Which tent belongs to Jake?" he asked his mother, who shook her head.

"Jake's family had a trailer," she replied, pointing. "That one."

"We should go there first, before we get swamped by kids." Marcus had noted, with growing alarm, that many of the converging children were carrying sticks and Boogie boards and fishing rods. "If Jake's not there right now, he might drop by later. And when we go inside, we can shut the kids out."

"Hear! Hear!" Newt's vote of confidence was unexpected, to say the least. "Good call! Let's shut the kids out!"

Edison showed his support by saluting Marcus. Coco nodded. Sterling said, "What if we split into a couple of teams, one for each trailer, and meet back here in ten minutes?"

But Holly wasn't listening. She was already half-way across the parking lot, heading for Jake's trailer.

31.

"You're not allowed in there...."

*K*nock-knock-knock.

"Hello? Jake? It's Holly Bradshaw...."

There was no reply. As Holly pulled open the trailer door, Marcus stood behind her, anxiously watching wave upon wave of sandy, sunburned kids close in on them from every direction. So far, only Little Coco and Little Holly had reached Jake's trailer; they were tugging at Sterling's Hawaiian shirt, nagging him to come and play, to buy them some ice cream, to leave Jake alone. "You're not allowed in there," they whined. "Jake said so. He'll get mad. He always gets mad...."

Marcus tried not to look at Little Holly. He found her freckles and her pointed chin extremely disconcerting, because he wasn't used to seeing them on such a small face.

"Just *go*!" he urged his mother, who didn't need any encouragement. She yanked open the door and plunged inside, closely followed by Coco, Newt, and Marcus. Edison soon joined them, with his father in tow.

When Little Coco tried to bring up the rear, it was Newt who pushed her back outside and slammed the door.

"You were such a pest," she informed her step-mother.

Jake's trailer was one of the largest in the camp-ground. It had a separate bedroom at one end, with a bathroom off that—plus all kinds of extra luxuries. There were fly screens, clothes cupboards, wall-mounted fans, a dining nook, a separate lounge area, a picture window, and a built-in china cabinet. Despite the wood-grain Formica plastered over nearly every available surface, including the fridge, it would have been a nice place to live if it hadn't been so untidy. Junk was piled up everywhere: rags, nets, shells, bottles, barbecue grills, gas cylinders, baseball bats, buckets and spades, broken umbrellas, comic books, animal bones.

Coco was appalled.

"How can anyone *live* like this?" she exclaimed, shocked out of her teary-eyed stupor. "It's a pigsty!"

"It's not that bad," was Edison's view. "It's not super dirty or anything. *I* could live here."

"That's because you're a boy," Newt said, pronouncing the word *boy* with utter disdain. "Maybe this guy is, too. A boy, I mean. Maybe he hasn't grown up after all."

"Then why did that other Coco say he'd got so big?" Marcus objected as his mother gingerly picked up a soiled bandanna.

"I remember this," she whispered. "He used to wear it all the time. Coco, do you remember this?"

Coco nodded. Edison, meanwhile, had slipped into the bedroom, where he was pulling open doors. "No one in here!" he announced, peering into a cramped little cupboard that contained a toilet and nothing else. "Doesn't look like he's at home, eh?"

BANG-BANG-BANG! Someone pounded on the trailer's exterior. "Come out!" a muffled voice demanded. "Come out and play!"

Sterling looked at his wife. "That's you, isn't it, Cokes?" he asked.

BANG-BANG-BANG! More thumping followed, involving more than one fist. Then came a chorus of high-pitched voices, echoing Little Coco's entreaties.

"Come out.... Come and play.... You're no fun.... You're not allowed in there...."

Newt scowled at the two women. "Can't you please tell yourselves to shut up?" she said.

But Holly wasn't listening. She had discarded the bandanna and pounced on something else: a dog-eared notebook. "Oh no," she croaked, flipping through its pages. "I just found Jake's diary!"

"Yeah?" Even Sterling was interested to hear *that*. Marcus gasped, while Newt raised her eyebrows. Edison came scurrying back from the bedroom just as another volley of thumps hit the side of the trailer.

"'I don't know what day it is. The days don't matter anymore. They're all the same. I went fishing as usual,'" Holly read aloud. "Oh, Coco, will you look at his spelling? Even Marcus can spell better than this!"

"What do you mean?" Marcus was offended. "I'm a really good speller!"

"Marcus goes to school," Coco pointed out, as if he hadn't spoken. "I bet there's no school around here."

THOMP! This time the noise wasn't caused by a fist, or even by a collection of fists. It was caused by something large and solid, and its impact made the whole trailer shudder.

"Hey!" Sterling boomed with a touch of annoyance. "Stop that!"

"You'd better come out!" was someone's squeaky retort. Then the trailer started to rock and sway so vigorously that Marcus almost fell.

"What on earth—" said Holly.

"They're trying to push us over!" Marcus exclaimed.

"Hey! *Hey, stop!*" Sterling lunged for the front

door but lost his footing as the floor dipped, and was thrown against the china cabinet.

"*Stop it!*" Holly shrilled. *"Holly Bradshaw, you stop that immediately!"*

A burst of excited laughter was the only response. Then the trailer bounced again, before tipping sharply to one side.

With the floor on such a slope, it was impossible for anybody to reach the door.

"They'll roll us!" Newt yelled, grabbing a bench-top. Outside, the cheering and chanting had swelled in volume; Marcus could no longer count the number of voices being raised, but he could tell that they all belonged to children—children who were happy and busy and having a lot of fun.

Then another voice cut through the din: a loud, deep, angry voice. *"Hey!"* it thundered. *"What do you think you're doing?"*

And suddenly the trailer dropped back into place. *CRASH!*

It took Marcus a few seconds to recover his wits. During that time, the shocked silence outside was succeeded by a babble of plaintive explanations. "It's not our fault. . . . They wouldn't come out. . . . We're sorry, Jake. . . ."

"Get lost!" the deep voice roared. *"Get out before I lose my temper!"*

"We were just trying to help. . . ."

But Jake wasn't impressed. "I'll count to three," he warned. "One." A pause. "Two!"

He didn't have to say "three." After a short burst of scuffling and squeaking, there were no more noises from the mob of children. All Marcus could hear as he pulled himself to his feet again was the sound of someone tall and heavy thudding up the trailer steps and jerking open the door.

"Who's in there?" Jake barked. "You'd better come out, or I'll come in after you!"

32.

The terrible truth

Jake Borazio was a big guy. With his broad shoulders, great height, and shaggy head, he filled the entire doorway. It was easy to see how well developed his muscles were—because he wore only a pair of frayed denim shorts, a rope belt, and a necklace made of shells, bones, and teeth.

He took one look at Holly and the color drained from his face.

"H-Holly Bradshaw?" he stammered.

"Jake." Holly would have turned white, too, if she hadn't been covered in fake tan. "Jake. Oh my—"

"You're still the same," Jake said, awestruck. "You haven't changed a bit."

"Neither have you," Holly replied, her voice cracking on a sob.

Marcus snorted. He knew for a fact that Holly had changed; he'd seen the difference with his own eyes. And as for Jake . . . well, Jake now had a raggedly trimmed beard, as well as hair down to his shoulders. He looked like a cross between a pirate and a pro wrestler, with a bit of rock star thrown into the mix.

In the Diamond Beach brochure, he was just a skinny kid wearing board shorts.

"Do you remember *me*, Jake?" asked Coco. "It's Coco della Robbia. The one in the purple-hippo swimsuit."

"*Coco?*" This time Jake sounded utterly gobsmacked. "*You're* Coco?"

"And this is my husband, Sterling. And these are my children, Newt and Eddie."

"Stepchildren." Newt corrected her in a surly kind of way.

"And this is *my* son, Marcus," Holly croaked. "We've come to save you, Jake."

Jake blinked. "*Your* son?" he said hoarsely, staring at Marcus as he addressed Holly. "You got married?"

"Well—uh—yes, but I'm not married now. Anymore." Holly flushed. "It's complicated."

"Did you hear what she said, Jake?" asked Coco, obviously surprised by his lack of enthusiasm. "We've come to take you home."

Jake's stunned gaze shifted in her direction, but he didn't respond.

"Maybe he doesn't want to go home," Edison remarked. "It's pretty nice here."

"No." Holly shook her head. "Jake, you can't stay. This is a bad choice. This isn't real."

"Are *you* real?" he interrupted, then frowned and glanced away, murmuring, "You must be. You must. I never could have imagined this. . . ."

"Of course I'm real!" Holly seized his hand. "There! See? Feel that! I'm as real as you are."

"We're from the outside world," said Marcus, who felt that the time had come to supply Jake with a clear and precise explanation. "Me and Mom bought Miss Molpe's old trailer to go camping in. We didn't know it was hers when we bought it. We didn't know about the cellar. But we found the office, and then we got on the elevator—"

"The elevator?" Jake cut him off. "You came in the *elevator*?"

"Yes." Marcus was surprised. "You know about that?"

"Of course. I know about everything here." Jake's tone was flat and bitter. "I've been in this place so long I know every rock. Every tree. Every blade of grass. But the elevator doesn't work. Nothing happens when I push the button."

"That's because you need a robot." Edison weighed in.

And when Jake's jaw dropped, Holly added gently, "Things have changed since we were kids. There are robots and . . . and other things. . . ."

"Like computers!" Edison supplied, much to Coco's disgust.

"We're not *that* old!" she snapped. "There were computers around when we were your age—they just weren't as good as they are now!"

"Yeah. Well, I guess a lot of things have changed while you've been down here," Marcus said to Jake, steering the conversation back toward more urgent matters. "But the important thing is that we're all trying to get out now. And since we found your brochure in the office—"

"This brochure," Holly interjected, producing the crumpled Diamond Beach Paradise pamphlet and passing it to Jake. It was a clumsy gesture, because of her remaining false fingernails.

Jake didn't take the brochure. He simply stared at it dumbly.

"When we found that," Marcus continued, "we thought we'd come and get you before we tried to go home. Just in case you wanted to leave."

"Because you *should* leave," advised Edison, who must have thought that Jake needed persuading. "I didn't want to leave my dream holiday, either, but I'm glad I did. You'll be glad, too. It's nice to visit, but you have to go home sometime."

Jake's lips began to tremble as he gazed at Edison in wide-eyed disbelief.

"You think I don't want to go home?" Jake rasped. "Are you *crazy*?"

"Shhh." Holly tried to calm him down—worrying, perhaps, that someone as big as Jake could do a lot of damage if he became overwrought. "Edison's so young he doesn't understand how hard it can be when you're away from your family—"

But Jake didn't let her finish.

"Of course I want to go home!" he cried. "I've been trying to leave since day one! The minute I got here, I wanted to leave!"

"Really?" Marcus was puzzled. "That's weird."

Holly was also confused. "But wasn't this your dream holiday?" she asked Jake, whose shoulders slumped as he became more subdued.

"Yeah," he confessed. "It was. Until I realized that you weren't here with me."

Holly frowned. So did Marcus. Coco said, "But Holly *is* here. I saw her. She's just outside." Then, as Edison opened his mouth to correct her, she quickly forestalled him. "I mean, obviously the one outside is a younger version, but—"

"I knew that kid out there wasn't you," Jake cut in, as if Coco hadn't spoken. He was talking to Holly. "As soon as I saw her diary, I realized I'd made a mistake. Remember how you used to keep a diary? You were always scribbling away."

Once again, Holly flushed. "Yes," she replied. "I remember."

"You'd never let me look at it," Jake went on. "So when I got here, that's the first thing I did. I asked to see your diary—and you gave it to me. *That* Holly gave it to me. The fake one." He pointed at the door. "But then I opened it up and there was nothing. Blank pages. Because I couldn't fill it myself, you see. I didn't really know what was going on inside your head. That's when I realized that all of this . . . this whole setup . . . it was all my own creation, some-how. It wasn't a copy of the real thing; it was just a dream of mine. And people in dreams are never any good. They're like cotton candy—they just melt away. I wanted the *real* you. I wanted to know what you'd written in your diary."

Holly was gulping and sniffing. "I wrote about *you*, Jake," she whispered. By this time Coco was wiping tears from her eyes (and dried goo from her face) with the sleeve of her bathrobe. Even Newt wore a slightly soppy expression.

Marcus scowled. He didn't much care for the way his mother was holding Jake's hand. "So if you wanted to leave, why didn't you?" he asked sharply.

"I tried," Jake revealed. "I went to see if Miss Molpe would send me back. She was the one who conjured up this place when I complained that I didn't want to leave Diamond Beach. She told me I'd never have to go away. So I packed a suitcase with things like a towel and a sleeping bag, snuck back to her place one night, and when she sent me down into her cellar—"

"You opened a door!" Edison concluded. "And you stepped into your dream holiday!"

"Yeah." Jake gave a nod. "But when I looked for the door again, it had disappeared. That's why I went to her trailer. Her false trailer, I mean. I went there, and I found out what Miss Molpe *really* wanted."

He paused, as if expecting instant and total comprehension from his audience. Instead, all he got was a series of blank looks.

"Oh yeah?" Newt said at last. "And what was that?"

"You mean you don't know?" Jake sounded genuinely taken aback. When no one answered him, he took a deep breath and said, "She wanted to kill me. That's what she does. She kills children."

33.
"They don't exist. . . ."

Everyone goggled at Jake.

"It's true!" he insisted. "She's a witch of some kind!"

Newt pulled a skeptical face. Edison uttered an awestruck "Wow!" as Sterling's forehead creased.

"Are you sure you don't mean 'siren'?" Marcus proposed, eliciting a snort from Newt.

"I told you, sirens were made up by the ancient Greeks," Newt scoffed. "Sirens don't exist! They never existed!"

"Oh, really?" said Marcus. He couldn't keep the scorn out of his voice. "So sirens don't exist, but magic elevators do? This isn't a computer game, in case you haven't noticed."

"Isn't it?" Edison peered up at Sterling from

beneath the rim of his pith helmet. "I thought you said it was."

"I'm pretty certain it is," his father assured him, then addressed Marcus in a sympathetic tone. "The trouble is it's such an advanced and complex computer game that it *feels* like magic."

Marcus cast up his eyes. "You wish," he growled before Jake suddenly hijacked the conversation.

"Listen to me!" Jake cried. "I know what I saw! You all think I'm crazy, but I'm not! She was going to build a beach house out of my bones—she said so!"

Everyone flinched.

"Oh my goodness." Coco was horrified. "How sick. She actually *told* you that?"

Jake hesitated. "Well . . . no. Not exactly," he was forced to admit. Seeing his audience exchange doubtful glances, he erupted again. "She was singing to herself! I overheard her!" He went on to explain how, on first entering Miss Molpe's trailer ("the one out there, not the real one"), he'd been planning to ask her if she'd send him home after all. He'd even packed his suitcase for the trip back. "But she wasn't in," he related, "so I had a look around. And I found all these . . . these bones." A muscle quivered in his jaw, and he had to swallow before continuing. "They were stacked in cupboards," he said faintly. "Laid out in drawers. Like a collection."

"Maybe they were animal bones," Holly speculated.

181

Jake shook his head. "Not these ones," he growled. "And there were piles of old clothes, too. Kids' clothes." Hearing a few indrawn breaths, he quickly explained, "She wasn't collecting for charity, either, because all the clothes had bloodstains on them."

Marcus didn't like the sound of that. Neither did Holly, from the look on her face.

But Coco wasn't convinced.

"Well, *I* used to go into Miss Molpe's trailer all the time," she objected, "and *I* never saw anything weird."

"Because you were in the real trailer. Not the one over there." Jake gestured at the door. "The one over there is inside the real one—like the rest of this place. The real one wasn't full of bones, either. Not like the one over there. And do you know what I found under the seats of the fake one, when I was looking for another staircase? Photograph albums. There was no cellar, but there were loads and loads of photograph albums, full of really old travel snapshots. Only they were pictures of bones. Charnel houses in France and crypts in Italy and piles of skulls in Cambodia . . ." He shuddered. "I was looking at the pictures when I heard her coming," he continued. "So I hid under a seat. She was crooning to herself, saying she had to sharpen her knives. *'He's a big boy,'* she kept singing. *'He's a big, juicy boy with great big bones.'*"

"Eeew. Gross," Edison murmured. Marcus's skin was beginning to crawl.

"And then she saw my suitcase." Jake paused for effect. "It was a big suitcase," he explained. "It belonged to my parents. I'd left it on the floor by accident, and when she saw it, she knew I was in her trailer. '*So,*' she sang, *'you've come to visit me? Come out, come out, wherever you are.*' She sounded so nice, but then her voice cracked, like a harp exploding. It was a real shock."

Newt laughed and said, "You're making this up."

"I am *not!*" Jake rounded on her, his dark eyes blazing. "If you don't believe me, go and look! She's over there right now! In the suitcase!"

Everybody gasped. There was a long, shocked silence.

Then Coco squeaked, "I *beg* your pardon?"

As Jake glanced from face to face, his own face slowly turned red.

"What else could I do?" he pleaded in a strangled voice. "She'd picked up a knife and was searching for me. Under the bed. In the cupboards. I was watching her—I'd pushed open the seat, and I was peeking out through the crack—"

"So what did you do?" Marcus broke in. He was anxious to hear the end of the story.

Jake shrugged and spread his hands.

"I didn't have a choice," he replied. "When she stopped in front of the suitcase, she had her back to me. And she was still singing, so she didn't hear me climb out from under the seat. She was too busy open-ing my suitcase. I guess she thought I might be hiding in there." He cracked a sour little smile. "That's how she ended up in there herself," he finished. "I came up behind her and gave her a shove."

For a moment no one said anything. Holly sat down abruptly, putting her head in her hands. "Wow," Edison squeaked. Marcus licked his dry lips.

"And you locked her in your suitcase?" Sterling demanded, sounding shaken. "That's really what you did?"

"Yeah," said Jake. "Then I piled a whole bunch of photograph albums on top so she couldn't get out."

"Oh , Jake . . ." Holly looked as if she was about to vomit. Even Marcus felt a little queasy.

"Did you give her any airholes?" he asked.

"She doesn't need airholes. She's a witch." Once again Jake reddened as his audience grimaced. "She told me! I mean, she *as good as* told me, when I wouldn't let her out and she was trying to make me feel sorry for her." He scowled. "She told me she used to have four sisters," he continued, "and they used to sing so beautifully that no one could resist them, but one day someone finally did—"

"Odysseus," Holly interrupted. "It was in Homer's *Odyssey*. He tied himself to the mast."

"Whatever. And when that happened, she and her sisters all had to throw themselves into the sea. I don't know why." *And I don't care, either,* his tone seemed to indicate. "But she didn't drown, like her sisters did— she just got a really, really bad cold that ruined her voice. She sounded pretty upset about that. I was supposed to think it was okay for her to lure people in with tricks and scams because she'd lost this mighty, beautiful voice that was a gift to the world for a thousand years, blah, blah, blah. . . ." He wrinkled his nose, then shrugged again. "So I figured: a thousand years? Only a witch would live that long."

"She's not a witch," Marcus interrupted. "She's a siren."

"If you say so. Anyway, she keeps scratching and singing to me whenever I go anywhere near the trailer, so I know she's perfectly all right."

"But she can't be. She must be dead by now," Newt argued. "Are you sure that's not a voice in your head?"

Jake's thick black eyebrows snapped together. He opened his mouth. Before he could speak, however, Edison cried, "Let's go and look! Can we go and look?"

"No." Holly stood up. "No. We're leaving right now."

"Oh, *please?*" Edison implored, jigging from foot to foot. "Can't we—"

"No!" Holly was adamant. "Come on. We have to leave. We have to get to the elevator."

"And then what?" asked Marcus, who was already thinking ahead, even if his mother wasn't.

"Then we take a ride up to the office," she rejoined. "And from there we go back to the cellar."

"How?" As she stared at him, he elaborated. "We don't know what buttons to push. We don't have a code number for the office, so how can we get back there?"

Holly blinked. Then she swallowed and gave herself a brisk little shake. "We'll figure something out," she declared before leading Jake to the door.

34.

The last resort

Nobody tried to stop them as they made their way from Jake's trailer to the public toilets. Though Marcus spied several groups of children huddled behind cars and trees and bushes, he quickly concluded that none of these children posed any kind of threat—not while Jake was around, anyway. Every time Jake even glanced in their direction, the kids would cringe and scatter.

At one point, when a snot-nosed toddler began to trail after Newt (who was last in line), Jake lunged at the poor little boy like a guard dog, yelling, *"Get lost or I'll punch your head in!"*

Coco was scandalized. "For heavens's sake!" she scolded. "What's the matter with you?"

"They're just children, Jake," Holly gently reminded him.

"No, they're not," Jake growled.

Marcus had to agree. "They can't be real kids, Mom," he pointed out, "because one of them is you, remember?"

"I used to let them push me around, but not anymore," Jake said on his way into the ladies' room. "They don't exist. They're nothing. They make me sick."

He was still heaping abuse on the children when he suddenly spied Prot—and was startled into silence. The robot hadn't moved. It was patiently holding the elevator door, awaiting new instructions.

Sterling seemed pleased. "There. What did I tell you?" he remarked to no one in particular. "It's reliable enough."

Coco gave a snort. She and her stepchildren piled into the elevator, just ahead of Sterling and Marcus. When Holly stepped inside, tugging Jake along with her, the narrow box began to feel very cramped.

"Right," said Coco. "So where to now?"

All eyes swiveled toward the panel of buttons, which were numbered zero to nine. There were also four control buttons: open door, close door, alarm, and stop. The alarm button was inscribed with an exclamation mark; the stop button bore a cross inside an octagon.

"Press zero," Marcus suggested. "Prot? Push that button there."

The robot obeyed, but nothing happened.

"Okay." Sterling's tone was thoughtful. "What about button number one?"

Again, nothing happened. Prot tried every single number, slowly and deliberately, without success.

"We need a code," Sterling muttered. "There must be a code number for that travel agent's office."

"What about the alarm button?" Coco weighed in. "Maybe if we press that, someone will come and save us."

When Prot pushed the alarm button, a high-pitched bell rang. But after a tense five-minute wait, everyone began to lose hope. "There would have been a response by now, if it was working at all," said Sterling.

"I knew it!" Newt broke into a wail of despair. "We're stuck! We could be here forever!"

"Don't be silly," her stepmother snapped. "There has to be a way out. . . ."

"All we need is the code for that office," Sterling reiterated, much to Newt's annoyance.

"But we *don't* have it, do we?" Her tone was sullen. "And we don't know how to get it, either!"

"Yes, we do," said Marcus. When everyone turned to stare at him, he cleared his throat, took a deep breath, and announced, "Miss Molpe can tell us the code number."

Jake hissed. "Oh, no." He shook his head. "No way. You can't do that."

"Do what?" asked Edison.

"Are you proposing we lift the lid on that suitcase?" Coco said to Marcus, wrinkling her nose in disgust. "I don't think so."

"Are you *kidding* me? Yuck!" cried Newt. "She'll be a gooey old skeleton by now! No *thanks!*"

Marcus stubbornly held his ground. "Jake says she's still alive," he insisted. "We should at least try talking to her."

"But she's a witch!" Jake was raking his fingers through his hair. "You can't trust her! She lies! This whole place is a lie, because it's her creation! And she has special powers. . . ."

"I know. Magical powers." Marcus had no doubts on that score. He was a total convert when it came to magic. "The thing is, though, you locked her in a suitcase. So she can't be *that* powerful, can she?"

It was a good point. It certainly had an impact on Jake, who briefly looked confused.

"And if she really is a siren but she's lost her voice, then she can't persuade us to stay here," Marcus went on, clinching the matter, as Holly caught Jake's wrist.

"I think we should do what Marcus said," Holly quietly recommended. "I think we should go and see if this . . . this Molpe creature is still alive. And if she is, we can ask her for a code number."

"Which you won't get," Jake warned.

"Then we won't let her out." Coco's tone was brisk. "And if we *do* let her out, we'll keep her in a headlock or something. You can take care of that, Jake. I'm sure you've got the muscles for it."

"It'll be all right, Jake," Holly promised. She took his hand and squeezed it in a gesture of reassurance. "You're not a little boy now—you're a big, strong man. And we're all here with you, backing you up." As he gazed down at her anxiously, she smiled and murmured, "You can take a few risks now. You can confront your old fears. Because you're not alone anymore."

35.
Inside the suitcase

Jake wanted to take a baseball bat into Miss Molpe's trailer, but Holly wouldn't let him. "If you think I'm going to stand by while you brain some little old lady with a piece of wood, then you don't know me very well," she declared. So when he finally jerked open the trailer door and charged inside, he was wielding his clenched fist and nothing else.

Luckily, he met with no resistance. No lurking predator tried to ambush him. And when Marcus finally edged into the trailer after his mother, he saw that it was tidy and peaceful, its floors neatly swept, its pillows plumped, its kitchenette spotless.

"There isn't a speck of dust," Coco whispered as she followed Marcus over the threshold. "I wonder who does the cleaning around here? *I'd* certainly hire them."

But the pristine condition of the place didn't interest Holly. She was more impressed by its layout and furnishings. "Look at this!" she hissed at Marcus. "This is our trailer! Look at the curtains! Look at the stove!"

Marcus grunted. His gaze was fixed on the only grubby, dilapidated item in the whole room: Jake's suitcase. It was big and brown and weighed down by dozens of heavy books. Its latches were rusty and its corners were dented.

Jake gave it a kick with his bare foot, which was hard and leathery.

"Hey!" he yelled. "Wake up!"

Marcus caught his breath. So did everyone else. There was a brief agonized silence.

Then a muffled voice trilled, "Is that you, little Jake?"

Holly squeaked. Marcus felt sick.

"Oh no," said Coco. "That's her! That's Miss Molpe!"

"It's *big* Jake now, you old bat," Jake snarled. He kicked the suitcase again. "So shut up and listen."

"She's still alive!" Coco was talking through both hands, which she'd clapped over her mouth. "How *awful*!"

"She can't be real," Newt argued, triggering a

sudden, excited response from her brother.

"Maybe she isn't real!" Edison cried. "Maybe she's part of Jake's dream holiday!" Seizing Jake's belt, he gabbled, "Isn't your Diamond Beach supposed to be a copy of the real Diamond Beach? Well, maybe *this* Miss Molpe is just a copy of the *real* Miss Molpe!"

"You're right, you're right, I'm just a creation. I sprang from Jake's imagination," Miss Molpe caroled from inside the suitcase—which received yet another swift kick from Jake.

"Shut up!" he barked. "Stop lying!" To Edison he said, "What do you think I am, a weirdo? Why would I want a cannibal witch in my dream holiday?"

There was no arguing with logic like that. Edison immediately subsided as Jake addressed Newt.

"She's as real as you are," Jake insisted. "And she's still alive because she's a witch. Now, what do you want to ask her?"

Newt, however, was sulking. It was Marcus who replied.

"We want to know the code for Siren Song Travel," he said. "So we can take that elevator back to the office where we first started."

"Did you hear that?" asked Jake, directing his raised voice at the suitcase. "We want the code for your office! Right now! Or we'll set you on fire!"

There was shifting, scraping noise. Then Miss Molpe warned sweetly, "You'll be trapped here forever if you set me on fire. Let me out and you'll have your heart's desire."

"Oh, will you stop with the *rhymes*?" Newt exploded. "They're so *irritating*!"

"We're not going to let you out," Jake growled. "Why should we do that?"

"To make sure that she gives us the right code." Marcus jumped in before the siren could respond. Seeing Jake's confusion, he quickly elaborated. "What if she lies to us? What if she deliberately sends us somewhere really dangerous? If we don't bring her along, we won't stand a chance." As Jake chewed at his bottom lip, pondering this advice, Marcus concluded glumly, "We shouldn't let her out of our sight until we get home."

"Yes, and then we should call the police," Coco suggested. When everyone turned to stare at her, she exclaimed, "It's a perfectly legitimate way of dealing with sociopaths!"

Newt gave a snort. "Yeah, right," she scoffed. "Like the police are going to believe a story like this one."

"If we tell the police, they'll probably arrest us for unlawful restraint," Holly said, at which point Miss Molpe spoke up.

"I'm old and I'm weak. I'm a friend, not a foe. It's not vengeance I seek—won't you please let me go?" she begged.

"Shut up," snapped Jake. Marcus, however, was more accommodating.

"We'll let you go once we're back in the cellar," he promised Miss Molpe. "The sooner you tell us the right code, the sooner you'll get out."

His mother gasped. "You mean you want to take her with us in that *suitcase*?" she protested. "Oh, no. No. That's horrible."

"We have to, Mom."

"I'm strong enough to carry her; don't worry," said Jake. But Holly didn't look convinced.

"I make children happy. I make dreams come true. You've no cause to entrap me if that's all I do," Miss Molpe warbled.

"You're not fooling anyone," Jake retorted. "We know what you *really* are."

"I'm a songstress, a wise woman, kind and meek. Let me out and I'll give you whatever you seek."

Jake ignored her. "I guess your plan does make sense," he said to Marcus grudgingly. "She won't help us unless she's got a reason to. Otherwise she'll send us straight down a live volcano or something."

"That's right," Marcus affirmed.

"And maybe when we get home, we can hand her over to the police," Jake concluded. Suddenly he bent down to yell at the suitcase. "Did you hear that, you old bag? If you tell us the code *right now*, we'll let you out when we get home. Otherwise you're going to be locked up forever and ever."

There was more creepy scratching. At last Miss

Molpe sang, "How do I know you're not lying to me? What will you give as a guarantee?"

Jake and Marcus looked at each other. Then Jake winked at Marcus—who realized Jake had no intention of freeing the captive.

Perhaps Holly reached a similar conclusion, because she promptly announced in a firm tone, "Don't you worry about that, Miss Molpe. I'll have you out of there just as soon as we get home. If you keep your side of the bargain, we'll keep ours. I give you my word." Having reassured the siren, Holly fixed Jake with a reproving glare and murmured, "Heaven knows I don't intend to stash a little old lady on the top shelf of my linen cupboard until the day I die."

For a moment Miss Molpe said nothing. Then she abruptly capitulated. "Thank you, my dear, your word will suffice. I'm deeply grateful—you're very nice."

"Oh, for Pete's *sake!*" Newt screamed. As everyone gaped at her, she pointed a trembling finger at the suitcase. "If she doesn't stop all that *rhyming*, I'll kick her teeth in, I swear!"

Jake laughed. "Did you hear that?" he asked the suitcase. "If you don't stop all that rhyming, you're going to get your teeth kicked in. Now . . ." He took a deep breath. "What's the code number?"

After a moment's pause, Miss Molpe gave it to him.

36.

Leaving at last

Jake had been telling the truth. Every one of the albums piled on top of his suitcase was stuffed to bursting with grisly photographs showing chandeliers made from ribs and vertebrae, skulls stacked up like profiteroles, bones arranged neatly on shelves, and bones dumped in ditches or scattered around like garden ornaments.

"I've been there," Coco remarked, pointing at a rosette constructed entirely out of knee joints. "That's in Rome, under a church. The whole place is decorated with hip bones and things."

"Look at this!" Holly had picked up the oldest-looking album of all. It was bound in vellum, and the pictures inside weren't photographs, though they *looked* realistic. Instead, they were engraved in gold on colored glass, and they showed a rocky seashore covered in rags and rib cages, with five beaming bird-like creatures perched on a cliff-top aerie. "Do you think these are the sirens?"

"I don't know," Coco responded, squinting at the group portrait, "but I have to tell you, that sure looks like Capri. I had a *lovely* holiday in Naples once, and we took a boat to Capri for a day trip. Fabulous shopping."

"Who cares?" Jake dumped the last books on the floor. "Let's go."

But when he tried to lift the suitcase, it was too heavy for him. Even after he'd kicked it a few times, accusing Miss Molpe of purposely 'stacking on the weight," he still couldn't hoist it more than a few inches off the ground. Finally he and Sterling had to take one end of the suitcase each and carry it between them like a trunk, gasping and straining as they shuffled along, out of the trailer, into the sunshine.

"She thinks she's going to *sweat* us into letting her out early," Jake groaned during a brief rest stop near the snack bar. "Like we're stupid enough to fall for that kind of trick."

Miss Molpe said nothing, but Marcus heard her sigh.

"Are there any adults around here?" asked Coco. She was keeping her eye on all the scruffy, silent kids who were drifting along behind Jake. They looked slightly lost, as if they didn't know what to do next. "*I* certainly haven't seen any."

"Me neither," Jake admitted. "I guess I must have wanted an all-kids holiday back when I first arrived."

"So the holiday doesn't change when your dream changes?" Holly seemed to be turning things over in her head. "That's interesting."

Marcus thought so, too. Then something occurred to him—something that made his heart sink. As the rest of the party moved off again, heading for the restrooms, he plucked at his mother's sleeve.

"Mom," he whispered. "Hey, Mom."

"What?" Her tone was distracted. "We mustn't get left behind, Marcus."

"Yeah, but I was just thinking—what if this *isn't* Jake's dream holiday? What if it's yours?"

Holly stared at him. "How do you mean?" she asked.

"Well, you were really keen to see Jake again—and here he is." Marcus glanced nervously at Jake's retreating back. "I don't know how it could have happened, but you were going on and on about the old Diamond Beach, and I suddenly thought . . . well, you know. This might be *your* dream come true. Not his."

"Oh no," Holly tensed. "Oh no, do you think so?"

"I—I dunno."

"*My* dream holiday? No. It can't be. Can it?" She stood for a moment, knitting her brow and chewing on her bottom lip. Then she brightened. "No," she concluded. "No, it's not mine. Because I'm here already. As a little kid. And it's very upsetting." Placing one hand on her breast, she heaved a great sigh of relief. "No, it's all right. I never would have put a mini-me in my own dream holiday."

Marcus wasn't so sure. If Holly's dream was to rescue Jake from twenty-odd years of captivity in *his* dream holiday, wouldn't there have to be a little Holly around somewhere? Marcus was certain that if Jake hadn't wanted Little Holly in his own beach-paradise scenario, Big Holly would have been brokenhearted.

But Marcus didn't say anything. There was no point. If he was right, they would find out soon enough. If he was wrong, he didn't want everybody knowing it. Instead of pursuing the matter, he followed his mother into the ladies' room, where Prot was still doggedly guarding the elevator door.

"Right!" said Jake after he and Sterling had dropped their burden onto the floor of the elevator with a mighty *thump*. "So what was that code, again?"

Sterling had memorized the number given to them by Miss Molpe. "Press the buttons zero-zero-zero-zero-one-zero-zero-zero-zero-zero-zero-one," he told the robot, which promptly obeyed. The door slid shut. The elevator began to move.

"This can't be right," said Coco. "It's going up again."

"Give it a chance. It always goes up. It's magic," Marcus reminded her as Newt sat down on the suitcase. Sterling hadn't recovered from his recent exertions; he was leaning against the wall, trying to get his breath back. Edison had produced a half-eaten granola bar from his pants pocket.

"I brought it from home," he explained when his mother asked him where it had come from. "I'm *starving*."

"Me too," Newt growled.

"This is taking an awfully long time," Jake grumbled. He gave the suitcase a nudge with his foot. "You'd better be telling the truth in there, or I'm going to dance on your head."

"It always takes a long time," Holly assured him. "Don't worry."

Marcus suddenly wondered about the food Jake had been eating for so many years. If it was magic food, what did that mean for Jake? Was magic keeping him alive? Would he shrivel up like a snake skin the minute he returned to the real world?

"Hey—um . . . Jake?" Marcus didn't know if he should warn Jake. "I was just thinking, um, about the food. Maybe we should ask her . . ." He hesitated.

"Ask her what?" said Coco when Marcus didn't finish. But before he could reply, the elevator stopped. There was a sharp *ping* as the door opened to reveal a familiar beige carpet and a set of well-stocked display shelves.

They were back at Siren Song Travel.

37.
Nearly home

"**O**h, thank goodness!" Holly exclaimed.

Coco surveyed the room in front of her. "Is this it?" she asked. "Is this the office you were talking about?"

"This is it," her husband confirmed.

Edison jumped out of the elevator, then scurried toward the only door in sight before Marcus could grab him.

"Wait!" cried Marcus. "Don't! Let Prot do that!"

But it was too late. Edison had dashed past the desk and yanked open the door—to reveal a rickety wooden staircase in a brick-lined cellar.

Marcus felt limp with relief. He'd been expecting the amusement park again.

"Oh, wow!" Edison shrilled. "We're back! Look! We did it!"

"Edison!" Coco ordered. "Stay *right* where you are, young man!"

Edison didn't listen, though; he just kept moving. Newt, meanwhile, had hauled herself to her feet.

"I am *so* out of here," she declared, stepping into the office without a backward glance. Coco quickly followed her. As for Sterling, he looked at Jake, who was blinking back tears, and said in a hesitant voice, "Do you want to help me with this suitcase, or... um...?"

"Just give him a minute," Holly advised. She gently touched Jake's arm. "It's all right," she murmured. "You're nearly home."

"I can't..." He choked on a sob.

"It must be very hard," Holly said sympathetically.

"I can't believe it. I can't believe I'm out."

"You're not out yet. Not until you leave the cellar," Marcus warned. He hovered at his mother's elbow, reluctant to set foot outside the elevator unless she was with him.

Prot, by this time, was buzzing toward Coco, who stood at the door of the office. "Come on, Sterling!" Coco nagged. "We've been down here long enough!"

"I'm coming," her husband replied. But still he lingered, his gaze fixed on Jake's hunched form.

"I'm fine. I'll be right there," Jake said hoarsely. He doubled over to lift his end of the suitcase while

Marcus pursued Prot into the cellar, which hadn't changed much. Marcus recognized the flagstone floor and trailing cobwebs, which were illuminated by a faint wash of light from the top of the stairs. Only one door was visible now, perhaps because everyone was going out, rather than in; he wasn't quite sure of the reason, and it didn't matter anyway. What mattered was getting out.

He waited impatiently for his mother at the foot of the stairs while Edison, who had already reached the top, shouted the good news down to him. "It's okay! We're home!" he announced. "Everything's normal up here!"

"Really? Thank goodness," said Coco. Unlike Newt, however, she didn't immediately rush to join Edison. Even though Sterling and Jake were moving very slowly, weighed down by the load they were carrying, Coco chose to wait for her husband.

Sterling complained. "Am I nuts, or has this thing got even heavier?"

Jake grunted. From her post at his side, Holly said, "You can't possibly carry it all the way up those stairs. You'll kill yourselves. Why don't you let the poor woman get out and walk?"

"That's not a bad notion," Sterling agreed. And from within the suitcase, Miss Molpe's tiny voice quavered, "Release me now and you won't regret it. Your heart will guide you, if you'll only let it."

"Shut up!" Jake barked. He then dropped his end of the suitcase with a *thump* that shook the whole cellar.

"Ow," said Miss Molpe.

"Just give me a minute." Ignoring her, Jake flexed his shoulders and took a few deep, reviving breaths. "All I need is a quick break and I'll get the suitcase up those stairs, no problem."

Holly frowned. "But—"

"We can't let her out down here," Jake insisted. And Marcus backed him up.

"Jake's right," said Marcus. "We can't risk it. We need to get her into the real world first."

"I don't see why," his mother argued. "What difference will it make?"

"The real world doesn't belong to her." Marcus had been giving the matter some careful thought. "That's probably why she can't get out of Jake's suitcase. If that suitcase had come from the world *she* created, I bet she could have got out of it quick smart." He glanced at the suitcase in question. "Once we're in the real world," he added, "we'll have a much better chance. Because she can only hurt people after she lures them into *her* world."

Holly sighed and gave up. The others nodded, and Sterling beamed his approval, saying, "That's very ingenious. I bet you'll be designing computer games when you get older."

Only Miss Molpe wasn't impressed.

"You're wrong; I'm weak wherever I go. You could knock me out with a single blow," she sang from inside the suitcase. At that point something else occurred to Marcus. Was there a chance that she would simply *turn to dust* in the real world?

"Hey!" Newt suddenly bawled from the top of the staircase, making everybody jump. *"Are you guys coming, or what?"*

"We're on our way!" Coco yelled back. She briskly patted her husband's arm. "Don't give yourself a hernia," she told him before padding upstairs in her grimy slippers.

Marcus hurried after her. He didn't want to hang around and blurt out all the terrible things that were on his mind. As he crawled out of the banquette seat, he heard Miss Molpe behind him brokenly crooning, "I've kept my promise; won't you keep yours? You're jailing me without a cause." He also heard the sound of someone's heavy, dragging tread together with Holly's worried voice, warning Jake, "Please be careful—watch that step—*slow down*, Jake, or you'll hurt yourself!"

Gazing around the trailer, Marcus derived some comfort from the fact that everything looked shabby and soiled. Edison's amusement park had been spotless, as had Coco's spa and Jake's version of Diamond Beach. The sight of so much ingrained dirt was therefore very reassuring; Marcus had learned to distrust perfection.

But then Sterling exclaimed from under the floor, "Am I double-nuts, or is this suitcase getting lighter again?" And Marcus felt his heart skip a beat.

Maybe the siren had *already* turned to dust!

"I don't know if this is going to work," he faltered with growing alarm. What if *Jake* started to disintegrate before his very eyes?

He was about to suggest that Jake might want to think twice about leaving the cellar when Edison cut him off.

"It's okay," said Edison, misinterpreting Marcus's concern. "There's *just* enough room for the suitcase to fit through this hole." Leaning down into the seat, he bellowed, *"Hey, Dad! We can pull that thing through from our side if you give it a big shove!"*

"Okay!" Sterling's answer was muffled. "I think we can do that! It's not so heavy all of a sudden!"

"Wait," Marcus protested. "Hang on. I was just wondering . . ."

Thudda-thudda-thump! Without warning, the suitcase suddenly reared into view, toppled over the rim of the seat, and somersaulted onto the floor of the trailer—just as a thunderous knock on the door made everyone freeze like rabbits in a spotlight.

"This is park security!" a deep voice boomed. "Is anybody in there?"

38.
"Let her go!"

Everyone exchanged horrified looks. Then Miss Molpe fluted, "Come in, come in, and set me free! I need your help—they've captured me!"

"Hello?" Once again, a meaty fist pounded on the door. "Are you in there? Hello?"

Newt and Coco clutched each other.

"What'll we do?" Coco whispered.

"Let her out! Quick!" Newt cried.

"He's not the police. He can't arrest us."

"He'll *call* the police if he hears *that*," Newt hissed, jerking her chin at the suitcase, which was emitting low, sinister noises. Meanwhile, Sterling had hauled himself over the edge of the seat, clearing the way for Holly and Jake to climb out.

Edison peered up at Marcus, who was very worried.

"Are we allowed to open the suitcase?" Edison inquired under his breath.

"I dunno."

Knock-knock-knock. "We've had a complaint about a missing dog!" the security officer announced as Holly joined Sterling. "Do you have a dog in there, by any chance?"

"Um—hang on a minute!" Coco pleaded. Then she lowered her voice, appealing to Holly. "We can't open this door until something's done about *that*." Coco was referring to the suitcase. Before anyone else could do more than glance at it, she addressed the security officer again. "There's no dog in here!" she assured him.

Marcus sucked air through his teeth. "Actually . . . there is. Sort of," he mumbled. "It's downstairs. In its own dream holiday."

"We've had a report that a small white dog wearing goggles and water wings was last seen entering this trailer!" the security officer continued. "Could I talk to you about that, please? Could you open the door?"

Newt pulled a face at her stepmother. Coco turned to Holly, who took a deep breath and squared her shoulders.

"Just give us one minute," she requested before marching toward the suitcase.

"No!" rasped Jake. "Wait! Not yet!"

"We have to let her out," said Holly, as quietly as she could.

"Okay, okay! Just wait till I'm ready!" Jake swerved in front of her. "I'll grab her when you open the lid, all right? On the count of three . . ."

"Jake—" Holly began.

"One," said Jake, but he was interrupted by the security officer.

"There's a little girl out here who's very upset about her missing dog!" the disembodied voice warned, much to Newt's disgust.

"Oh, for— *Can you hold on, please? We're getting dressed!*" she screeched before muttering, "For Pete's sake, what's the matter with this guy?"

"Two." Jake positioned himself beside the suitcase.

"I'm not accusing anyone," the security officer went on, "but if your actions suggest to me that you're disposing of illegal substances in there, I'm going to have to call the police!"

"*Three!*" Jake barked. As Holly lifted the lid of the suitcase, he lunged forward, ready to seize whatever might spring out of it.

But nothing did. Instead, after several seconds, the featureless bundle inside began to shift and unfold. A tiny clawlike hand slowly appeared. It was soon joined by another hand, which hooked itself over the side of the suitcase. Joints popped and crackled. Two beady little black eyes were suddenly blinking at everyone from behind a pair of Coke-bottle glasses.

"Help me up, I'm stiff and sore. I'm not a youngster anymore," the siren gurgled.

Jake's fingers immediately clamped around her brittle arm; he yanked her to her feet, which were shod in lamb's wool slippers. She had skinny legs, a beaky nose, and thick, feathery white hair. She was wearing a flowered apron over a powder-blue housedress.

Marcus couldn't believe how small she was. She barely reached his nose.

"Oh my," Coco breathed. "She hasn't changed a bit!"

Outside, the security officer was fast losing patience. "If I have reasonable grounds to believe that you've failed to comply with park rules," he began, "I have a right of entry as representative of the property owner—"

"All right, all right, you can come in now!" Without waiting for her mother's permission, Newt opened the door. "See? I told you. No dogs in here."

As Jake froze—and Coco cast her eyes to the ceiling in despair—a short, stocky uniformed man entered the room, just ahead of a little blonde girl with braces. Ignoring everyone else, the little girl headed straight for the kitchen cupboards, which she promptly started to search. The uniformed man put his hands on his hips.

"You're not *all* residents of this trailer, are you?"

212

he demanded. "Because there are rules about over-crowding."

"I'm a visitor. They kidnapped me. I'd rather leave, if they'd set me free," Miss Molpe sang.

Marcus saw Holly cover her face. It was a stupid thing to do; it made her look horribly guilty. Sterling looked bewildered. Newt was trying to slip out but couldn't edge past the security officer. Jake gave Miss Molpe a little shake and snapped, "Don't be stupid!"

Coco tried to offer an explanation. "She's forget-ful. Don't worry. She's fine."

"I'm not, I'm not, I'm very ill. They've held me here against my will," the siren insisted feebly.

"Okay, nobody move." The security officer was frowning. He nodded at Jake. "You—the big guy. Let her go!"

Jake flushed. "I can't," he said. "You don't understand—"

"Let her go! Now!"

"But—"

"What's wrong with you? Can't you see she's sick? *Let her go*, or I'll call the cops!" When Jake reluctantly obeyed, the security officer approached Miss Molpe and took her elbow, helping her out of the suitcase. "Come on, love. You sit down and tell me what the problem is."

"*I'll* tell you what the problem is!" cried Jake. "She's been holding *me* against *my* will!"

The security officer snorted. "Yeah, right," he drawled with a sidelong glance at Jake's muscles. Marcus, meanwhile, was getting nervous.

"Please, sir—not over there," he begged. "Can't she sit down on the bed or something?"

"Oh no," Coco suddenly realized that Miss Molpe was being guided straight toward the cellar stairs. "Wait! Stop! Don't let her sit on *that* seat!"

"It's all right; I'll put the lid down," was all the security officer had time to say before Jake suddenly darted toward him. There were a scuffle, a grunt, and a shove that sent the officer reeling.

He dropped Miss Molpe's elbow.

"Look out!" Marcus yelled. But it was no good.

Free at last, Miss Molpe didn't waste a second. After nimbly dodging Edison, who had rushed to intercept her, she threw herself at the open seat and hopped inside like a sparrow. Marcus caught a glimpse of her venomous, triumphant glance as it flashed toward him. Then the lid fell. *Bang!*

And she was gone.

39.
Nightmare holiday

All at once, Marcus noticed something very, very ominous.

"Hey," he said. "This place doesn't smell like old gym clothes. It used to smell like old gym clothes."

No one paid any attention. Jake was wrestling with the security officer. Holly was making a brave attempt to break up the fight as Sterling hovered helplessly on the sidelines, pleading, "Hey, hey, let's cool it!" The little blonde girl was on her hands and knees under the table.

Edison looked at Marcus with a frown. "But it's *never* smelled like gym clothes in here," the younger boy objected. "It's always smelled like my grandad."

"Not to me," Marcus rejoined. "What does your grandad smell like, anyway?"

Edison wrinkled his nose in concentration. "My grandad smells a bit like mothballs, and a bit like bacon, and a bit like the boys' toilets at school," he told Marcus, who snuffed the air. Sure enough, it was filled with an acrid mixture of aromas: mothballs, bacon, toilets.

Meanwhile, Jake had floored the security officer with a giant shove, nearly knocking down Newt in the process. Coco had opened the seat, but before she could climb through it, Jake pushed past her, swinging himself over the side and onto the top step.

"I'll get her!" he promised as he dived downstairs. "I'll bring her back!"

"Wait!" Marcus warned. His mother took up the refrain, jostling Coco in an effort to follow Jake. "Wait! Be careful! Wait for us!" Holly entreated.

"This isn't the real world!" Marcus bawled. But it was too late. Holly had vanished. Coco would have done the same if the security officer hadn't reached out to grab her ankle.

"Leave that old lady alone!" he ordered.

Newt kicked him. *"You* leave *us* alone!" she spat. Her father began to remonstrate but was distracted when Marcus cried, "Edison opened the downstairs door when we first came in! This is what *Edison* wanted! More than anything else, he wanted—"

"To go home! Right!" Edison began to nod furiously. "It's like my dream come true! Except that

Miss Molpe has escaped. She must have set it up so she could do that."

"Sterling!" By this time Coco was struggling to release Newt from the security officer's grasp. *"I need you, quick!"*

On seeing Sterling join the tussle, Marcus seized Edison's hand and picked up the empty suitcase. "Come on. We have to get Miss Molpe," said Marcus. The two boys ducked past the rest of Edison's family and scrambled into the open seat. When the little blonde girl tried to block their path, they trod on her. They couldn't help it. Downstairs, Holly was desperately calling to them. From his vantage point on the top step, Marcus could see her leaning against a half-open door, struggling to stop it from slamming shut.

Prot was also visible in the light spilling from this door. The robot seemed to be waiting patiently where it had been left, in a corner of the cellar. But Jake and Miss Molpe were nowhere in sight.

"Come and hold this!" Holly screamed at her son over the roar of a cyclone. Her hair was whipping around her head. "I have to go get him!"

"Jake, you mean?" Marcus clattered downstairs, dragging Jake's suitcase, with Edison at his heels. "Where is he? Where's Miss Molpe?"

"She closed this door behind her, just ahead of Jake!" Holly answered Marcus at the top of her voice. "He followed her before I could stop him!"

Marcus was horrified. "Oh, no," he groaned, throwing his shoulder against the door, which was being pushed from the other side by a howling gale. "You mean he *opened this door himself*?"

Holly didn't reply. She rushed straight into the shrieking wind and lashing rain. "I'll fetch him back—" she began, then screamed as her feet slid out from under her. Marcus saw her tumble across a steel deck, which was now tipping steeply away from the threshold on which he stood.

"*Mom!*" he shouted, vaguely aware of gunwales and scuppers and hawsers and other maritime objects that were familiar to him after many hours spent racking up enormous scores on Cruising for a Bruising. Jake had plunged straight onto a passenger ship—but it was a foundering ship, being battered by a monstrous storm. Marcus couldn't see Jake anywhere. He could barely see his mother through all the driving spray. She had fallen against a bulwark and was clinging to a rail. Around her everything was in violent motion: waves, clouds, cables, deck.

Glancing over his shoulder, Marcus couldn't believe the contrast. The cellar behind him was solid and still; only the Hucksteps were moving. They were galloping down the stairs, yelling instructions.

"Hold that door open, Prot! Hold that door!" Sterling roared at the robot, which immediately headed toward Marcus.

Marcus put down Jake's suitcase. Then, clasping the doorjamb and leaning into the wind and water, he stretched out his hand to Holly, who was trying to crawl back in his direction. Little by little, as the deck slowly righted itself, she closed the gap between them until her fingertips were almost brushing his. But at that instant the Hucksteps all threw themselves at the door, knocking it open with such force that it banged off the bulkhead to which it was attached.

At the same time, Newt bumped into Marcus, loosening his grip. He had to grab her when he lost his footing.

They didn't slide as far as Holly had, because the slope of the deck wasn't as steep anymore. But they still rolled toward the bulwark. Coco was shrieking. So was Newt. Marcus managed to hook his arm around a cable.

Holly was pointing at a nearby lifeboat.

"*There's Jake!*" she cried. "*Jake, we're over here!*"

Jake was clasping the lifeboat's canvas cover. He looked terrified. Something about the expression on his face made Marcus think, *This is his worst fear come true. This is his nightmare holiday.*

The Hucksteps, meanwhile, had formed a chain, with Prot at one end and Coco at the other. Lurching and staggering, Edison's parents inched their way toward Newt; Coco was hanging on to Sterling, who was hanging on to Edison, who was hanging on to

219

Prot. The robot was parked on the basement threshold, having attached itself firmly to the doorjamb with one set of steel fingers.

"Take my hand, Newt!" Coco exclaimed just as a towering wave crashed across the deck.

Coco went spinning. Sterling was knocked off his feet. Edison's pith helmet was washed out to sea through a scupper—and he might have suffered the same fate, if Holly hadn't caught him. Suddenly they were all wallowing in foamy water, on a deck that was almost level.

The ship, however, was already starting to roll the other way.

"Prot! Stay right there!" Sterling screeched. Marcus realized that the robot was still at its post—minus a hand. The missing hand had been ripped off. It was twined around Edison's.

Jake's suitcase was now bobbing against Marcus's leg, having been sucked on board by the freak wave.

"Please clarify 'Prot's day ride there,'" the robot said tonelessly.

"Just hold that door!" begged Sterling, who was already sliding back in Prot's direction. He couldn't stop himself. As the deck tipped, everyone except Jake went slithering straight toward the open door—and toward the reassuring glimpse of brown brick directly behind Prot's head.

Torrents of water swirled along with them,

piling up against the bulkhead. Marcus found himself gasping for breath.

"Jake! Let go!" Holly wailed. "If you let go, you can come back with us!"

After a moment's hesitation, Jake let go. He immediately slipped down the slanting deck, landing on the bulkhead just a few yards away from Prot. Gasping and choking, he began to half crawl, half swim toward the robot.

Then a sudden gust of wind slammed the door shut in Prot's blank face.

40.

The last place you'd ever want to be

"**O**h, no, no!" cried Holly.

Marcus plowed into her from behind; they both hit the bulkhead just ahead of Newt. But it was Sterling who collided with the door itself and yanked it open, only to reveal a vast room full of plush carpet and swaying chandeliers. Prot had vanished. The cellar had vanished.

Marcus realized that he and the others were still on board the ship.

"This way!" Sterling seized a handful of his daughter's T-shirt. "Eddie! Cokes! In here!"

The deck was at such a steep angle that Marcus found it hard to *avoid* the open door. He practically fell into the room that lay on the other side of it, flailing about until he fetched up against the well-padded flank of an overstuffed armchair. Holly skidded into him, closely followed by Edison. Coco managed to halt her headlong fall by throwing her arms around a granite-topped bar, while Sterling stayed on his feet by keeping a firm hold on the door handle.

Jake was the last one inside. When the door swung shut behind him, the noise level finally dropped—though the floor remained unsteady. Coco whimpered, "We're stranded! What are we going to *do*?"

"Shh." Her husband tried to calm her. "It's all right. We can use the elevator."

"Not if we don't know where it is," Holly pointed out. And Marcus said, "We don't have Prot to push the buttons."

There was a gasp of horror. Then Edison, who had the sodden, wrung-out appearance of someone put through a spin cycle, held up Prot's hand. "We've got this," he croaked.

Marcus doubted very much that a disembodied piece of metal would work half as well as a whole robot. But he remained silent, because everyone else seemed both comforted and relieved by the sight of Prot's hand—unless their sudden change of mood had something to do with the ship, which was slowly righting itself again. As it did so, all the empty glasses and billiard balls that were rolling around on the carpet changed direction. There was a crashing noise from inside the big steel refrigerator behind the bar.

Marcus realized suddenly that he was in some kind of onboard cocktail lounge. It had its own stage and pool table; there were even a couple of poker machines. The whole place smelled of brine and spilled alcohol.

I shouldn't be in here, he thought. *I'm underage.* Then he reached for Jake's suitcase, which had beached itself on the parquet dance floor.

"You know what?" said Newt, pushing the wet hair out of her eyes. "I bet *I* know where that elevator is." Seeing all the raised eyebrows and creased foreheads that greeted this announcement, she continued in a more strident, waspish tone. "At Diamond Beach, it was in the toilets. At Ed's fairground, it was in the dingiest part of the ghost train. At my club, it was in the quietest corner, where you couldn't hear the music properly—"

"And at the Crystal Hibiscus, it was in the caretaker's hut!" Marcus instantly grasped what she was trying to say. "You're right! It's always in the *last place* you'd ever want to be!"

"Which is where?" asked Holly. "I've never been on a cruise ship before."

Sterling and Coco looked at each other. At last Coco said, "The engine room. Those engine room cabins are always dirt cheap. It's the noise, I expect. And the vibration."

"Then let's go straight to the engine room,"

Sterling declared, almost cheerfully. His wife, however, wasn't so confident.

"Do you know where the engine room actually *is*?" she quavered. "Because I don't."

"I do," said Marcus. When the others stared at him, he added, "I mean, I can guess. Most of these cruise ships are pretty much the same."

"How do you know?" Holly's voice was hoarse; she was still coughing and spluttering from all the water she'd inhaled. "You've never been on a cruise ship, either."

"Not a *real* one," Marcus conceded. "I've been on a lot of virtual ones, though." Then something occurred to him. Turning to Jake, he said, "Unless *you* know where everything is. Because I reckon this whole thing probably came out of your imagination, somehow."

Jake had anchored himself to a fake-marble pillar. He looked dazed and waterlogged. "I-I dunno," he mumbled. "Maybe . . ."

"Is this your worst nightmare, Jake?" Holly pressed. "If someone asked you what kind of holiday you'd hate the most, would it be a cruise ship in a storm?"

"Or would it be a *sinking* cruise ship?" Newt interrupted. As the deck started to tip again, everyone waited anxiously for Jake's response. But he shook his head.

"I try not to think about stuff like this," he rasped. "I just—I can't."

Marcus swallowed. Holly closed her eyes. Sterling licked his lips and Newt growled, "In other words, you don't know where the engine room is."

"It'll be down below the waterline," Marcus insisted. "We just have to go downstairs and follow the noise."

"Then we'd better hurry," warned Edison. "Because we might not have much time left."

41.

Belowdecks

So they went in search of the engine room, bouncing off bulkheads as the vessel heaved from side to side. Though Marcus was too busy keeping upright to worry much about the ship's amenities, he did notice that they weren't a patch on the ones he'd seen in Cruising for a Bruising. Where was the ice rink? The driving range? The ten-storied atrium? As he and his companions descended from deck to deck, they spent most of their time in dingy, narrow passages lined with cabin doors, picking their way past creeping tides of vomit.

Luckily, Marcus was used to dodging vomit. In Cruising for a Bruising, the puke was usually flying through the air; more than once, his avatar had been splattered by a whole row of seasick passengers in evening clothes projectile-vomiting onto a lower deck. He knew how to clear a path through the computer-generated puddles with a fire hose. He was also very good at avoiding runaway dessert trolleys, popped champagne corks, golf balls on the driving range, galley fires, freak waves, machete-wielding stowaways, high-kicking chorus lines, gushes of scalding steam, and drunken passengers careening around in stiletto heels.

Not that any corks were popping on board this particular ship. But his virtual training stood him in good stead. He had perfect judgment when it came to threading his way through an obstacle course in a heavy sea, thanks to all the practice he'd had; he was like a pilot finally taking off after months spent on a flight simulator. The only difference between this and the game was that slamming into a virtual bulkhead didn't actually hurt.

Magic bulkheads were different.

"We can't really sink, though, can we?" Holly asked as they all clung to a handrail, waiting for the right moment to descend another companionway. "I mean, this ship doesn't exist. How can it hurt us if it doesn't exist?"

No one answered. Jake was too upset. Coco was feeling too sick. Edison was still coughing up water, and Sterling, at the rear of their group, was fending off a panicky steward. "Where are your life jackets?" the steward was demanding. He had an armful of life jackets, one of which he thrust at Marcus. "Put on your life jackets and report to your muster station!"

"That's what we're doing," Sterling assured him. But the steward wasn't buying that.

"Not below, you're not!" he exclaimed. "Passengers muster on the *upper* decks—" He broke off suddenly, interrupted by the arrival of a woman in a sparkly evening gown. She banged through the nearest swinging door, wide-eyed and hysterical.

"We're going to die!" she shrieked. "We're all going to die!"

"Miss? Miss!" The steward ran to intercept her. "You have to put on your life jacket—"

"Save me!" When she flung herself at him, he lost his footing; they both collapsed in a heap.

Marcus, meanwhile, was concentrating on the task in front of him. He had to get downstairs without falling off the companionway—and without tripping on the avalanche of oranges that swirled around its bottom step. The move called for split-second timing. . . .

"Now!" he barked, then rushed to take advantage of that fleeting moment when the ship was more or less horizontal. By the time he reached the deck below, it was on just enough of a slope to make the oranges roll away from the spot where he landed. He realized

that they must have spilled out of the dry store.

"Quick!" he cried. "We're getting close!"

"This place is huge!" said Holly, who was just behind him. She gazed around in despair at a long, irregular space lined with bins and cupboards and fridges. Many of the cupboards were open, their doors flapping dangerously, their contents strewn across the deck. "How are we going to find one little elevator?"

"We could use *that*," Edison suggested. He had joined Holly at the foot of the companionway, where a handy evacuation chart was attached to one of the bulkheads. "Look," he continued, pointing at a red dot. "It says we're right here. . . ."

"But there's no engine room on this level!" Coco was peering over her stepson's shoulder. "It's all galleys and health spas. . . ."

"We have to keep going down," said Marcus just as a giant tub of maple syrup crashed to the deck behind him. It wasn't easy wading through a slick of maple syrup in rough weather, but they all managed it somehow. And when a couple of enraged crewmen suddenly charged around the corner, the maple syrup turned out to be a blessing. The two men ended up with their feet in the air, spinning around and around on their backs before crashing into a pallet of canned tomatoes. Marcus and the others escaped through a minefield of broken glass.

Upon reaching the next companionway, they

found its lowest portion wreathed in something that looked a lot like smoke.

"Uh-oh," said Sterling.

"It's okay." Marcus had faced a lot of virtual fires. He knew the drill. "All engine rooms have fire extinguishers. It's against the law not to."

Newt gave a snort. "Uh—hello?" she spluttered. "What law would that be, exactly? The law of Myth World?"

Coco, by this time, was at the end of her tether, wet and cold and bruised and queasy. "We shouldn't be here. We *really* shouldn't be here," she moaned. "We should go back upstairs right now!"

"But there's nothing up there, Coco. Not for us," Holly reminded her. Edison nodded in agreement.

"We need to get to the elevator. It's our only chance," he assured his stepmother.

Jake said nothing. His face was white and drawn, his gaze dull, his jaw clenched. Having taken charge of the suitcase again, he was clutching it as if it were a life preserver. He gave the impression of someone working very hard not to curl up into a tight little ball.

"That elevator's not far away. I know it isn't," said Marcus. "I mean, just look at the smoke down there. It's the *last* place you'd want to be. The worse things get, the closer we are."

He'd hardly finished speaking before the deck dipped abruptly, dropping from under their feet. They all bumped and slid to the bottom of the companion-way, yelping and screeching and grabbing at the rail. After disentangling themselves, however, they found that no one had broken anything; despite a few sore knees and elbows, they'd survived the fall practically unscathed.

"This isn't smoke," Holly announced hoarsely, scrambling to her feet as she sniffed the air. "It's steam, thank goodness."

"And *this* is the engine room," Marcus said. "It has to be." He peered through the whitish haze at a vast tangle of chains, valves, switches, cables, dials, taps, and pipes—pipes of every size, from tubes the width of his finger to cylinders as big as factory chimneys. Amid all the humming, clanking machinery were a couple of red fire extinguishers, a metal walkway, a roll of duct tape, an empty soft drink can, and a sign that read ON HEARING CO_2 ALARM, EVACUATE IMMEDIATELY.

"Okay. Here's what we do," said Marcus. "We look for the bilge pump."

Everyone gaped at him. Even Sterling said, "Huh?"

"The bilge pump is full of bilge. Which comes from the bilge wells." Thanks to Cruising for a Bruising, Marcus knew quite a lot about the workings of an engine room. "Bilge is slimy black stuff that sits at the bottom of the ship," he explained. "It's a combination of water, oil, sludge, and chemicals."

"So it's disgusting?" asked Newt.

"Yes," Marcus replied.

"And smelly?"

"Very smelly."

"Then that's exactly what we want!" Edison squeaked. "Something you'd never, ever want to see in a billion years!"

The words were barely out of his mouth when there was a deafening *crack*—and a roaring jet of seawater burst through a tear in the hull.

42.
Sinking

Everyone screamed. Coco yelled something about lifeboats. But Marcus cried, "No, wait! This is good!"

"Are you *insane*?" Newt squawked. "We have to get out!"

"No, we don't! This is the worst place on board!" Marcus looked around, desperate for a glimpse of the elevator. "It's got to be here somewhere!"

"This way, Marcus, quick!" When Holly tried to grab him and pull him back toward the companionway, Marcus managed to shake her off. He darted toward the stern, past what he knew to be the main-engine cylinder-head pistons. Behind him, Holly uttered a howl of despair. *"Marcus! Come back!"*

The water was already surging around his ankles.

He found an elevator near the alarm panel, but it was a freight elevator. The door was standing open and he could see its scratched paint, its warning notices, its clearly marked escape hatch. Next to it was a break room full of torn carpet and shabby couches. Then came a generator, then a compressor, then . . .

Someone clamped an arm around his chest.

"You moron!" Jake screeched into his ear before lifting him clear off the ground. As Marcus struggled, he caught a scary glimpse of Jake's red face and bulging eyes. Jake was still carrying the suitcase in his other hand. Behind him, some distance away, Holly was knee-deep in water, waving her arms. Marcus couldn't see anyone else.

"It's gotta be here!" he pleaded. "It's *gotta* be!"

At that very instant, a steep roll of the ship knocked Jake off his feet. He dropped Marcus, who was carried down the walkway by a foaming green torrent. Gulping and thrashing, Marcus grabbed at the first available pipe. He wedged his body against it—and found himself staring straight at a familiar door, tucked between the bilge pump and the fuel-oil drain tank.

"Here it is!" he shrieked. "Here's our elevator!"

But its door was shut. And when Marcus pushed the up button, nothing happened.

"Where's Edison?" Marcus shouted at Jake, who was trying to retrieve his floating suitcase. *"We need Prot's hand!"*

Jake couldn't seem to absorb this information. He faltered, looking confused. It was Holly who responded, from much farther away.

"I'll get him!" Her voice was barely audible above all the rushing, creaking, groaning noises. "I'll get all of them! *Coco! Sterling!"*

She turned and waded back toward the companionway—much to Jake's alarm. "No! Holly! Don't!" he begged, forgetting his suitcase as he lunged after her. By now the water was waist-high on Jake, sloshing against door handles and lapping at light switches. Marcus's legs were sucked out from under him by the turbulence. His glasses were snatched from his nose and would have floated off if he hadn't seized them. He had to kick his way up the pipe to which he was clinging, vaguely aware of Jake's suitcase nudging his ribs.

The suitcase had taken on a life of its own. It was caught in a kind of whirlpool that swallowed it up and spat it out and spun it around and finally tossed it straight at the elevator button. When Marcus heard a faint *ping*, he couldn't believe his ears.

He gasped as the door opened.

"Mom! Jake! Come back!" he bellowed. *"It's our elevator!"*

He hurled himself into the metal box, landing on his hands and knees. The carpet beneath him was bone-dry. Glancing around, he saw a hissing, churning, bubbling wall of water arrested on the threshold by some invisible barrier. It was freakish, and unnatural, but Marcus didn't have time to wonder what it meant. Because a stainless steel panel was already beginning to clank across his view of the chaos.

"Hurry, Mom!" He caught the door just in time. Then he reached past it and snared Jake's suitcase.

He was amazed to find that he could lean into the water as he would have leaned into a curtain.

"Marcus!" yelled Holly. She was being towed along by Jake, who was half wading, half swimming toward the elevator. Marcus dragged Jake's suitcase over the threshold before tossing it behind him. Then he braced himself against the edge of the door, using his whole body as a doorstop.

"Oh thank goodness!" Holly was coughing and gasping. When Jake pushed her inside, she tripped over her son's leg and fell down as Jake burst into the elevator like a breaching whale, almost thudding off its rear wall in his eagerness to jump ship. Once he'd steadied himself, however, he turned back to help Holly.

Only after she was on her feet did he throw himself against the door, adding his weight to Marcus's.

"Where's Sterling? Where's Edison?" Marcus demanded. "Mom? Where are they?"

"They're coming," Holly replied. Sure enough, Coco suddenly appeared, paddling in their direction. Newt and Sterling were already behind her, though Sterling, being taller than Newt, wasn't so much swimming as plowing through the waves.

He was giving Edison a piggyback ride.

"Edison! Hey! Do you still have Prot's hand?" Marcus called across the surface of the deluge. "We can't lose Prot's hand!"

Edison's arms were wrapped around his father's neck. But as Coco collapsed into the elevator ahead of them both, her stepson unlocked one arm and raised Prot's hydraulic hand with an air of weary triumph.

Then he slid off Sterling's back onto the elevator floor. "Still got it!" he wheezed.

By now the level of the water outside the elevator was way above Marcus's head. It didn't matter, though; all he had to do was let go of the door and retreat a few steps, tugging Jake along with him. A steel curtain was immediately drawn across the doomed ship's final moments. There was a grinding, snapping, rending sound. Then blessed silence fell.

At first no one spoke. Holly couldn't stop hugging Marcus. Jake was sitting slumped in a corner. Sterling had crouched beside Coco, who was sprawled across the carpet, her hairdo ruined and her herbal mask completely expunged. They were all shaky, breathless, and dripping wet.

At last Newt opened her eyes, lifted her head, and croaked, "So how do we get out of *here*?"

43.
Where to now?

It was a while before anybody answered. Marcus felt too drained to talk. Edison was retching up seawater and Coco was sobbing pathetically.

At last Jake asked, "What was that number? The one for the office?"

"Zero-zero-zero-zero-one-zero-zero-zero-zero-zero-zero-one," Sterling recited.

"Are you sure?"

"I'm sure." Though Sterling looked pale and wrung-out, he sounded absolutely confident. "I'm good with numbers."

Marcus, meanwhile, was trying to wriggle out of his mother's viselike hug. "That might not have been the real office," he warned. "It might have been a fake."

Jake shrugged. "So what?" he rejoined. "It has to be better than this."

No one tried to argue. Even Marcus couldn't disagree. So Sterling gently took Prot's hand from Edison and used one lifeless steel finger to key Miss Molpe's office code in to the panel of wall-mounted buttons.

But the elevator didn't respond. It just sat there.

"Oh no," Newt groaned. Holly buried her face in Marcus's shoulder as Coco sniveled.

Edison looked anxiously at Sterling. "Dad?" he squeaked. "It's going to work, isn't it?"

Sterling hesitated, clearly at a loss. Marcus, however, refused to give up. After playing so many computer games, he knew that there was *always* another way out. You just had to know the secret password or complete the right sequence of tasks.

"Try another code," Marcus suggested. "That one might be a dud. I don't trust Miss Molpe."

"What code should I use?" asked Sterling. "Does anyone still have a pamphlet on them?"

There was a sudden murmur of protest. "Oh, no," said Jake. "No, I'm not going back to Diamond Beach."

Holly muttered something about homicidal pink cats. Only Edison seemed open to the prospect. "I did promise those clowns that I'd be seeing them again . . . ," he reminded the assembled company.

But Marcus had a better idea. He pulled away from his mother.

"Pick any set of numbers," he advised Sterling. "Just pull them out of your head."

"*You* try." Sterling offered him the robot's hand. "It might work for you."

"Okay." Marcus took Prot's hand from Sterling. "I'm not going to *choose* anything," Marcus announced on reaching the panel of buttons. "I'm just going to shut my eyes and wave this hand around until it lands on a number."

"What if it doesn't land on a number?" Newt objected. "What if it lands on the alarm button?"

"In that case I'll try again," said Marcus. Then he closed his eyes and jabbed Prot's finger at the panel. After connecting with blank steel a couple of times, he finally hit plastic.

"Six," Sterling muttered.

"Shh." Marcus scowled without opening his eyes. "Don't tell me, okay? I don't want to know. This is meant to be random."

Again and again he poked at the wall as the others whispered together behind him. Sometimes he was lucky. Sometimes he missed. It was a tedious and time-consuming process, but at last the elevator sprang to life.

It shuddered, bounced, and began to ascend while the others erupted into a triumphant cheer.

"Yay, Marcus!" cried Edison.

"Well done," said Jake.

"Oh, Marcus, I'm so proud of you." Holly wrapped her arms around Marcus all over again. "You're such a clever boy. . . ."

Marcus flushed, while trying not to grin. But Newt promptly spoiled the mood of congratulation by observing in a sour tone, "Don't get too excited. We haven't arrived yet."

Silence fell. Jake sniffed. Sterling cleared his throat. Coco said, "Where *are* we going, anyway?"

"We don't know," Newt snapped. "That's the whole point."

"I hope it's somewhere with lots of food," whined Edison. "Because I'm really, really hungry."

All at once, without warning, the elevator stopped. Jake jumped to his feet, and Newt stood up more slowly. Everyone turned to face the door, which slid open to reveal a big log cabin set on a mangy patch of grass. Behind the cabin lay a basketball court; in front stood a rack of fiberglass canoes. The sign over the cabin's screen door read DORMITORY B. There were identical cabins nearby, scattered around a lightly wooded clearing.

The setting sun cast long shadows across the peaks of a distant mountain range.

"Uh—you know what?" said Marcus. "This is no good."

Heads jerked around. Jake blinked. Edison goggled.

"What do you mean?" Coco asked.

"This is no good," Marcus repeated. "We should leave. Right now."

"Why?" Newt spoke crossly. "It looks fine."

"It's not," Marcus assured her. Holly, meanwhile, was carefully studying his face.

"What's wrong, Marcus?" she asked. "Do you know where we are?"

"I sure do." Marcus swallowed before adding, "It's *my* nightmare holiday."

"Your what?" Holly was puzzled—but Edison wasn't. His jaw dropped.

"*Camp* is your nightmare holiday?" he spluttered. "Boy, that's weird. Don't you like having fun?"

"It's not just any old camp," Marcus explained. "It's Vampire Camp." He pointed at the closest log cabin. "See the way all those windows are boarded up on the inside?" he continued. "See how there's no dining hall? It's Vampire Camp, all right. I used to dream about it a *lot*."

There followed a long, tense pause. Then Jake said tersely, "Let's get out of here."

Luckily, Marcus didn't have to push any buttons. The elevator door closed of its own accord, responding to some built-in timer.

After that, once again, nothing happened.

44.

"This is a job for emergency services...."

Marcus was stumped. He didn't know what to do next.

Clearly, things had changed since Miss Molpe's escape. Her trap had once worked automatically, churning out dream holidays without her direct input. Now, however, she was back in the driver's seat. Now the horror was becoming visible, like the piles of bones in the fake trailer. And her evil essence was beginning to taint the world of her creation, the way the bones of her victims had transformed the fake trailer from a cheerful haven into a charnel house.

"Great. Terrific." There was a hint of panic in Newt's voice. "As if our dream holidays weren't bad enough, now we have nightmares!"

"What's *your* nightmare holiday, Newt?" Edison asked. He seemed genuinely interested.

"This is," she spat. "What's yours? A giant brussels sprout?"

Edison had to think for a moment before answering. "My fairground, I guess. Except that all the clowns and aliens and bumper cars would have been tortured by Miss Molpe because they let me go."

Coco shuddered. "Well, we certainly won't be going back to the fairground," she decreed. "I couldn't cope with *that*."

"My nightmare holiday would probably be a skiing trip with my ex-wife," Sterling suddenly volunteered. "Last time I went on one of those, I had to be airlifted off a glacier." Seeing his son's slightly hurt expression, Sterling hastened to add, "My ex-wife's much braver than I am. And a lot fitter, too."

"Oh, no. No way. No ski trips with Janice." Though scared and bedraggled, Coco was still able to put her foot down. "I couldn't cope with that, either."

"I could," growled Jake. "A ski trip sounds fine to me." He was hovering on the sidelines, looking sullen. Marcus was about to point out that a pair of shorts and a rope belt weren't the right kind of clothes for a ski resort when Holly jumped in.

"Before we do anything drastic," she declared, "I've had an idea." She produced her cell phone. "If Jake's suitcase was more powerful than the witch, maybe my phone is, too," she continued. "I mean, we haven't tried it yet, have we? Maybe I should just call someone."

"Oh, wow," breathed Newt. "Oh, you're *right!*" Her face lit up. Sterling, however, simply frowned.

"Are you sure it's working?" he asked Holly.

"I don't know. We'll soon find out." When Holly turned it on, the phone beeped in a reassuring way. "Looks okay to me," she remarked. "And the reception's pretty good."

"But who should we call?" asked Coco. "Who's close enough to get us out of here?" Without waiting for a reply, she offered to call her Diamond Beach massage therapist. "Except that I can't remember her details. . . ."

"We'll call the police," Holly interrupted. She was already tapping a three-digit number into her keypad. "This is a job for emergency services."

Marcus wasn't so sure. Wouldn't his mother just be luring another set of victims into Miss Molpe's trap? He was about to suggest that they call directory assistance to ask if there were any paranormal investigators living nearby when Holly caught her breath.

Marcus saw her grim expression dissolve into one full of hope and excitement.

"Oh—oh, yes!" she cried into the phone. "Yes, we need help! It's an emergency! We need to talk to the police!" A pause. "What? You *what?* Oh . . ."

Everyone stared at Holly as she listened to the voice at the other end of the line. Though Marcus couldn't hear what was being said, he deduced that it was both puzzling and unexpected—because the light in her eyes was slowly replaced by a dazed, disappointed look. "Well, yes," she finally admitted, "we can't get back. We're stuck here and—what?" Another pause. "I see. Well, yes, I suppose so. But how . . . ?" She glanced toward the panel of buttons. "But there *isn't* a minus one," she protested. "How can we . . . Hello? *Hello?*" She blinked and lowered the phone. "He hung up on me!" she complained.

"Who did?" Newt asked. "Was it the operator?"

"I don't know. I don't think so." Holly swallowed before reluctantly adding, "He told us to go to the embassy."

"The *embassy?*" Coco's tone was shrill with disbelief. "What embassy?"

"*Our* embassy," Holly replied. "Because we're stranded tourists."

"That's weird," said Jake.

"And where exactly is our so-called embassy?" was Newt's next question. "Did he tell you that?"

"It's on level minus one." Seeing the blank stares that greeted this news, Holly burst out, "I told him there *wasn't* a level minus one, but he wouldn't listen!"

"There's no minus-one button . . . ," Edison began.

"I know!"

"Maybe it was the siren," Marcus suggested. "Maybe she's teasing us."

"It was a man. I told you. A man with a foreign accent."

"Wait a second!" Sterling spoke so sharply that everybody else jumped. He put a hand to his forehead and stood for a moment, thinking hard. Then he whirled around and pointed at the panel of buttons. "That exclamation mark!" he said. "It's an upside-down i!"

"So?"

"So the square root of i is negative one!" Sterling paused, as if expecting an eager chorus of agreement. When no one reacted, he sighed and began to explain. "It's an irrational number, like pi. If I press the alarm button, and then I press the emergency stop button, and then I press the alarm button again, it's i x i— which equals minus one!"

Newt wasn't impressed. She just scowled at him. "Yuck! Algebra!" was all she said.

It was Jake who seemed to grasp the importance of Sterling's brain wave. "Well? Go on," Jake urged, shifting restlessly from foot to foot. "Why don't you push the buttons?"

"With Prot's hand," Marcus added quickly. "Don't forget Prot's hand."

He passed the hand back to Sterling, who promptly used it. *Click. Click. Click.* As soon as the last button

249

was pushed, the elevator jerked and clanged. Then it started to drop.

"This is good," Coco said nervously. She appealed to her husband. "This is good, isn't it? It's never gone down before."

"We'll see," he replied.

"What's an embassy, Dad?" Edison asked. "Is it some kind of ship?"

"It's . . . um . . ." Sterling trailed off, scratching his head as he tried to think of a good definition.

At last Holly supplied one for him. "It's a little bit of your own country in a foreign place," she told Edison, slipping her phone back into her pocket. "You go there when you want to be protected from the country you're in."

"Oh."

"Where's *my* phone, by the way?" Newt demanded, turning to Marcus. "You had it last."

"It broke," Marcus confessed. "I dropped it."

Newt flushed—but before she could say anything, the elevator stopped with a bounce. *Ping!* went the door. It trundled open.

They found themselves staring at a dull, drab, stuffy, ill-lit, unoccupied, thoroughly dismal waiting room.

45.
The Perfect Escape

The room was a plain gray box. It had been fitted out with gray carpet, gray plastic seats, and a drooping grayish plant in a stainless-steel pot. The only splash of color was a poster advertising GETAWAY ISLAND— THE PERFECT ESCAPE.

Opposite the elevator was a service window with a metal grille over it. A dark-gray door beside the window was firmly shut.

Marcus was reminded of the office where his mother sometimes went to pay her car insurance.

"Is this the embassy?" Edison inquired.

"I don't know." Holly peered at a sign on the counter, which said IF UNATTENDED, PLEASE RING BELL. "We'd better ask."

"I'll do that," Jake offered. He picked up his suitcase and strode across the room to the service window, where he vigorously rang a small silver bell. After about half a minute, someone answered his summons—but the grille over the window was so heavy, and the glass behind it was so thick and smeared, that Marcus could make out only a vague, dark silhouette hovering behind the counter.

"Can I help you?" a woman's voice queried.

"Yes," Jake replied as Holly rushed to join him. "We need to get out of here."

"We need to go home!" Holly interrupted. "We're completely lost and looking for a way back to the real Diamond Beach, which is where we originally came from."

"We were kidnapped by Miss Molpe," Marcus added from the elevator. He had a feeling that the woman behind the counter might know Miss Molpe.

And he was right.

"Ah. Yes. Miss Molpe," the woman said. She had a young, gentle, heavily accented voice. "I understand."

"Can you help us?" Holly implored her. "Can you send us back home?"

"You will need a visa for Getaway Island." The young woman pushed a bundle of paper through the narrow slot between the grille and the counter. "Just fill in these forms and we will process them for you."

"Forms?" Holly echoed as if she couldn't believe her ears.

"How do you mean 'process' them?" Newt demanded from the safety of the elevator. "How long is that going to take?"

"Who are you, please?" asked Coco. When there was no response, she marched over to the service window, where she jostled Jake aside so she could rap on the grille. "Hello?" she snapped. "I'd like to know *exactly* where we are and who's in charge here."

But the young woman had already vanished into the shadows from which she'd emerged. Jake, meanwhile, had picked up the topmost form.

"'Application for visa to Getaway Island,'" he read aloud, rather slowly and awkwardly. "'Please complete questions one to thirteen in *black or blue pen only* and submit to embassy staff.'"

"How can we do that when we don't have any pens?" Coco exclaimed. She put her mouth to the slot under the grille. "Hey! Excuse me! We don't have anything to write with!"

"I do," Jake remarked. When Coco and Holly turned to stare at him, he patted his suitcase. "I packed a bunch of stuff in here when I first ran away—fishing line, and a flashlight, and some pens, and a cigarette lighter—"

"How many pens?" asked Coco.

"I'm not sure. I'll have a look."

"Maybe we should try phoning someone else," Marcus suggested. He felt very uneasy. "Maybe this is just another nightmare holiday. . . ."

But Holly wasn't convinced. "It's not my nightmare," she informed him.

"Or mine." Coco was watching Jake unload his few scrappy possessions from the suitcase. "One . . . two . . . three . . ."

"Four pens," said Jake.

"We can double up," Holly told him. "I'll fill in both our forms, Marcus—and you can do the same for Newt, Coco."

"And I'll do Edison's," Sterling offered. He went to retrieve the piece of paper Coco waved at him. "I hope they don't ask for proof of identity. . . ."

Marcus was amazed. He couldn't understand why the adults seemed so happy to fill in forms. *They probably like it because it feels normal,* he concluded, knowing that Holly's life was always full of forms to file.

"I'll just stay here and hold the door open, shall I?" he said.

Holly gave a preoccupied grunt; she was already scribbling away. So was Coco, who stood at the counter beside her. Jake was using his suitcase to write on. He didn't seem very confident and kept looking sideways at Sterling's answers.

"'Do you have any criminal convictions?' No."

Coco ticked a box. "'Are you carrying goods received or purchased from Miss Molpe?' No." She ticked another box.

"'Which false realities have you visited in the last two weeks? Please attach complete list.'" Holly chewed at her pen. "Well, let's see now. . . . There was Diamond Beach Paradise, and the Crystal Hibiscus Health Spa, and the sinking ship—"

"And my fairground." Edison weighed in. He was helping Marcus prop open the elevator door. "And Newt's dance club. And the fake trailer."

"Does the elevator count as a false reality?" wondered Sterling, who was sitting beside Jake with Prot's hand on his lap.

"I'm going to include it," said Holly. "Along with the cellar."

Marcus sighed. "Don't forget this place," he observed. "This is fake, too."

"Yes, but it might be good fake, not bad fake," Edison pointed out. Marcus wasn't convinced, though—and neither was Newt. She stomped over to the closed door, which she tried to open. When it wouldn't budge, she gave it a sharp kick.

"Hey!" she shouted. "Let us out, or we'll set fire to this place!"

"Newt! Hush!" Holly was scandalized. "You know very well we can't do that!"

"Yes, we can. Jake just said he had a cigarette

255

lighter," Newt rejoined as her stepmother rang the little silver bell.

"I'm finished," Coco announced. *"Hello! Are you there? I'm finished!"*

"Me too," said Sterling. He passed his completed forms to Coco, who pushed them under the metal grille.

Holly's forms soon followed, but there was a slight delay before Jake was ready to surrender his. "How do you spell 'parallel universe'?" he asked.

Only after his form had been signed, dated, and returned to the pile were all seven forms suddenly whisked away by the faceless young woman, who had reappeared from some unseen back room. "Thank you," she murmured. "Could you take a seat, please? We'll be with you shortly."

"Who will?" Coco snapped. "You and who else? Hello? *Hello?"*

"It's no good," said Jake. "She's gone again."

"Hey!" Newt banged on the door with her fist. *"Hey! Open up!"*

"I hope this doesn't take too long." Holly fretted. "I mean, it's not as if there's a line. . . ."

Sterling shook his head. "In my experience, when people talk about 'processing,' you should always be prepared for a bit of wait," was his view. "An hour or two at least."

"I'm not waiting here for an hour!" his wife

protested. "They don't even have any magazines!"

Holly seemed resigned. "At least they didn't tell us to go away and have a coffee. If they'd done that, we'd have been looking at half a day minimum."

"Half a day? Are you kidding?" Marcus was beginning to lose patience. Didn't they understand? This was magic, not red tape. "We could be here for days!" he cried. "Weeks! *Months!* We could be here *forever!*"

It was at this precise moment that the gray door opened to reveal a beautiful black-haired gypsy girl.

"Will you come in, please?" she asked. "The ambassador will see you now."

46.
Martiya

"That was quick," said Sterling.

The gypsy girl smiled. She had a wonderful smile. Her eyes were big and brown and she wore colorful gypsy clothes: hoop earrings, a long skirt, a ruffled blouse, lots of scarves. She was the prettiest girl Marcus had ever seen.

He still didn't trust her, though. He suspected that she might be the siren in disguise, even though she wasn't rhyming everything she said.

"I don't think we should *all* go and see the ambassador," he advised warily. "Maybe some of us should stay here, just in case."

"If you stay, you will never leave," warned the gypsy girl. "The only exit is through this door." She gestured gracefully at the long gray hallway behind her. "Come. Shibilis awaits."

"Shibilis?" Coco had trouble pronouncing the word. "Is that the ambassador?"

"Yes," the girl replied. "Shibilis is the ambassador of travelers and the king of the gypsies—the *Bulibasha*, as we call him. He has much power. He can help you. Only he."

"Was he the one I spoke to?" asked Holly.

"You spoke to him," the girl confirmed. "He heard your plea from the shadows and summoned you into the half-light."

Holly blinked. Then she rephrased her question. "No—I mean, was he the one on the phone?"

The girl cocked her head. "What is a 'phone'?" she inquired.

"Oh, come *on*." Newt's tone was a mixture of disgust and disbelief. "You don't know what a phone is?"

"Shibilis will know. He knows all. He sees all. He heard you in the whistling wind and saw you in the smoke from his fire." The girl laid a hand on her breast. "I am his *martiya*—his spirit of the night. I am his messenger, sent to find you. Without his help, you will never escape this curse."

"Curse?" Holly echoed. And Coco said, "What curse?"

"The curse that entraps you. The curse of Miss

Molpe." When everyone continued to stare at her doubtfully, the gypsy girl tried to explain further. "Miss Molpe is a monster. A *chovexani*. We call her *Trushal odji*—the Hungry Soul. Shibilis has fought her many times."

"With magic, you mean?" Marcus suddenly began to feel more hopeful. "Is he a wizard or something?"

"He is a seer. *Drabarno*. Also a warrior, a healer, and a judge. He communes with the spirits and with captive souls like yourselves." Without warning, the girl leaned toward Jake and gently touched his elbow. "Come," she urged. "Speak to him. He will show you the right door and tell you how to open it."

Jake flushed as he shook her off. He then retreated a few steps. Marcus and Holly exchanged questioning glances. Newt was wearing her usual scowl, while Edison was leaning against his father, looking pale and pinched and ready for a nap.

Sterling scratched his neck. "I don't know," he murmured. "It's tempting. . . ."

"Does anyone recognize this?" Marcus asked quietly. "Is this anyone's dream or nightmare holiday?"

"No," said Sterling.

"No," said Coco.

"No," said Holly.

"Are you kidding?" said Newt. "What kind of loser would come up with a dumb idea like this?"

"Not me!" her brother protested as if he'd been accused of something. And then Jake spoke, his voice deep and harsh.

"We've got my suitcase," he declared, "and your steel hand, too. If this girl does turn out to be Miss Molpe, we can smash her skull with the hand and throw her in the suitcase again."

Holly winced. "Oh, Jake . . . ," she remonstrated. But no one else seemed troubled by Jake's plan. Marcus, in fact, found it quite reassuring.

"I vote we talk to this Shibilis guy," Sterling proposed. "Unless someone's got a better idea? Because *I* certainly haven't."

"Me neither," said Newt.

"I don't think we've got much choice," Coco agreed.

Holly looked at Marcus, who nodded. She then addressed the gypsy girl, announcing tartly, "We'll only come if you *promise* to get us home."

The gypsy girl laughed. "How can I make such a promise?" she rejoined. "Shibilis will show you the portal, but only you can pass through it." She lifted a hand as she turned her back on them. "If you wish, you may follow. If not—farewell," she concluded.

"Wait!" Coco rushed forward to catch the gray door, which was starting to swing shut. "We're coming, okay? We're coming right now. Aren't we?" She appealed to the rest of her family, who mumbled in agreement. So did Holly and Marcus and Jake. "Let's go," Coco instructed. "Kids at the back, men at the front."

They set off after the gypsy girl, who led them down a very drab, narrow hallway. Fluorescent lights in the ceiling leached everything of color; a worn gray carpet deadened their footfalls. At the end of the hallway was another door, which the gypsy girl opened with a flourish.

"Welcome!" she cried. "Welcome to the *vardo* of *Bulibasha* Shibilis!"

And she flung out her arm invitingly.

The room beyond her shapely silhouette was very dark, though Marcus could just make out the glint of brass and the firelit sheen of leather. He could smell smoke and cooked meat. He could hear the crackle of flames and the sighing of the wind. But he couldn't see Shibilis—not from his vantage point.

"Give me that," said Jake, snatching Prot's metal hand from Sterling's grip. He then approached the gypsy girl. "Ladies first," he ordered. "In you go."

She obeyed with a simper and a sidelong glance, her hips swaying as she crossed the threshold ahead of him. Jake followed her cautiously, braced for an ambush, his suitcase in one hand and his raised weapon in the other. The shadows soon swallowed him up completely. There was a brief, tense wait.

262

At last, however, his voice came floating back to them, clear and firm and confident.

"It's all right! You can come in!" he shouted.

So they did.

47.

The ambassador

Shibilis was sitting beside a brazier, surrounded by what looked like the contents of a secondhand shop; there were stools, boots, pots, cushions, saddles, books, lamps, jewelry, embroidered quilts, musical instruments, and antique guns. The flickering light of the brazier picked out a gleam of silver here, a shimmer of silk there. Smoke drifted up toward a low wooden ceiling. Two large dogs slumbered on the floor.

Shibilis himself was a big, swarthy, unshaven man with lots of wild black hair and a nose like an eagle's beak. He wore a bulky fur cloak and gold earrings. When he lifted his gaze from the red-hot coals in the brazier, the dogs twitched and whimpered in their sleep.

"Martiya," he said to the gypsy girl.

"Bulibasha," the girl replied with a half curtsy. Then she added something Marcus couldn't understand before retiring into a corner.

Shibilis squinted at his guests through a pall of smoke. He had dark, haunted eyes. *"Besh!"* he commanded. "Sit!"

Everyone looked around. There wasn't much to sit on. Sterling lifted a cocked hat off one of the stools, then passed the stool to Coco.

"I can hardly see you," Shibilis went on. "You are like *mule*—spirits of the dead. You are like morning mist. Can you speak to me?"

"Of course we can speak to you," Newt snapped. "We're not comatose."

Shibilis nodded. "Good," he said. "You have a strong voice. That is why I heard you. Who spoke to me from behind the veil?"

"Um . . . that was me, I guess," Holly volunteered. Then she cleared her throat and added, "Can you show us the way home, please?"

"Of course." Shibilis cocked his thumb. "It's over there."

Everyone else gasped—except Martiya. She just giggled.

"What?" said Coco.

"Over where?" asked Newt. "*I* can't see anything."

Marcus was peering at a blank stretch of wall,

which was made of wood, just like the floor and ceiling. It occurred to him suddenly that they were in a caravan—a gypsy caravan.

"You can see nothing because you are blinded by the curse of Miss Molpe," Shibilis explained. "But I have a *draba*—a charm—that will open your eyes." With the toe of his boot he nudged at a plain earthenware pot that was sitting next to the larger of his two snoring dogs. "Here," he continued. "Each of you must reach inside and draw out your own key, for it will unlock the door to your *slobuzenja*."

When he didn't go on to translate, Coco said, "Our what?" She sounded suspicious, as if she thought he might be talking about a toilet cubicle.

"Your freedom," Martiya supplied. "'*Slobuzenja*' is 'freedom.'"

There was an awkward pause. Marcus glanced at Holly, who glanced at Jake. No one really wanted to reach into the pot.

"It isn't a trick, is it?" Edison piped up. "You haven't put a mousetrap in there, have you?"

Shibilis smiled. "Are you such a little mouse, to be afraid of a mousetrap?" he teased.

Newt scowled at him. "That's not an answer!" she said sharply. Then her father stepped forward.

"I'll go first," Sterling offered. "Just give me Prot's hand, Jake, will you?"

266

Jake promptly surrendered the hand, which aroused great interest in Shibilis.

"Ah!" the gypsy exclaimed. "A talisman! Clever."

"It's not a talisman." Marcus couldn't help correcting him. "It's part of a robot."

"But you brought it from the real world, did you not?" Shibilis inquired. When Marcus nodded, the gypsy king said, "Then it is a talisman. A talisman against Miss Molpe. She has no power over objects from the real world, because she is weak—physically weak. That is why she likes to prey on children. That is why she must trick them with elaborate snares. Instead of hunting her victims, like a wolf, she must lure them, like a spider. Once she had her sweet songs to trap them with. Now she has only her magical tricks."

Sterling, meanwhile, had inserted Prot's hand into the pot. On encountering nothing squishy or sharp or otherwise unpleasant, he reached in with his own hand—and uttered a yelp of surprise. "This isn't a key!" he spluttered, withdrawing a long, rectangular card. "This is an airline ticket!"

"Keys may come in all shapes and sizes," Shibilis pointed out.

"Let *me* see that." Coco wrested the ticket from her husband. "'RepAir'?" she read. "I've never heard of RepAir."

"Yes, but look at the destination," said Sterling. "'Home.' That's where we want to go."

"Terminal One," murmured Holly, who was studying the ticket over Sterling's shoulder. "I don't get it. Where's Terminal One?"

Again Shibilis gestured at the blank wall. "Through there," he replied. And Coco suddenly caught her breath.

"I can see it!" she squeaked.

"See what?" asked Holly.

"The door! I can see the door!" Coco was jiggling with excitement, her damp curls bouncing and her hands flapping. "Quick! All of you, get a ticket! When you've got a ticket, you can see the door!"

Hearing this, Jake immediately reached into the earthenware pot—and pulled out another rectangular card. Then he stepped aside so that Coco and Holly could fish around for their own tickets.

As the Huckstepps lined up behind Holly, Marcus found himself hanging back. "Did you hear Mom's voice because she called you on her phone?" he asked Shibilis, who seemed quite happy to answer questions. "Is her phone a talisman, too?"

"No doubt," said the gypsy in a careless sort of way.

"I guess that's why Jake could lock Miss Molpe in his suitcase. Because his suitcase is a talisman." Without waiting for a response, Marcus muttered to himself, "I thought so. I figured it had to be something like that."

"Marcus!" Holly beckoned to him. "Come and get your ticket, please."

"Yeah, okay." Before joining the end of the line, however, Marcus had one last query for Shibilis. "Do we really have to fly home? I don't get it. Why can't we just take an elevator? It can't be very far."

The gypsy stared at him for a moment before remarking quietly and solemnly, "There is no greater distance than that between night and day."

"Marcus!" Holly reached over to grab his arm. "Hurry up, we're waiting!"

"*Okay*, Mom!" Yielding to her pressure, Marcus squatted down and plunged his hand into the pot. When he drew out his ticket, he saw his name printed on it.

"Oh, wow," he said. Then he spotted a pair of automatic doors, made from steel and frosted glass, embedded in the caravan wall under a sign that read DEPARTURES. "Oh, *wow*!"

"So our flight's through there?" Coco asked Shibilis. "Our flight home?"

The gypsy inclined his head. "It is your *drom*," he replied. "Your way back."

"I still don't get it." Newt's tone as she addressed him was anxious and irritable. "We're supposed to walk through there, get on a plane, take off, land, and . . . then what? Walk through another door into the Bradshaws' cellar?"

Shibilis sighed. "Please understand, this is *your* way back, not mine. I gave you the key. You must do with it as you wish." After a moment's pause, he added, "What is a 'plane'?"

"Auugh!" Newt turned on her heel and marched toward the double doors, which parted smoothly in front of her. Beyond them lay the walls of glass, rows of desks, and endless expanses of carpet that characterize airports everywhere.

"Newt! Wait!" cried Coco, sprinting after her stepdaughter. Sterling grabbed Edison and set off in pursuit. Jake looked at Holly. Holly seized Marcus.

"Bye!" said Marcus as he was towed toward the door. "Thanks for helping!"

"Good-bye," Martiya crooned, smiling at Marcus. Shibilis, however, looked grave.

"Tread softly," he advised Marcus. "Miss Molpe may be weak now, but she will grow bigger and stronger with every child she consumes. Remember that. Only your blood will satisfy Miss Molpe. Only your death will bring her life."

Having issued this warning, he raised his hand in farewell. Then the smoke billowed up and engulfed him.

48.
Terminal One

"**I** didn't have enough time to ask about Miss Molpe," Marcus complained. "Maybe that guy could have told us about her. We should have talked to him. . . ."

No one was listening. They had emerged into a gigantic airport terminal, where it seemed to be the middle of the night. Impenetrable darkness lay beyond the vast sweep of floor-to-ceiling windows. There were no slow-moving lines or heaps of luggage scattered around. The rows of check-in counters stretched almost as far as the horizon, yet only one of them was staffed.

"Look!" said Holly, pointing. "There's RepAir! And the check-in's open!"

Everyone immediately hurried toward the only human being in sight. When Marcus finally reached the RepAir check-in, however, he began to wonder if the woman behind the desk really *was* a human being. She looked a bit like a shop mannequin, with her heavy makeup, glossy hair, cheery smile, and perfect proportions.

The badge on her teal uniform blazer read CANDI.

"Good evening!" she chirped. "Where are you folks heading tonight?"

"Uh . . . home." Holly presented her ticket, then reached for her son's.

"And you're a party of . . . ?"

"Seven," Coco supplied. As she placed her own family's tickets on the counter, she asked, "Are we in business or economy?"

Holly pulled a face. *"Coco . . ."*

"I never travel economy," Coco insisted. "It's inhumane."

"These are all first-class tickets," Candi assured her. "Do you have any luggage to check?"

Every eye swiveled toward Jake, who shuffled forward, suitcase in hand.

"Only one piece?" asked Candi, on accepting his ticket.

Jake nodded. Sterling cleared his throat. "I guess it's too big to take on as cabin baggage?" he inquired.

"Yes, sir, I'm afraid it is," Candi confirmed. "And

272

you'll also have to check that other item you're carrying."

"This?" Sterling waggled Prot's hand. "But—"

"That would be classified as a dangerous article, being a weapon or tool," Candi explained. "It can be stowed in your luggage, though."

Jake looked at Holly, who gave an apologetic shrug.

"Airport security has got really tough," she murmured. "You can hardly take *anything* on planes these days."

While Sterling packed Prot's hand into the suitcase, Candi issued them all boarding passes. "You'll be leaving from Gate Number One," she revealed, "and the scheduled boarding time is in approximately one hour, though there might be a slight delay."

"Is there a special lounge for first-class passengers where we can relax in the meantime?" asked Coco.

Candi's wide smile grew wider still. "Ma'am, there's a special *terminal*," she responded. "Terminal One caters to first-class passengers only." She indicated the nearest exit. "If you go straight down there and turn right, you'll pass through the baggage screening. Then Gate Number One is to your left."

"Thank you," said Holly, moving away. But Coco hadn't finished.

"Is there somewhere we can eat?" she demanded. "Or buy toiletries?"

Candi's smile didn't flicker. "Most of our outlets are closed at this hour," she admitted. "However, there are vending machines near every restroom."

"And what about foot massages?" Coco asked—triggering a chorus of impatient sighs from everyone except Candi and Sterling.

"Oh, come *on!*" groaned Newt. Marcus rolled his eyes. Holly said, "I'm sure we'll manage, Coco. I'm sure it won't be a very long flight. Will it?" This question was aimed at Candi, who shook her head.

"But we'll be getting on a plane, right? A plane back to Diamond Beach?" Marcus was anxious to clear this up. "It's an actual flight, isn't it?"

"Yes, sir," Candi trilled. "I think the word *flight* defines it very nicely, though you could also call it an escape, a getaway, or a retreat."

"Good! Terrific! Let's go, then!" Newt forged ahead, stomping toward a distant sign that read PASSENGERS ONLY BEYOND THIS POINT. The rest of her family set off in pursuit, leaving Holly, Jake, and Marcus with no choice but to follow.

"Can you tell me who actually booked these tickets?" was Marcus's final question, thrown back over his shoulder as Holly dragged him away from the check-in counter. "Was it someone called Shibilis?"

"I'm sorry, sir." Candi sounded genuinely apologetic. "This station is closed now. I just logged off the system and can't access those booking files."

"Oh."

"But I hope you enjoy your trip!"

"So do I," Jake muttered. He didn't sound too confident, though—and when he reached the security screening area, the sight of it failed to reassure him. In fact, he scowled.

"What *is* all this?" he demanded.

"Haven't you been on a plane before? I have." Marcus couldn't help preening a little. "It was five years ago, but I can still remember it. I went to visit my dad."

"Don't worry, Jake," Holly said. "We don't have any bags, so it'll be easy. Just walk through that gate and they'll scan you for concealed weapons."

Jake blinked. Then he peered down at his naked midriff, his bare feet, and his ragged shorts. "Can't they tell just by looking?" he grumbled.

"Jake! Holly!" Coco was waving to them; she and her family had already passed through the screening process without tripping any alarms. "You have to take off your shoes!" she warned. And when Holly glanced up at the rock-faced guard near the machine, he confirmed what Coco had just told her.

"Please remove all shoes and metal items," he said, grinding the words out.

Marcus was annoyed. He didn't like having to take off his shoes. Holly, on the other hand, seemed resigned to the process.

By the time she and her son had been scanned and cleared to go, they were a long way behind Jake and the Huckstepps, who had wandered off down a wide, carpeted passage to stare at a bank of TV screens.

"Departures," said Coco when Holly and Marcus finally joined her. "Just departures. No arrivals."

"And there are so many. . . ." Even Newt was awe-struck. "How come there are so many?"

Inspecting the TV screens, Marcus saw a very odd departure board. All the flights had the same destination—"home"—but they weren't departing from Terminal One. Instead, they were leaving from all kinds of weird places: Antarctica, the moon, Mount Everest, Atlantis, Toytown . . .

Suddenly Marcus had a flash of insight.

"These are all dream holidays!" he exclaimed. "They must be!"

"And they've all been canceled. Every one of them. Except ours." Sterling reached up to tap on a screen. "See that? Crystal Hibiscus Island, departing from Gate One . . . and the flight number is the same as the original brochure code."

"Which means we must all have different flight numbers," said Holly.

"Yeah, but we're still leaving from the same gate at the same time," Sterling pointed out. "You know how the airlines often combine two different flights on the same plane? It must be like that."

Marcus could see what Sterling meant. There was a flight from Diamond Beach, which had a number identical to the code on Jake's brochure. There were also flights from Fairground Valley, from Party Central, and from . . .

"'Lysitte Run'?" Marcus read aloud. "Where on earth is that?"

49.
Waiting

"Why, Lysitte Run might be *your* dream holiday, Marcus," Holly proposed. "Surely you must have one. Even if you've not been there yet . . ."

Marcus rubbed his chin and wrinkled his nose. "Lysitte Run?" he said. "That doesn't sound like the sort of place I'd want to go for a holiday."

"No. You're right. Because it isn't." Sterling had been comparing flight numbers; now he checked the ticket in Marcus's hand. "Mmmph. I thought so."

"What?" Marcus didn't like Sterling's frown. "What's the matter?"

"Oh, nothing. Nothing really. But look how the number on Coco's boarding pass is identical to the one up there on the screen." Thrusting his wife's ticket at

Marcus, Sterling added, "Ed's and Newt's and Jake's are the same. They match the numbers on the departure board. But that Lysitte Run number—it's not on your pass. Or mine."

"Or mine." Holly weighed in a little anxiously. "Mine hasn't got a number at all. It just says 'Flight Reserved.'"

"So does mine." Marcus squinted through his glasses at Sterling. "Does that mean we can't leave? Because we didn't visit our own dream holidays?"

Jake hissed. Newt looked alarmed. But Holly refused to accept such an awful possibility.

"Of course we can leave," she insisted. "We're all on the same plane, remember?"

"And we weren't told that anyone would be left behind," Coco reminded Marcus. "At least, that's not the impression *I* got."

Marcus grunted.

"So what about Lysitte Run, then?" Newt asked Holly. "If it's not your dream holiday, and it's not Dad's, and it's not his"—she jerked her chin at Marcus—"then who wants to hang out at this Lysitte Run place?"

There was a brief silence as everyone gazed blankly at the TV screens. Finally Jake said, "I guess all the other flights have been canceled because Miss Molpe killed the passengers."

Holly flinched. "Some of those people might have escaped," she objected.

"Maybe." Jake didn't seem convinced. "But that Lysitte Run person is still here, because their flight's only been delayed. If they were dead, or gone, it would have been canceled."

Suddenly Marcus had a brain wave.

"Wait!" he cried. "Lysitte Run! Get it? *Lie, sit, run!*" He couldn't help laughing. "It's the little white dog!"

"What little white dog?" Sterling asked.

Newt, however, understood instantly. "Oh, no!" she exclaimed, her sulky expression changing to one of tenderness and concern. "Don't tell me the little white dog is stuck in here somewhere."

Marcus had to admit that it probably was. "I told you before, it's in its own dream holiday," he said. "It went through a doggie door in the cellar."

"Poor thing!" Newt began to plead with her father. "Can't we rescue the dog, Dad? Can't we get it out? Maybe it's here at the airport. . . ."

"I think we should focus on getting ourselves out first," was Coco's opinion—and only Newt disagreed with her. Even Edison was more concerned about finding the restrooms than he was about the little white dog.

"I really need to pee," he announced in a strained voice. "I'm hungry, too, and there are snack machines near the toilets. That's what the lady out front said, anyway."

"She did, didn't she?" Coco glanced around. "Can anyone see the men's room?"

"I think it might be down there," Holly replied, pointing.

So they all trudged down the wide, empty hallway toward Gate One, pausing briefly when they reached the restrooms. Sterling, Coco, and Edison peeled off from the main group to relieve themselves, while Newt collected change for the only vending machine in sight—which dispensed jelly beans and chocolate bars, but no salty snacks.

"We've got just enough money for two chocolate bars," Newt grumbled. "I guess it'll be chocolate for dinner, followed by a drink out of a bathroom tap."

"And they call this a first-class terminal!" Holly wasn't impressed. "It doesn't look any different from a normal airport to me."

Marcus grunted. He was feeling very tired, perhaps because of the late hour, stale air, and fluorescent lights. The chairs at Gate Number One looked uninviting; made of hard blue plastic, they were grouped so that you couldn't lie across them. Outside the windows, a few scattered greenish lights made fitful appearances through a thick veil of snowflakes. Marcus couldn't see any planes. He couldn't see any people, either. There were no TV channels, no ceaseless announcements from the PA system. The only sign of life was another set of electronic screens displaying the computerized departure board.

"Look," Marcus said as he gazed out the window. "It's snowing."

But Holly didn't reply. She was talking to Jake, who had settled down beside her in one of the uncomfortable plastic chairs. "Your parents will be so happy to see you after all these years," she remarked. "You might have a bit of trouble finding them, but you can stay with us until you do."

"Thanks," Jake mumbled, staring down at his hands.

"We'll get you some clothes, because you can't go around looking like that—not once you've left Diamond Beach." Holly was struck by a sudden thought. "Didn't you have a couple of older brothers? I seem to recall they were always jumping on your back. . . ."

Jake nodded. "Three," he answered.

"Three!" Holly gave a low whistle. "Four boys! Wow! Your poor mother!"

Jake sniffed. "She didn't worry about it," he retorted. "She just drank more booze and passed out."

"Oh."

"I don't even know if I *want* to find my parents," Jake added darkly. "It's not like they enjoyed having me around when I was actually there."

"I'm sure they did." Holly's tone was encouraging. "It probably just felt like that sometimes, because you were competing for their attention."

With a grunt, Jake fell silent. Marcus, meanwhile, was scanning the departure board. "You know what I can't work out?" he said. "I can't work out why Jake's nightmare holiday isn't up there on the screen. Diamond Beach is, so why not all the other places we visited?"

"Not to mention the ones we *didn't* visit," Newt remarked. Having extracted two chocolate bars from the vending machine, she threw herself onto a plastic seat and began to break each bar into small chunks. "Like *your* dream holiday, for instance," she said to Marcus. "What is it, anyway? You never told us."

"I dunno." Marcus pondered for a moment. "I guess . . . I guess it would be a holiday with my dad. Just the two of us. That would be great."

Newt sniffed. "You think so?" she said. "I don't. Sounds like another nightmare holiday to me." Then she turned to Holly, who was staring at Marcus with a troubled expression on her face. "So what about *your* nightmare holiday? Jake's was the ship. Marcus came up with that dumb Vampire Camp. What about you?"

Holly sighed. For one fleeting instant, Marcus thought she was going to say, "A holiday with my ex-husband." He could almost see the words forming on her lips. But then she seemed to change her mind, making a choice that wouldn't upset him.

"My nightmare holiday would be getting stuck in a foreign airport terminal with small children for days on end, waiting for a flight that keeps getting delayed for some reason," she revealed. "I'd have no change of clothes, and no money, and hardly any food, and everyone would be grizzly and tired, and we couldn't even go outside because of a hurricane or a snowstorm—"

Suddenly she stopped. Her eyes widened.

All four of them turned to gaze out the window.

"Oh, no," Newt whispered. Jake groaned. Marcus checked the departure board.

Sure enough, he saw that the word DELAYED had popped up next to every flight that hadn't already been canceled.

50.
Ambushed

"**O**h, *nuts*." Marcus was filled with despair. "I *knew* it! Right from the start I was worried about Martiya, but then Shibilis was so convincing. . . ."

He trailed off as Newt covered her eyes.

"I don't believe this," she whimpered. "Can you believe this?"

"Believe what?" asked her stepmother, who had finally rejoined them after freshening up in the ladies' room. "What's the matter?"

Without even looking at Coco, Holly explained dully, "We've been tricked again. This is just another nightmare holiday."

"*This* is?" Coco gaped in disbelief. "How do you know?"

Jake suddenly jumped up and began to kick the nearest chair, incoherent with rage.

Coco ignored him. "I don't understand," she said, growing shriller with every word.

"Neither do I." Marcus was trying to swallow the lump in his throat. "Why would Miss Molpe go to all this trouble? She could have left us in the elevator—we'd never have gotten out. Why set up this whole thing with the phone call and the gypsies and the airline tickets—"

"Are you kidding?" Jake interrupted. "She wanted to disarm us! We've *checked our luggage*, remember?"

Marcus caught his breath. "Oh, man . . ."

"I still don't get it," Coco complained. Meanwhile, Sterling appeared behind her, wiping his hands on a paper towel.

Holly stared at him, horrified.

"Where's Edison?" she demanded.

"Eddie?" Sterling was taken aback. "He hasn't finished yet."

"You mean you left him *alone*?" Jake yelped. Without waiting for an answer, he vaulted over several rows of seats before pushing past Sterling, who looked around in confusion.

"What's the big deal?" Sterling asked.

"We've been suckered!" wailed his daughter. And Coco added, "Holly says this is just another nightmare holiday—"

She was cut off by a muffled scream from inside the men's room.

There was a moment's pause. Then everyone stampeded after Jake, skidding around the nearest corner at top speed. In a tightly packed group, they all burst through a door marked with a faceless trousered silhouette. Not even Holly thought twice about invading the men's room. She and Newt and Coco followed Marcus and Sterling; they all galloped past the hand dryers and threw themselves at the line of cubicles like a pack of ravening wolves. They nearly trampled Jake, who had arrived just ahead of them. He was trying to break down the only locked door, behind which Edison could be heard screaming for help.

"On the count of three!" Jake roared. "One, two—"

Wham! Four shoulders hit the door simultaneously. When it didn't budge, Jake spun around to address Sterling.

"Gimme a leg up!" he ordered. As Sterling laced his fingers together, Coco cried, "Eddie! We're coming! Hold on!"

Edison screamed again—and the sound pierced Marcus's rib cage like a dagger. Newt dropped to her knees so that she could peer under the cubicle door, which was several inches off the ground.

"I think I might be able to wriggle through there," she offered hoarsely. But Coco bent down to stop her.

"No!" Coco screeched. "Not you!"

By this time Jake had been hoisted to the top of the door. He flung his leg over it, yelled, "Hey!" then rolled out of sight into the cubicle. There was a *crash*, followed by a squawk, followed by a thundering "Gotcha!"

"Open up!" Sterling banged on the door with both fists. "Let us in, for goodness' sake!"

Click went the latch. The door swung open, and Edison stumbled out, sobbing and rubbing his left wrist.

"She came—she came—I didn't . . . ," he hiccuped. Behind him, Jake was grappling with something long and thin that seemed to be emerging from (or disappearing down) the toilet.

"Oh no," Holly croaked.

Coco released Newt so she could grab Edison. "Are you all right, sweetie? Are you okay?" Coco quavered. Edison promptly buried his face in her slightly damp robe.

Jake turned *his* face toward Sterling. "Help! Quick! Don't let her get away!" Jake pleaded breathlessly. That was when Marcus realized who was trying to escape down the S-bend.

"Miss *Molpe*?" he squeaked from his post by the door of the stall.

It was Miss Molpe, all right—and yet it wasn't. The writhing, slippery shape being hauled out of the plumbing looked longer and bonier than Miss Molpe, with scalier skin and a much bigger nose. Marcus hadn't noticed it before, but Miss Molpe had only four talon-tipped digits on each hand. There weren't any bumps where her ears should have been, and her neck was as long as a heron's. Around her little black eyes, the skin was creased and gray, like an elephant's.

Bit by bit, as she was dragged into view, her flattened hair fluffed up and her limbs unfolded.

"Someone *grab her*!" yelled Jake, who was finding it difficult to keep a firm grip on the slimier parts of Miss Molpe's thrashing body. Sterling immediately dashed into the cubicle, with Holly at his heels. By this time, there were so many people crammed into the tiny space that Marcus couldn't squeeze in there himself.

Newt pulled a face and retreated. "Eww!" she said. "Gross."

"Heave!" Jake had braced one foot against the porcelain pan. "Okay, all together now, *heave!*" There was a slurping sound, followed by a wet *pop*—and all at once Miss Molpe was sprawled on the tiled floor, half inside and half outside the cubicle, with Jake sitting on her back.

She tried to talk, but she was coughing too hard.

"Who's got a belt?" Jake barked. "Everyone take off their belts! We need to tie her up!" He began to pluck at the rope that was wrapped around his own waist. "I can use this. It's from the real world. Who else has something?"

Sterling began to unbuckle his belt. Marcus wasn't wearing one.

"Come and sit on her while I tie her hands," Jake told Holly, whose momentary hesitation seemed to annoy him. "What's wrong? She's not a little old lady—she's some kind of *creature*. Can't you see?"

"She came up the pipe," Edison volunteered, his voice thin and breathless. "She tried to drag me down with her—" He broke off, shuddering.

"I didn't try to drag him down; I simply didn't want to drown!" Miss Molpe croaked. She was trying to sing, but her voice sounded like an old hen's.

She looked a bit like an old hen, too, Marcus thought. Or an evil, ancient vulture.

"Ow!" Jake reared back suddenly, clutching his forearm. "She's got *spurs*! On her *wrists*!" he exclaimed. Sure enough, Marcus spotted a trickle of blood oozing from beneath Jake's hand.

"I can't breathe; I can't see; I'm fainting; I'm dying! What can I say to prove I'm not lying?" Miss Molpe lamented.

"Shut up," said Jake; then he appealed to Sterling. "Put your knee on her neck, okay? Holly can sit on her legs."

"Oh, no . . ." Holly didn't like any of this. Marcus could tell. But she kept Miss Molpe pinned down until

Jake had finished tying the siren's leathery, clawlike hands. Only when he needed access to Miss Molpe's feet did Holly rise again.

The siren, meanwhile, was pleading tunefully. "You're monsters! You're heartless! I'm old and I'm ill! I was drowning in there, not trying to kill!"

"For Pete's sake, somebody gag her!" Jake snapped, yanking hard at a knot to make sure that it was tight enough. Everyone else exchanged questioning glances.

"With what?" asked Holly.

"I don't know! A sock?"

"A *sock*?"

"Just *do* it, okay?"

Coco sighed. "We'll need a big sock," she said to Sterling, who obediently kicked off his shoe.

Miss Molpe began to keen like a mourner. "*Please no, I beg of you, not as a gag! Don't stuff my mouth with that filthy rag!*" she warbled. Her tone was piteous, but when Marcus caught her eye, it was cold and bright and hard.

He felt a shiver run down his spine.

"Maybe she *was* drowning . . . ," Holly murmered, as Sterling wrestled his sock around Miss Molpe's mouth. It wasn't easy, though; the siren's small, bony head kept lashing from side to side, and her nose was so big and sharp that her mouth was hard to find.

"Don't be stupid." Jake spoke through his teeth. "She just can't resist little kids. But she's too much

291

of a wimp to pick 'em off unless they're alone and unprotected. So she sets up a big, complicated trap like this one." Sitting back on his heels, he surveyed his handiwork with fierce satisfaction. "*Now* we've got her, though," he concluded. "Now we've got her just where we want her."

"So what?" Newt growled. "What's the big deal? I mean, it's not like we can believe anything she says."

"That's true." Coco began to nod. "Newt's right. We might as well flush her back down the toilet, for all the use she is."

But Jake hadn't finished.

"No," he reasoned, "you don't understand. It's not her advice we need. That's just rubbish. We know that now. What we need . . ." He clamped a wiry brown hand around her brittle arm. "What we *need* is one of her fingers."

51.

"I hate everything about airports...."

Miss Molpe gave a hiss through her gag. "Mmmh! Mmmm-mmmnn ... ," she protested.

"One of her *fingers*?" Holly echoed, aghast. But Marcus knew what Jake was getting at. He knew that Jake wasn't suggesting that they lop off any digits.

"You mean for the buttons? In the elevator?" asked Marcus.

Jake nodded. "That elevator's gotta be here somewhere," he pointed out. "If *she* presses the buttons, it'll have to move."

There was a moment's silence as everyone tried to think of a likely location for the elevator. Marcus was stumped; the only possibility that occurred to him was the men's room, but they were already inside the men's room.

At last Jake observed, "If this is your nightmare holiday, Holly, then it's your call. Where would you really hate to go?"

Holly's brow puckered. She seemed preoccupied with the bound captive gurgling away under Sterling's knee.

"Oh—ah—gosh . . . I don't know," she replied. "I hate everything about airports. There isn't a specific place."

"There must be," Jake insisted. "Think hard."

"A cleaning closet?" was Coco's suggestion. "A transit lounge?"

"Out on the tarmac in a howling subzero wind?" Sterling asked, shivering like a man familiar with such an experience. Holly shook her head, frowning. Then she blinked and sucked air through her teeth.

"Oh!" she exclaimed, her eyes widening. "I know!"

"What?" said Marcus.

"It was at the Bangkok airport, years ago," Holly recalled. "When I spotted it, I remember thinking, 'That must be the worst place on earth—'"

"*What* was?" Newt interrupted. "Hurry up and tell us!"

"It was the smoking room." Holly looked from face to face, her own face creased into an expression of pure disgust. "It was a glassed-in box where all the smokers had to go if they wanted to light up a cigarette. I swear, you could hardly see them through the pall of smoke and the nicotine stains on the glass—"

"That's it, then." Newt cut her off. "We have to find the smoking room. Any ideas?"

Jake shrugged. "We'll just follow the signs," he said. Then he elbowed Sterling out of his way, hooked an arm around Miss Molpe, heaved himself upright with a grunt, and threw her over his shoulder like a bag of wet laundry.

When she growled deep in her throat, the rumble seemed to reverberate right through the floor.

"Oh, Jake!" Holly protested. "Be careful!"

"It's okay." He staggered slightly. "I can manage."

"You'll hurt yourself!"

"Nah. She doesn't weigh a thing." Jake's voice was gruff and his eyes were bulging with the effort of keeping his balance. "So are we going or not?"

"I—I guess so. . . ." Holly draped her arm around Marcus's shoulders. Then she looked at Coco, who looked at Sterling, who climbed to his feet and took Edison's hand. Together they made their way out of the men's room into a larger, brighter, emptier, more exposed space.

The hallway seemed endless. The numbered departure gates stretched on to infinity, or so it appeared; between each gate, acres of window held back snow flurries that were swallowed up, again and again, by a dense, enveloping darkness. The flurries made odd shapes. *Very* odd shapes.

Marcus felt his heart skip a beat as he caught a glimpse of something out of the corner of his eye. Was it . . . ? Could it be . . . ?

Was that an *open hand* sliding down the glass?

"I hate these stupid signs that have pictures on them," Newt complained with a hysterical edge to her voice. She was staring up at an information sign that was covered in arrows and icons: the symbol for male and female toilets, with a universal man and a universal woman standing side by side; the symbol for food service, a stylized knife and fork; the symbol for an elevator, with two universal men wedged into a square.

"That won't be the elevator *we* want." Holly decided as Jake staggered again. He was hunched over, gasping and red in the face. But when Sterling offered to help, Jake simply snapped at Miss Molpe.

"Hey! You! I know what you're up to! If you make yourself any heavier, I'll drag you along by the *hair*! Got it?"

Miss Molpe didn't reply, of course. She couldn't. But Marcus figured that she must have got it, because after a few seconds, Jake straightened up and said, "That's better."

"What do you think the one at the end means?"

Coco asked. She'd been squinting at the sign above her, trying to interpret some of the more obscure icons displayed there. "Is it a thermometer or a baby's bottle? I can't tell."

"Me neither," Sterling confessed. "But that one means a telephone, and that means a luggage cart. . . ."

"What about that one?" Newt pointed to a white horizontal line with a black tip. "That looks like a cigarette, don't you think?"

"Yeah, but so does that," said Marcus, drawing her attention to a straight black horizontal line with a wiggly vertical line attached to one end. "That looks like a *smoking* cigarette."

"And that looks like a cigarette lighter." Jake nodded at a leaf shape on top of a rectangle.

Holly, who had been nervously eyeing Miss Molpe's beaky, malevolent face, cut a quick glance at the sign and observed, "They're all in the same direction. Why don't we just see what they are when we reach them?"

"Yeah," Jake agreed. "Good idea." He set off at an unsteady trot, clearly anxious to find the smoking room before his back gave out.

Marcus hurried after him, trying not to look at the windows. The view from these windows was beginning to disturb Marcus. He wanted to ask the others if they'd spotted a face emerging from the snow flurries, its eyes shadowed and its mouth hanging open in a yawn or a scream, but he was afraid that the answer might be yes. So he kept his gaze fixed firmly on the overhead signs as Holly and the Huckstepps caught up with him.

"You know what? I've had an idea," Sterling announced, puffing a little. "It's about your phone, Holly."

"My phone doesn't work," Holly reminded Sterling. "Whoever answered my call wasn't real. He was . . ." She flapped her hand. "He was in this world somewhere."

"Exactly. That's what I mean. You got through to another part of this . . . whatever it is. Program. Scenario." Sterling increased his pace to match Holly's. "What I'm saying is that Prot has a Bluetooth function—and so does your phone. If he's not far away, I can make contact with him."

"Really?" Marcus stopped in his tracks just as Jake, who was a yard or two in front of him, exclaimed, "Here it is! Here's the first one!"

They had drawn level with a purple door set into a featureless stretch of pale-blue wall. The door had a symbol on it: two lines, one straight and horizontal, the other wiggly and vertical.

"It's that smoking-cigarette sign," said Marcus.

Coco promptly stepped forward. "Let's have a look, then," she remarked before pushing open the door.

There was no smoke. That was the first thing Marcus noticed. Though the room beyond the threshold was dim and reeking, it didn't stink of smoke. Marcus was trying to work out what it *did* smell like when a whip lashed out of the darkness and wrapped itself around Coco's wrist.

She screamed like a gibbon.

52.

The search for the smoking room

Sterling grabbed Coco just in time. A sudden tug on the whip nearly jerked her off her feet; it would have yanked her over the threshold if Sterling hadn't caught her.

Miss Molpe chuckled deep in her throat, her black eyes glittering.

"Cut it! Cut the cord!" Sterling yelled.

"With what?" wailed Newt. No one had any knives or scissors. Edison began to cry as Marcus groped around in his pockets.

Luckily, Holly knew just what to do. She pushed past Sterling and slammed the door with such force that the whip was severed. *Snap!* Sterling and Coco reeled backwards, bumping into Jake—who nearly dropped Miss Molpe. The siren bucked and twisted, trying to dig her spurs into his neck.

Jake had to squeeze her tightly until she squeaked and stopped thrashing about. For a few seconds, there was no sound except the rasp of people catching their breath.

"Sorry," Marcus said at last. "I guess it's a whip sign, not a smoking-cigarette sign."

"A whip? *A whip?*" Newt screeched. "Why would there be a *whip room* at an *airport?*"

No one replied. Coco was too busy tearing the leather strap off her wrist, which was now disfigured by a raised reddish welt. Sterling was trying to calm her down. Edison was sucking his thumb for comfort, and Marcus couldn't think of a sensible answer.

But when Miss Molpe tried to hum a little tune, Jake turned to Newt and growled, "Just punch her in the face for me, will you? I can't reach around that far."

The humming immediately stopped.

"Jake, *don't*," Holly chided. Then she took a deep breath. "Okay, we're all in one piece and everything's fine. Obviously that's not the smoking room, so we'd better keep moving."

"I'm not opening any more doors," whimpered Coco. "In fact, I don't think *anyone* should."

"We have to," said Marcus. He was about to go on when Jake suddenly announced, "I'll do it. I'll open the doors. In fact, I might even use this evil old bag as a battering ram."

Holly clicked her tongue. "Jake—"

"Or as a shield, perhaps. If anything comes at me, it'll hit her first."

"Uh—before you do that," Sterling interjected, "maybe I should try calling Prot. For all we know, he's in this terminal somewhere. And if he is, he can open some doors for us."

Since no one could find a flaw in his plan, Holly gave Sterling her cell phone. And as they all trudged along, past gate after gate, Sterling busily tapped codes and commands into its keypad.

"Look," Edison suddenly remarked. "There's that cigarette." He'd been clinging to Newt with both hands. Now he raised one of them to point at a familiar symbol: the white line with the black tip. "Except that it might not even *be* a cigarette . . . ," he had to admit.

Everyone slowed, then halted in front of another purple door. Sterling, meanwhile, connected with Prot. "Prot?" he said. "Where are you?" There was a brief pause. "Really? You *are*?" Sterling covered the mouthpiece of Holly's phone. "Prot's at Siren Song Travel!" he exclaimed. "He took the elevator back there!"

"Oh, wow." Marcus brightened. "That's *fantastic*!" But when he beamed at his mother, he saw that she was wrinkling her brow and chewing on her bottom lip. The others wore the same troubled look; they were either too tired, too stunned, or too stupid the grasp the importance of what Sterling had just told them.

"It might not be the real Siren Song Travel," was Coco's immediate concern.

"It has to be," Marcus insisted. "Prot's a robot. Robots don't have dreams or nightmares." To Sterling he said, "Ask if there's an airport brochure."

"Good thinking!" Sterling proceeded to interrogate Prot. "Prot? Is there a brochure for an airport? An *airport* . . ."

Jake, by this time, had come to a decision. "I'm going to take a look," he declared, adjusting the weight on his shoulder. Then he strode forward and reached for the purple door.

"Be careful, Jake," warned Holly as he turned the handle. Everyone else retreated a step—except Sterling, who was still doggedly questioning his robot.

"Have you searched the whole room?" he asked. "What about the desk? Yes, I want you to check all the drawers in that desk. . . ."

"*Yuck!*" cried Newt, slapping a hand over her nose. The smell was overwhelming; it seemed to engulf them like a tidal wave before Jake could shut the door again. He gagged and coughed and gasped. So did Holly and Coco. Marcus felt dizzy. Staggering backwards, he nearly fell.

"Read it to me. Okay. And the next one? And what about—" When the stench hit Sterling, he was cut off in midsentence. "Oohh . . . arrgh . . . gaak!" he choked.

Around him his family were scattering in every direction, fleeing from the smell as if it were poison gas. Even Jake moved away once the door had been shut. It took a while for the noxious fumes to dissipate—and even longer for Jake to find his voice again.

"Maggots," he wheezed.

"Hnnn?" Holly's eyes were brimming with tears. She was holding her breath and couldn't speak.

"Giant maggots. In there." Jake jabbed a finger at the door. "White body . . . black head . . ." Propped against a wall, he was doubled over beneath Miss Molpe's oddly misshapen frame, with its stalklike neck and small, bobbing skull. "That picture wasn't a cigarette. It was a maggot."

Miss Molpe snickered.

"A maggot room. Great." Newt was holding her nose. "No *way* should we be opening any more doors! Not unless we know what's on the other side!"

"But we have to," Marcus objected. And Sterling backed him up.

"That's right, because Prot—*hack-hack*—Prot's found a drawer full of—*hack-hack-hack* . . ."

When her father dissolved into a fit of coughing, Newt cried, "Prot's found a drawer full of *what?*"

"Ahh . . . ahh . . . a drawer full of files," Sterling croaked at last. "Each one's got a number and each one deals with a specific complaint."

"*Complaint?*" Holly echoed hoarsely. "What kind of complaint?"

"A complaint about a disastrous holiday." After clearing his throat and wiping his eyes, Sterling continued. "According to Prot, there's a sunken-ship complaint, and a vampire-infested-camp complaint—"

"And a delayed-flight complaint?" Marcus interrupted breathlessly.

Sterling gave a nod. "Yes," he confirmed. "Which has to be the file for this airport."

"And it's got a number? Is that what you said?" asked Holly.

"A file number. Yes."

"Which Prot can key into the office phone!" Marcus seized Sterling's arm. "Then he can program the elevator to come straight down here!"

"But he shouldn't come down here with it." Sterling seemed to be thinking aloud. "He's to send the elevator to us, and when we get into it, I'll call him—"

"And he can use the office phone again," Marcus finished, "which means the elevator will go back there to pick him up!"

"Exactly." Sterling and Marcus surveyed each other for a moment, full of mutual respect and mounting

305

excitement. Then Sterling put the phone to his ear again. "Prot?" he said. "Listen carefully. I want you to lift that phone receiver . . ."

Marcus was thrilled. *This time,* he thought, *I know it's going to work.* When he looked around, however, he was surprised to see no answering gleam of anticipation in the eyes of those people who had the most cause to celebrate. "Don't you get it?" he demanded. "The elevator's coming! It means we can go!"

Newt sniffed. "We're not going anywhere unless we can *find* the thing," she spat. "Which is not going to happen if we can't find the smoking room." She obviously wanted to pick a fight, but as she folded her arms defensively, her brother suddenly pointed.

"You mean *that* smoking room?" he asked.

53.
Choking

Sterling was still on the phone to Prot.

"You have? Excellent. Then wait right there until I call you." With a *beep* he hung up. "The elevator's coming!" he cried before he realized that everyone else was staring down the hallway. "What is it?" he asked. "What's wrong?"

"Look." Coco drew his attention to a distant glass box about half the size of a single-car garage. It was tucked into a corner between a wall and a window. "We think that might be the smoking room."

"That's *definitely* the smoking room," Marcus decreed. He could just make out the sign on the glass box, which showed a universal hand holding a black stick between two fingers. "Apart from anything else, it's full of smoke."

"Is it?" Holly squinted. "You mean that isn't *frosted glass?*"

"We'll soon find out," said Jake, marching ahead briskly. Soon, however, he began to slow down—and by the time he reached his destination, the others had caught up with him. "This is it, all right," he announced, panting and sweating. "Because old ferret-face here has decided to stack on the pounds again."

"But I can't see an elevator." Newt had pressed her nose against the glass wall of the box, beyond which lay a swirling gray cloud. "I can't see *anything.*"

"There must be some pretty heavy smokers inside," said Marcus. Coco wasn't persuaded, though.

"That's an awful lot of smoke to be coming out of a few smokers," was her opinion. "Maybe it's a fire. Maybe we shouldn't go in."

"Oh, we're going in. We're not backing off now." Jake's tone was hard and firm. Though his knees were trembling with the effort of supporting Miss Molpe, he barged straight through the door of the smoking room.

Then he started to cough.

"Aw—*huck-huck*—I can't see a thing—*huck-huck-huck . . .*"

"I'm coming, Jake! I'll help you!" Holly pursued him into the smoke, which immediately swallowed her up. Marcus couldn't see her anymore.

He could hear her, though. She was coughing her lungs out.

"Jake—*cough-cough*—where are you?"

"They'll suffocate in there," Coco muttered. Then she raised her voice. "Jake! Holly! Come out before you die of smoke inhalation!"

By this time smoke was billowing into the hallway; Marcus couldn't believe how much of it there was. He, too, began to cough—and wonder what would happen if they opened a window. Would something nasty try to get in?

Suddenly a loud *ping* made his heart leap.

"That's it!" he exclaimed. "That's the elevator! It's arrived!"

"Come on." Sterling seized his hand. "We have to go in."

"Everybody hold hands so we don't lose each other!" Coco instructed. "Newt! Take Eddie's hand, please!"

Together they formed a chain, with Sterling at its head. As they crossed the smoke-blurred threshold, choking and gasping, Marcus heard his mother's cracked voice drifting out of the gray haze. "I found a—*cough-cough*—wall!" she was saying. "Jake? Where are you?"

"I'm here!" Jake's response was muffled. "This place is so—*huck–huck–huck*—big!"

"Wait! Listen!" cried Holly. Straining his ears, Marcus caught the rattle of a metal sliding door before the noise was drowned by a fit of coughing.

"I hear it!" Jake rasped. "It's just over there!"

"Hurry, before it closes again!" croaked Sterling. The smoke was so thick that Marcus could barely see him, even though the two of them were holding hands. It was impossible to tell which way they were facing or how far away the glass door was.

Marcus felt sick and dizzy. He couldn't breathe. *The siren is doing this somehow,* he concluded. *She's trying to stop us from finding her elevator.* His knees were beginning to buckle when Jake suddenly screeched, "I've got it! I found it!" After that, there was total confusion.

Marcus was vaguely aware of a thump and a swish. His vision seemed to be darkening at the edges—or was that just the smoke closing in? He nearly lost his balance as he was tugged forward; then someone bumped into him and said, "Ooof!" Newt and Sterling both let him go.

All at once Marcus staggered into a wall. It was a familiar wall. It was, in fact, the back wall of the elevator.

Looking around with watery eyes, he realized that the dense haze was lifting. He could see Coco,

Sterling, Newt, Jake, Miss Molpe, Holly and . . .

"Edison? Where's Edison?" Coco demanded.

"Here," squawked Edison.

"So everybody's present and accounted for? Yes?" Satisfied, Sterling started jabbing at Holly's phone again as Jake, who had been leaning against the elevator door, stepped aside and let it rumble shut. Holly was almost sobbing with gratitude.

"Jake, you're a—*cough-cough*—genius!" she spluttered. "I couldn't see a thing! How on earth did you find your way in here?"

"Simple," Jake replied gruffly. "This stupid old cow led me straight to it. The heavier she got, the closer I was."

With a shrug and a grunt he let Miss Molpe slide off his back, so that she landed heavily on the floor. *Thump!* Everyone else shrank against the walls in a general movement of revulsion.

Only Sterling seemed oblivious to Miss Molpe. He was on the phone, addressing his robot. "Hello? Prot?" he said. "You can pick up that phone again. Yes, please. And then you can key in the same number . . ."

After delivering his instructions, he signed off. "We won't have long to wait," he announced.

He was right, too. Because about ten seconds later, the elevator gave a sudden lurch—and dropped like a stone.

54.
Paper chase

*"A*aaaaaaaaaaaaaaaaaaaaaaaagh!"

A chorus of screams rang out. Marcus was thrown against a wall. For about two seconds he thought he was going to die.

But when Sterling fell on top of Miss Molpe, the elevator stopped abruptly. There was no devastating crash, though some of the passengers did bump their heads and bruise their elbows. Most of them ended up on the floor in a muddled heap.

As they slowly disentangled themselves, the door opened.

"Prot!" Coco exclaimed. "Hold that door! Don't let it close!"

The sight of Prot was a welcome one. Framed in

the doorway against a familiar backdrop of display shelves, the robot jerked to a halt before obediently wedging one steel hand against the elevator door. Prot's other (detached) hand was probably still inside Jake's suitcase, which sat right in front of them on the shabby beige carpet of Siren Song Travel.

"Look at that!" Holly quavered. "It's your bag, Jake! How on earth did it end up here?"

Jake didn't reply; he was wincing and rubbing his knee. Miss Molpe also failed to respond—perhaps because she was buried under Sterling's massive stomach.

It was Marcus who said, "Maybe the dangerous stuff always ends up here. So Miss Molpe can chuck it back into the real world." Adjusting his glasses, which had nearly been knocked off his face, he studied the closed door that stood a few yards across the room. "Maybe this is where she normally hangs out," he concluded, "and the real world's beyond that door at the top of the cellar stairs."

"I hope so," Newt whimpered. She had climbed stiffly to her feet. "But who's going to open the door and find out?"

"Prot will." Sterling was struggling to raise himself. "Not yet, though."

"No. Not yet," said Jake. "Before we do anything else, we need to lock up our *friend* here." He spat out the word *friend* like a mouthful of sour milk. "Then

313

we can take her with us and decide what to do with her later."

Marcus had no objection to this plan. Not even Holly kicked up a fuss; on the contrary, she was eyeing the siren's slightly flattened shape with the nervous disgust she usually reserved for slugs and cockroaches.

Lying on the floor, all damp and bent and angular, with her scaly blue limbs and wisps of feathery hair, Miss Molpe looked like plucked roadkill.

"Can't we just leave her?" Coco asked in a plaintive voice. But Jake shook his head.

"Not until we're *absolutely sure* that we're home," he insisted. Then he turned to address Holly. "Can you go get my suitcase? I'd do it myself if I didn't have to keep an eye on this sneaky pile of—"

"I'll do it," Newt volunteered, cutting him off mid-insult. Before anyone could object, she stepped out of the elevator and moved toward Jake's suitcase.

That was when the brochures on the shelves began to rustle as if they were caught in a strong breeze. At the same time, the door to the cellar remained tightly shut. So where, Marcus wondered, could the breeze be coming from?

"She's moving, Jake!" Holly spoke sharply, her gaze on Miss Molpe, who seemed to be shivering or clucking. It was hard to tell, because the siren's face was hidden. By now almost everyone was upright, including Sterling.

Inside the office, brochures were fluttering from their shelves like butterflies, flapping and snapping their colorful pages.

"Ow!" yelped Newt. A flying brochure had just grazed her cheek. She slapped at it, then bent to pick up Jake's suitcase. By now, more brochures were swooping from their perches like a flock of angry birds. *"Yeow!"* she cried. "Get off!"

"Oh, boy," said Jake. He sounded distinctly rattled.

Marcus, however, was encouraged by the sight of the many whirling, spiraling paper airplanes. "This is good," he said. "It means that someone's protecting that door over there."

"Because it leads to the outside world?" Holly inquired.

Marcus shrugged. Though he couldn't be sure, it certainly looked that way.

"Ouch!" As Newt ran back toward the elevator, suitcase in hand, she was pelted by dive-bombing brochures. When she swung at them with the suitcase, they swirled aside and attacked her from another angle.

But they didn't follow her into the elevator. The moment she crossed the threshold, nearly tripping over Prot, the brochures seemed to lose interest. They banked and turned and headed straight back into the room, where they tumbled about in midair like a giant cloud of confetti.

"Gimme that." Jake wrenched the suitcase from Newt and slammed it onto the floor. Then he flung it open, struggling with Miss Molpe at the same time. She was screeching like a banshee or a circular saw— or even like a chorus of fire alarms—and the noise was excruciating. It was like a needle in the brain. Marcus had to clap his hands over his ears. Everyone else did the same thing, except Jake. Both of *his* hands were busy, so he had to grit his teeth and turn his head away from her.

The gag wasn't enough to stifle Miss Molpe's wordless shriek.

"Somebody take the stuff outta my case!" Jake barked hoarsely. "Now! Quick!" To Sterling he shouted, "We've gotta lift her! On the count of three . . ."

While Marcus and Edison squatted down to scoop all Jake's old supplies out of the suitcase, Jake and Sterling tried to lift Miss Molpe. Unfortunately, she wouldn't budge. No matter how much the straining men heaved and grunted—no matter how firmly they grasped her writhing, squirming, howling shape—she was too heavy for them. At last Jake called a halt to the attempt.

"*What's in that suitcase?*" he roared over the noise.

"Um . . ." Edison surveyed his booty, his little face creased with discomfort. "There's Prot's hand, and a fishing line, and pens, and a cigarette lighter, and a packet of chewing gum—"

"Pass me the cigarette lighter," Jake interrupted grimly. "I'll make her talk."

Miss Molpe abruptly stopped screaming. In the sudden silence, Holly's gasp of horror was clearly audible, but before she could protest, Sterling exclaimed, "It's all right! She's losing weight! I can lift her now!"

Miss Molpe, in fact, had suddenly become so light that Sterling almost overbalanced as he yanked at her legs; he hadn't been expecting her to slide across the floor as easily as she did.

"How are we going to get out of here, though?" Holly demanded. She was peering at the flurry of brochures that hovered between the elevator and the door to the cellar. "We'll be cut to bits!"

"A paper cut never killed anybody," Jake rejoined. He had stooped to pick up Miss Molpe's shoulders, leaving her feet to Sterling. When the two men swung her toward Jake's suitcase, however, her tongue whipped out like a long blue serpent.

Jake dropped his end. *"Yechh!"* he squawked.

"Get her in! Just get her in!" cried Coco. She had flattened herself against a wall in abject terror. Marcus was also paralyzed; like Edison, he stood motionless, spellbound by the siren's transformation into a coiling, wriggling, hissing, boneless *thing*. Only Holly and Newt darted forward.

Miss Molpe tried to peck at them with her nose. She tried to cut them with her spurs. Thanks to the combined efforts of Newt, Holly, Jake, and Sterling, however, she was finally overcome. They managed to thrust her into the suitcase.

Then Jake slammed the lid shut and Holly sat on it.

"Okay!" Jake was breathless and damp with sweat. "Now we send Prot ahead to open the other door. When he's done that, we'll make a run for it. Agreed?"

"I don't know." Marcus was dubious. "One paper cut can really hurt. Imagine having fifty of them!"

"I don't like paper cuts," Edison whined.

"Okay, I tell you what." Jake tried again. "How about we get Prot to hold open that other door and then we send one person to fetch blankets or tarpaulins or something from the outside world, which the rest of us can use to shield ourselves when *we* leave. How about that?"

"Sounds good," said Sterling. Marcus gave Jake a thumbs-up sign, and his mother nodded. Coco made an approving noise as Edison relaxed against her.

Only Newt objected.

"Wait!" she shrilled. "Aren't you forgetting something?" When everyone stared at her blankly, she added, *"What about the little white dog?"*

55.
Inferno

"We're not going back for that dog," Coco declared.

"But we have to!" cried Newt. "It's *our* fault the poor thing's trapped!"

"No."

"But—"

"No!"

"We could send Prot," Marcus meekly suggested. "We could give him the flight number for Lysitte Run, and he could key it into the elevator."

When Coco hesitated, Jake put his foot down. "Later," he said. "First things first. We need Prot to open that door." Stooping, he addressed the robot. "Open that door, Prot," he said, pointing through the snowstorm of brochures. "And hold it open. Understand?"

"I understand," Prot droned in response. "I must open that door and hold it open."

"Correct." Jake turned to face the others as Prot trundled off to execute his command. "When the door's open, I'm going out to get blankets."

"No. Not you." Holly grabbed Jake's wrist. "You're hardly wearing anything, and you don't even know where my blankets are."

"So why don't you tell me?" He sounded impatient. Holly wouldn't yield, though; she shook her head.

"With any luck, it's my trailer out there," she replied. "And if it is, then I know just where to look for things. Wait here and let me do it. I'll be back in three seconds."

"But, Mom," Marcus protested, "have you *seen* what you'll be walking into?" He himself had been watching the robot plow through a whirlwind of bombarding brochures, which were hitting Prot's metal hide with such force that they made clinking noises as they bounced off. "Those things are really going to hurt!"

Holly simply smiled. "I've had a root canal, Marcus. Nothing else will ever come close to that," she assured him.

Prot, meanwhile, had reached the other side of the room—and had pulled open the door, as instructed.

When a sudden gust of fresh air blew a path through the paper, Holly saw her chance. "Off I go!" she cried, darting forward. But she wasn't quick enough. By the time she reached the desk, she was almost invisible; hundreds of brochures were swarming around her like bees. To protect her eyes, she had to fold her arms across her face.

Then she veered off course, because she couldn't see where she was going.

"Mom! No!" Marcus shouted. Jake didn't think twice. He plunged straight after her, with Marcus close behind him. There was an immediate reaction from the brochures, which descended on Marcus so thickly that he soon found it hard to breathe. They plastered themselves over his nose and mouth. They became tangled in his hair. No matter how many he pulled off or batted away, more and more kept coming.

"Newt! Stop!" Coco screamed. There was a flash of light and a smell of smoke. Jake gave Marcus a push, bawling, "Get out! That way! Quick!"

All at once Marcus found himself stumbling past Prot into a familiar brick-walled, stone-floored cellar.

"Oh!" He turned around. "Mom! Look! We're home!"

But Holly wasn't listening. She was too busy dodging the brochures, some of which were now on fire. They careened over her head, singeing the paint and igniting other brochures, until they dropped, blackened and shriveled, onto the office carpet. There they lay, smoldering like cigarette butts, while Coco shrieked and Prot made a high-pitched fire-alarm noise.

Squinting through the chaos, Marcus could just make out that Newt was holding the cigarette lighter.

"Newt!" Jake roared at her, "Did you set *fire* to the *pamphlets*?"

Holly, meanwhile, was crawling across the carpet, which had already begun to send up little plumes of smoke.

"Well, somebody had to do *something*!" Though Newt defended herself loudly and fervently, no one paid any attention. Her father was trying to lift Jake's suitcase, which had suddenly become much heavier. Jake had doubled back to help him. Holly was now on her feet, staggering toward the exit with her head down.

"Here, Mom!" called Marcus. "It's safe in here!"

He reached out and grabbed her sleeve, guiding her over the threshold. None of the burning brochures followed her; they seemed unable to. They were stuck inside the office, like fiery flecks inside a snow globe.

Beyond them, in the elevator, Coco was hanging back. She'd wrapped a fold of her robe around Edison and was staring, aghast, at the flames that were licking along the carpet near one of the display shelves.

"I'll get water!" Holly cried. "Water and blankets!" She whirled around and raced up the cellar stairs, just ahead of Marcus.

"Wait! Mom!" he protested. "Be careful! It might not be our trailer!"

But it was. Marcus *knew* it was. Because on finally emerging from the open bench, he found that he could smell sweaty gym clothes.

His mother was already pulling blankets out from under the bed. "Here!" she exclaimed, throwing them at Marcus. "Take these down! I'll get some water!"

"Mom? Hey, Mom." Before he did anything else, Marcus wanted to make absolutely sure that they weren't being taken for a ride. "What does this place smell like to you?" he asked.

"What?" Holly stared at him as if he were mad. "For heaven's sake, Marcus!"

"Just tell me."

Holly sniffed. "It smells like moldy baked beans," she declared. And her son heaved a sigh of relief.

"Then we're home," he said. "We really are back home."

56.
Excess baggage

"**W**ell, of course we're home!" Holly didn't seem to have the slightest doubt about *that*. "If we weren't, we'd be fending off the security guard, not to mention the little blonde girl."

"Do you think so?" Marcus couldn't agree with her. He was about to point out that the witch could have dreamed up any number of fake Diamond Beaches when Holly flapped an impatient hand at him.

"Go on! Quick!" she said. "I'll be right behind you!"

So Marcus retraced his steps—very, very carefully. With the bundle of blankets impeding his view, he couldn't exactly rush. In fact, he was only halfway downstairs when he almost collided with Coco and

Edison. Coco had used the hood of her robe to shield her head during a mad dash from the elevator.

"Are those blankets?" Coco extended her arms toward Marcus. "I'll take them! You take Eddie!"

Marcus hesitated. "But—"

"Hurry up!" Coco pleaded. "Before the whole place burns down!"

Sure enough, the basement was already filling with smoke. And although none of the flaming brochures had ventured past Prot, Marcus could see that the doorjamb was beginning to smolder.

"Go on, Eddie!" Coco urged him. With one hand she gave her stepson a prod up the stairs; with the other she seized the untidy clump of blankets from Marcus. "I'm going back to help Sterling—you boys wait in the trailer, okay?"

"I have some water!" Holly called from the topmost step. She tossed a plastic bottle into the basement as Coco scampered back downstairs. The bottle hit the floor and rolled but didn't break. Instead, it came to rest against the side of Newt's bare foot.

Newt had just emerged from the office, coughing and looked flustered. When she saw the bottle, she bent down, picked it up, and dumped its contents over her head.

Her stepmother was hurling blankets through the cellar door. "Here!" Coco screeched. "Put them on!"

Marcus could only assume that she was talking to Jake and Sterling.

"Why don't they come out?" he asked no one in particular. "What are they waiting for?"

"Nothing." It was Edison who replied, his voice thin and hoarse. He was on the same step as Marcus. "They're just slow. That suitcase is really heavy."

"*Stand aside*, boys, I need to get past you!" Holly interrupted. Then she threw another bottle onto the floor, screaming, *"More water, Coco! Use the water!"*

At that point Jake began to shuffle backwards into the basement. Though a blanket was draped over his head and shoulders, his bare calves were clearly visible. He seemed to be having trouble with his end of the suitcase, which he nearly dropped when Coco dumped half a pint of water onto his shrouded skull.

"Aaagh!" he spluttered. "Gerroff!"

"Dad! Hey, Dad!" Newt was still hovering near the door, coughing and choking and wiping her eyes. "What's that—*hack-hack*—flight number?"

"Huh?" It took Sterling a moment to catch on. Though he'd flung a blanket across his bald spot, his face wasn't covered, so it was easy to hear him, even from a distance. "Oh!" he said breathlessly, adjusting his grip on the suitcase. "You mean for Lysitte Run? It was eight-eight-two-three-zero-five-nine-eight . . ."

All at once, a mighty crackling roar nearly drowned out his voice. There was a *crash* and a shower of sparks just behind him. "It's the shelves!" cried Jake, who was face-to-face with Sterling and could see what Sterling couldn't. "Move! *Move!* Get outta there, quick!"

Holly panicked. She squeezed past the two boys and charged downstairs to join Coco. Luckily, Edison didn't lose his balance. He clung to Marcus, who began to hustle him upstairs. Sterling, meanwhile, had just entered the basement; his knuckles were almost dragging on the ground, thanks to the weight he was carrying. When Coco darted forward to help him, he gladly surrendered one corner of the suitcase.

Jake wasn't quite as eager to admit that he was struggling. But after a brief, scrappy exchange, he let Holly take another corner—and with four people supporting it, the suitcase was soon halfway to the stairs.

Newt didn't even try to lend a hand. She was too busy talking to Prot.

"Hey, *Newt!*" Marcus yelled, pausing on his climb. It was hard to see through all the billowing smoke, but Newt's dark silhouette stood out quite cleanly against the red-hot backdrop; fire was leaping from Miss Molpe's desk, which lay under the collapsed remains of a briskly burning display shelf. Though most of the dive-bombing brochures had already turned to ash, they'd been replaced by clouds of glowing embers, which were starting to drift into the basement. Ripples of white flame were lapping around the lintel.

"Coming!" cried Newt just as Prot spun around and plunged back into the heart of the inferno.

"*Prot!*" Marcus bawled. He started forward, clattering down the stairs and leaving Edison behind. "Prot, come back!"

But apparently the robot couldn't hear; it forged ahead implacably as Marcus reached Newt's side. Though he had to shade his eyes from the heat of the lapping flames, he caught a glimpse of Prot's small, stolid back receding toward the elevator.

"I've sent him to save the dog," Newt explained. "He's made of metal—he won't get hurt." The words had barely left her mouth when one panel of the cellar door collapsed into a blazing heap, scorching the basement floor and sending up another flurry of sparks. "Oh, no!" she wailed. "That poor dog!"

"Poor *dog*?" Sterling croaked from a spot near the bottom of the staircase. "What about my poor *robot*?"

"Newt! Marcus! *Move!*" snarled Jake. "We're waiting for you!"

Marcus took Newt's hand. Together they moved away from the cellar door and began to edge past the four laboring adults, who by now were bent double. The suitcase was such a dead weight that the two women, in particular, were finding it hard to lift their feet. Holly was certainly flagging. Her face was bright red and the veins stood out on her forehead like pieces of spaghetti.

"Hurry, kids!" she gasped. "We're really slow here, so you'd better go up ahead of us!"

She staggered slightly as she shuffled aside to give Newt and Marcus enough room. But she wasn't fast enough for Newt, who launched herself at the bottom step so abruptly that she knocked against her mother. And that was when Coco lost her grip on the suitcase.

CRASH! It fell through the floor.

Then it kept falling.

57.

"Is this the real thing?"

*C*RASH . . . CRASH . . . *crash* . . . crash . . .

The suitcase plummeted through the basement floor and through the floor beneath that, then punched its way through floor after floor, towing bits of debris with it, until it finally became a speck in the distance and was swallowed up by shadow.

Newt had nearly followed the suitcase. A flagstone had dropped from beneath her feet, but she'd managed to grab the edge of the hole just in time. Now she was dangling over a void, screaming her lungs out, as other things hurtled into the crumbling shaft beneath her: water, furniture, snow, fish, cakes, trees, tiles, chunks of footpath. Every punctured floor under the basement seemed to have its own landscape, climate, and ecology. And as oceans drained into go-kart tracks that collapsed onto herds of dinosaurs, the chaos spread like a virus. Distant buildings swayed and sagged and toppled into the hole. Rivers of chocolate poured over its edge. Ice shelves crumbled away as the hole sent cracks shooting across them.

For Marcus, it was like watching the apocalypse from the top of a very tall skyscraper—or through the wrong end of a telescope. But he wasn't too worried about the possible destruction of a hundred dream-worlds, especially when most of it was happening so very far away. He was much more concerned about Newt.

"Grab my hand!" he bawled, dropping to his knees. Around him, everyone else was doing the same thing. Since Marcus's hand was the closest, though, Newt seized it—and nearly pulled him into the hole with her.

"*Marcus!*" Holly shrieked. She caught him just in time, though even *she* was pulled toward the bottom-less pit, dragged by the combined weight of Newt and her son. Only when Jake threw his arms around her was Holly's accelerating slide arrested.

Marcus felt as if his arm was about to be pulled out of its socket. His hand was being crushed by Newt's frantic grip. He could hardly see because of all the blood that had rushed to his head, which seemed to be hanging upside down.

Newt was still screaming.

"Heave!" yelled Jake. Then someone clutched Marcus's T-shirt. Suddenly he found himself sitting on the basement floor again, with Newt lying next to him. Her feet, however, were still hanging over the edge of the hole. And once his vision had cleared, Marcus noticed that the floor was shedding more and more of its paving stones.

As each stone peeled away, pulled downward by the force of gravity—or by a peculiar wind-tunnel effect created by the hurtling suitcase—the yawning chasm grew wider and wider.

"Come on!" Jake cried, yanking Marcus to his feet. "This floor's caving in!"

Around them, the air was full of drifting embers. Above them, at the top of the stairs, Edison was shouting hysterically. Everyone stampeded toward him—and Marcus was carried along in the rush. He was pushed up the steps, just behind Coco, and pulled through the bench seat by Coco and Edison. As he stumbled into the caravan, dazed and coughing, he heard Newt's voice just behind him. "Get me out!" she was wailing. "Get me out! Get me out!"

She popped from the seat's narrow slot like a cork out of a bottle, closely followed by Holly, who was shoved from behind by Jake. Jake practically vaulted into the trailer. But he immediately whirled around and leaned down to help Sterling, who had gripped the edge of the seat just in time. Below him, the staircase had begun to sway, pulling away from the brick wall that supported it.

"Hold on, sweetie!" Coco cried. She and Jake both heaved and grunted until Sterling had enough elbow room to maneuver himself into the real world.

As he rolled onto the floor of the caravan, gasping and sweating, the lid of the seat slammed shut.

"It's okay . . . We're okay . . ." Holly hugged Marcus. "Thank heavens."

"Are you all right?" Coco asked Sterling, then glanced around. "Is everyone all right?"

"I'm fine," Sterling replied breathlessly. "What about you, Eddie? Are you okay?"

"Yes," said Edison, who was already gnawing on a chocolate bar he'd found in one of the kitchen cupboards. Marcus recognized this chocolate bar. He recognized the curtains and the cushions and the clock on the wall. Everything around him was comfortingly familiar, though none of it was quite as reassuring as the smell of sweaty gym clothes.

"What do you think?" Jake muttered. "Is this the real thing?"

"I think so." Marcus was still breathless with shock. He turned to his mother. "But I guess there's only one way to find out. Why don't you make a call, Mom?"

"Are you sure?" Holly dithered. She glanced at

the darkness beyond the window, then at the screen on her phone. "It's a bit late, don't you think?"

"Is it?" said Sterling with real interest. "How late?"

"It's after ten," Holly revealed, triggering a chorus of gasps.

"We were down there longer than I thought," Coco said, marveling. And Marcus said, "I still think you should call someone."

"Maybe Nicole," Holly murmured. "She's a night owl. . . ."

As Holly punched a number into her phone, Marcus swallowed, Jake tensed, and Coco licked her lips nervously. Sterling crossed his fingers. Edison stopped chewing.

"Oh—hello? Nicole?" A smile began to spread across Holly's face. "Yes, it's me," she continued, making a thumbs-up sign. "Yes, I'm calling from Diamond Beach. Oh, are you? That's good. . . ."

Coco threw her arms joyously around Sterling's neck. Jake sagged against the wall, limp with relief. Edison started chewing again, and Marcus felt his heart return to its normal rhythm.

But Newt didn't cheer up. Her face was as long as ever. And when Holly finally finished her call— breaking the connection to announce, "We must be back home, because I just talked to our next-door neighbor!"—Newt didn't join in the applause that erupted.

"What's the matter, Newt?" Edison asked. "Why aren't you happy?"

"Yes, Newt. Why not? After all, you're still alive." Holly's tone was a little waspish. "And you have Marcus to thank for that."

Newt sniffed. "I know," she mumbled. "Thanks, Marcus."

"That's okay," Marcus replied. He knew that Jake's strength had actually saved them both, but he didn't want to talk about it. He wanted to forget that it had ever happened.

"The trouble is, we didn't save the little white dog," Newt quavered, her voice cracking. "That's why I'm still upset. *We're* all right, but what about the little white dog?"

Everyone else exchanged guilty glances. "I'm sure the dog will be all right, Newt," Holly said at last. "It's in its dream vacation, remember?"

"Which has probably gone up in flames!" Newt tearfully retorted. "Or collapsed into a black hole or something!"

"We can't be sure of that, Newt."

"Yes, we can! The whole place was trashed! Didn't you see? Have a look, why don't you?" Newt pointed at the closed seat—just as something knocked against its lid from the inside.

Tap-tap. Tap-tap-tap.

For an instant nobody moved. It was Jake who

finally stepped forward; he flung the lid open before Marcus could cry, "No!"

Luckily, however, Miss Molpe didn't spring out of the seat. There were no giant pink cats or burning brochures. There wasn't even a staircase. Instead, Prot and the little white dog were sitting there, slightly singed but otherwise unharmed, inside an ordinary, wooden seat.

58.
The end of the holiday

Marcus spent the rest of his beach holiday in the Huckstepps' trailer.

He and his mother didn't want to stay in their own trailer, even though Sterling had examined it from top to bottom without finding a trace of Miss Molpe. The cellar had vanished; the staircase had vanished; there wasn't a cat hair or a flake of ash anywhere. Even the brochure in Sterling's pocket had either fallen out or evaporated. And when Coco went to retrieve her Crystal Hibiscus bathrobe from the wash, the robe couldn't be found. Though Sterling tore apart their washing machine, he came away empty-handed.

Everything was gone—except Jake.

Without Jake, it would have been impossible

to prove that the whole adventure had happened at all. And Jake didn't look like someone who'd been rescued from an updated version of Homer's *Odyssey*. He didn't look as if he'd just stepped out of a Greek myth. With his hair cut and a proper set of clothes, he looked more like a normal guy.

"So no one will *ever* believe you when you try to explain why you didn't go home all those years ago," Holly assured him sadly. "If you tell the truth, people will think you're mad. That's why you can't tell the truth, Jake."

"You'll just have to say that you lost your memory," Coco advised.

"Or that you stowed away on a ship," Edison suggested.

"The important thing is that the newspapers don't find out," Holly finished. "So we'll all have to keep our mouths shut and hope that your parents don't make a big fuss when you contact them. Otherwise the police might get involved."

But the police didn't get involved, because Jake's parents were already dead. Sterling discovered this when he ran an Internet search; Mr. and Mrs. Borazio had died in a car accident ten years earlier, leaving a sizable fortune to Jake's older brothers. And when Sterling finally tracked those brothers down, none of them would acknowledge Jake. They called him an impostor.

"That's because they don't want to share," Marcus deduced. "I bet they'd be nicer to you if they weren't so greedy."

"And if you tell them the truth, they'll say you're a *mad* imposter," Holly lamented. "I'm sorry, Jake. This is going to be harder than I thought—unless you fight them with a DNA test, and that will mean police involvement. . . ."

"I don't care," said Jake. And he really seemed to mean it. His brothers' rejection didn't appear to bother him. Neither did his epic struggle to prove who he was. Marcus found out why much later, after Jake had given up his job as the Huckstepps' gardener and moved out of the furnished loft that had been built over their six-car garage. Though his new boss didn't pay as well as the Huckstepps had—and his new digs were only half the size of his former residence—Jake was adamant that he preferred it that way.

"If things were too easy, I'd be back in fantasyland," he pointed out. "All these tough breaks *prove* that I'm in the real world. It's such a relief not being stuck in an endless loop where you always know what's going to happen next!"

According to Jake, the setbacks of his everyday life were good for him. He certainly thrived on challenge; even Marcus could see that. On first emerging from Miss Molpe's trailer, Jake had been unable to drive a car, use a computer, or identify an eggplant.

Within six months he had mastered all these skills and more. It was like watching someone grow up in fast-forward mode. Soon Marcus wasn't showing Jake what to do anymore. Soon Jake was giving advice to Marcus.

There was only one challenge that Jake wouldn't face. Though he cheerfully wrestled with unfamiliar technology, hostile lawyers, and grudging government departments, he wanted nothing to do with Miss Molpe. He wouldn't even discuss her—unlike the Huckstepps, who were always asking each other questions about every aspect of her existence. Had she really been a siren, or had some weird, birdlike being (an alien, perhaps) chosen to disguise itself as a mythological monster? And if she really *had* been a siren, why had she felt compelled to keep killing travelers? Could it have been because she missed the cadaver-strewn shores of her youth, where her voice had once ruled the waves and won every heart?

No one knew. No one could even agree on a likely explanation. And while Sterling was keen to pursue the matter, Jake definitely wasn't. "No," said Jake when Sterling proposed that they should try to discover Miss Molpe's present whereabouts. "I don't care where she is. Or what she is. I just want her to stay away from me."

"But aren't you interested in knowing what actually happened?" Sterling pressed.

"Not really," Jake retorted. And Newt backed him up.

"What happened is that she destroyed her own tourist trap," Newt theorized. "So she wouldn't get caught. And good riddance, too."

"Yes, but *how* did she destroy it? And what was actually destroyed? Prot wasn't; we know that. Was it because he belonged to the real world, or because of the alloy in his casing?" Sterling turned to the Bradshaws. "What I want to do is dismantle your trailer, piece by piece. I'd like to examine all of Prot's data banks, because there'll be quantifiable readings in there. I want to check police records for disappearances, and then I want to compare our own recollections of what we saw, and after that, I want to pursue the whole Shibilis angle—"

"Why?" Jake interrupted.

"Why?" Sterling looked astonished. "Because unless we find out what actually happened, we might not be able to stop it from happening again!"

"Do you think so?" Marcus wasn't sure. "Couldn't we just sell the trailer? Or destroy it?" He appealed to Holly. "I don't really want to go in there again—do you? I mean, even if Miss Molpe never comes back, it still smells horrible."

His mother sighed. "I know it does," she admitted. "But I paid so much for it, you see—"

"That's all right!" Sterling interrupted, beaming

enthusiastically. "I'll pay you double the original price! And you can buy yourselves something better!"

So Sterling bought the Bradshaws' old trailer, took it apart, and found nothing. He combed through Prot's data banks and found nothing of great interest in there, either. None of his research turned up any useful information, though he kept making inquiries long after his beach holiday had well and truly ended. Every so often, during the months that followed, he would call the Bradshaws with a question or invite them to evaluate his latest theory. Sometimes when Jake visited Holly, he would bring an update from Sterling. But nothing ever came of all this work—and eventually, even Sterling gave up.

As for Holly, she didn't use Sterling's money to buy a new trailer. She didn't need to, because the Hucksteps were always inviting her to stay in theirs. Instead, she used the money to pay for a very simple honeymoon once she'd finally married Jake. And with the small sum left over, she was able to take Marcus to see his dad.

For something Marcus had looked forward to for so long, it proved to be a disappointing trip. He soon realized that his father wasn't particularly interested in him—not half as interested as Jake was. And the journey itself was a disaster, what with the baggage handlers' strike, the unscheduled stopover, the endless rain, the bad cold Marcus picked up, and the earphones he lost. But he didn't mind, really. Disastrous holidays no longer worried him. On the contrary, he found them reassuring, because he knew he was safe from Miss Molpe just as long as things weren't perfect.

It was the dream holidays he had to avoid.

"Look at this," he remarked to his mother one day, on glancing at a magazine holiday promotion. "'Island Paradise Getaway Special. Four nights in a luxury spa resort, all meals included, complimentary champagne and snorkeling, swim with the dolphins, free kids' club.' That sounds too good to resist, don't you think?"

"Probably," Holly agreed.

"Do you think it's Miss Molpe again? Do you think it's one of her traps? 'Free kids' club'—that's just the kind of thing Miss Molpe would dream up."

"Perhaps," Holly allowed.

"Maybe we should warn people that she's still out there, waiting to pounce on them." Marcus was concerned about all the innocent little kids who might find themselves lured into Miss Molpe's paradise trap. "Maybe we should write a letter to the newspapers, saying that if it sounds too good to be true, then it's probably a lie."

"We can't do that, Marcus. We'd be sued for defamation."

"But—"

"People want to believe in paradise. They want to believe that they can escape into a perfect world where nothing will ever go wrong. It's why they pay so much money for these trips." Holly leaned down and hugged him. "Don't fret about it, sweetie. You don't have to worry about Miss Molpe. As long as you're sensible, you'll be safe from Miss Molpe and everyone like her. All you have to do is remember that the real world isn't *meant* to be perfect. And that there will always be ups and downs, no matter where you are."

Then she went off to watch the Powerball jackpot on TV, leaving Marcus to help Jake build a kennel for their little white dog.